HARD CORPS

Scott Hildreth

DEDICATION

Alec Jacob is a fictitious character, but there are many like him on earth. They are sheep dogs. They protect the sheep of this earth from the wolves who attempt to prey on them. Without the sheep dog, the sheep would certainly perish, one by one, until the flock is gone. The sheep dog does what he does not for pay, or even recognition, but because he was born a sheep dog.

Before you fall asleep, say a prayer for the sheep dog who allows you to relax into the state of slumber without worry, without fear, and without shedding a drop of blood. When you sleep, sleep soundly and without reservation.

Because the sheep dog is out there. Waiting.
For a wolf to make his move.

To the protectors. The sheep dogs.
This one is for you.

PROLOGUE

Unconditional love was something I deeply desired, but until I met Alec Jacob I wasn't sure actually existed. After meeting him and experiencing his ability to love first hand, I knew I could never live without him.

He was more kind than any man I had ever met, and as much as I expected his kindness to eventually diminish, it never did. The few who were foolish enough to cross him were always met with a warning, and if they chose not to heed it, were dealt with accordingly.

A predictable man in many ways and quite misunderstood in others, he was somewhat of an enigma. As much as we were in love and as close as we had become, I still found him to be the most intriguing individual I had ever encountered or expected I ever would encounter.

The first day I saw him ride up on his motorcycle I was attracted to him, but any woman would have been. His body was perfectly proportioned and his face was constructed in a way that any female would be drawn to him, but it was his mysterious eyes that provided a clear warning to proceed with caution.

And I did just that.

The more I learned about him, the more attracted to him I became. As handsome as he was, and as much as his chiseled torso made my mouth water, it was *who* Alec Jacob was that made him more attractive to me than any other man on earth.

He accepted me for who I was, never asked me to change one thing, and assured me he would always protect me from all of what was evil on this earth.

And the earth was filled with evil, there was no doubt in my mind of that.

Alec was a war hero and a highly decorated Marine. I was well aware not only that he had killed, but that he had killed many. Not all, as much as I hated to admit it, being a casualty of the war he fought in.

But as capable as he was of administering what he believed to be justice upon those he deemed to be the deserving recipients, he was not an evil man.

He was kind, he was caring, and he was loving.

And he was mine.

CHAPTER ONE

Summer 2003, Al-Anbar Province, Iraq

The days seemed to last forever and as much as I hoped I might be able to defend my life and the lives of the three men I was in charge of, I had no expectation all of us would make it home alive. My belief was that prior to the war ending, at least one of us would be shipped back to the states in a casket with a flag neatly draped over the top.

Deep in my mind, a picture was embedded. Taken from the tail end of a C-130 into the cargo area, the image was haunting. The sight itself, one coffin neatly positioned perfectly beside the other – each with an American flag covering the casket – was one of dignity, selflessness, sacrifice, and freedom. I fully realized the image should not have troubled me in the manner it did, but it tormented me nonetheless. As much as I was willing to fight, I didn't want to be shipped home in a box or a bag.

There weren't many assurances during war, but one remained true throughout all wars ever fought.

Men died.

Damned good men.

Truly believing any other option was possible, at least while in combat, was unrealistic.

I steadied my M4, glanced in Grayson's direction, and gave a slight nod of my head.

He kicked the door right beside the makeshift lock. So many of the homes didn't appear to be houses in a conventional sense. What seemed to be a commercial building may have an entire family living inside, most sleeping on a thin mat that had been tossed on a dirt floor. Other identical buildings may have half a dozen insurgents hiding inside, prepared to kill whoever entered without any warning whatsoever. Knowing what was on the other side of the door prior to entering was close to, if not totally, impossible.

Me again.

Keep my men safe.

The wooden door swung open with a bang, revealing what appeared to be sleeping quarters for six or more people. I entered first, with the other three Marines immediately following me. As my eyes darted around the room, a tingling sensation ran along my spine. Although there was no one visible in the room, there was *something* about it I didn't like. With the buttstock of the M4 against my right shoulder and my finger indexed along the side of the trigger guard, I quickly scanned the room for any signs of life. The floor was covered with bedrolls, blankets, clothes, and supplies, but there appeared to be no munitions or occupants.

The stucco-like inner structure of the building was cracked, damaged, and dirty. The blankets, positioned around the perimeter of the open room, were the only sign of life. Even seeing everything the room had to offer, it was unclear if it was an insurgent hideout or the home of a local family. As I stood, staring at the pile of dirty bedding, the smell of stale sweat filled my nostrils, providing only an indication of the space once being occupied, but nothing more.

I felt like spraying the piles of blankets with a few dozen rounds from my weapon, making certain no one stood from the piles of rubble and shot me or one of my fellow Marines, but I knew better than to do so. If I did, there would undoubtedly be women and children sleeping under them, and I would find myself being court-martialed for the murder of civilians. As Cunningham was turning toward the door, mumbling something about yet another lost opportunity to cleanse the world of all living al-Qaeda, I noticed one of the blankets move slightly. I raised my left hand in the air and clenched my fist as I lowered the barrel of my weapon toward the movement.

With the room eerily silent compared to the sound of our entry and quick search, the passage of time seemed to come to a complete stop. I suspected to whoever was beneath the blanket, the same was true. As much as I hoped the person hiding was friendly, my first tour had taught me to assume everyone was a threat.

I fixed my weapon on the pile of blankets. "Raweenee edeek."

Show me those hands, motherfucker.

The pile of bedding remained motionless.

"Raweenee edeek!" I said in a more demanding tone.

As the mound of blankets began to move ever so slightly, I recognized the unmistakable shape of the barrel of an AK-47 as it exposed itself from the cover of the bedding.

My vision narrowed to the threat, and I could actually hear my heart beating. My throat constricted and instantly went dry. Everything surrounding me became distant, and the only thing that mattered was the location of the barrel. The AK-47 was the weapon of choice for the majority of the resistance against us, and had become a common sight. Although there was no doubt whoever was beneath the blanket had the *means* to resist, so far they hadn't actually done so. The fine line we were required to walk regarding the use of deadly force had cost the life of many a Marine, but was a requirement nonetheless. Until the person with the rifle became an actual threat, the possibility existed that they were prepared to turn over the weapon and surrender, and we were required to treat them as such. Until he pointed the weapon at us or fired it, we were to treat him as if he were friendly.

I stood firm, anxiously waiting on whoever was beneath the blankets to reveal themselves.

"Weapon!" I heard Grayson shout.

"Shut the fuck up, Private. I see it," I said over my shoulder as I maintained focus on the tip of the barrel.

"Raweenee edeek!" I shouted in an attempt to get him to release the weapon and show his hands.

A thin man jumped from the blankets without any warning, and the barrel of the weapon swung toward where I was standing. It was all that was necessary for me to act in self-defense. Without thought, the tip of my index finger slipped inside the trigger guard and pulled against the trigger twice.

His body jolted from the impact of the two bullets, and his hand instinctively pulled the trigger, discharging a few rounds into the far wall. As he dropped his weapon to the floor and fell to his knees, his eyes revealed the unmistakable regret he felt for doing what he had done.

"Hold your fire," I said flatly as I watched him collapse.

On his knees, staring up at me with hopeful eyes, he held out his weathered hand.

Why?

Why didn't you fucking surrender?

I kicked the weapon to the side. "Someone secure that weapon, and get this bedding searched."

I shifted my gaze to meet the blank stare of the man I had shot. His eyes appeared to be that of a thirty-year-old man, but the sun damaged skin of his face seemed to be sixty, common for the people of Iraq.

"He's alive. Cunningham, get a Corpsman in here and see if you can find a Terp," I shouted.

"Fuck that Haji motherfucker," Grayson blurted as he kicked along the pile of blankets positioned around the perimeter of the room.

"Find me a Corpsman and a fucking interpreter!" I demanded.

Just hang on for a few minutes, I've got help en route.

I glanced down at his wounds. One of the rounds struck him in the left side of the upper chest, and the other slightly higher, closer to his clavicle. With quick medical attention, he might survive, but the chest wound needed immediate action if he was going to live. I reached for his outstretched hand, held it in mine, and waited for a Corpsman. As he looked into my eyes, he calmly spoke in a manner and tone I perceived as apologetic. Although I had learned a few of the necessary phrases, I was not fluent in Arabic, and needed an interpreter to not only understand what he was saying but to interview him before he died.

Determining the locations of any other resistance we were likely to encounter would be helpful, and I had learned a dying man was more willing to be truthful than one who believed he was free from the threat of death.

In seeing as many men die as I had, there seemed to be one common thread in the few seconds immediately preceding death – regardless of race, religion, or skin color.

Death took the dying to a peaceful place.

I positioned my weapon over my shoulder, knelt in front of him, and cut the front of his shirt open. The chest wound was considerably lower than I expected it to be, and was discharging blood with each heartbeat. If he didn't receive medical attention immediately, he would undoubtedly be added to the long list of men I had killed in my 16 months of combat.

"Anyone got a chest seal or catheter?" I asked over my shoulder as I studied the wound.

The sound of shuffling boots and a few light sighs was my only response.

With our eyes locked, he blinked a few times before his mouth curled into a shallow smile. It was a smile not of joy, but of comfort. I silently studied him, wondering if he had a family, kids, or a wife. I wondered if he was forced to fight, did so out of a feeling of need, or if he was simply guarding what was once his home. As he continued to gaze at me and smile lightly, I did my best to return the gesture. A few seconds later he released his grip on my hand and slumped against me.

Well, fuck.

Killing was not complicated, and had become more of an instinct than a decision I consciously made.

Dealing with death, however, was different.

I released his hand, frustrated that he had chosen to point the weapon at me, but feeling no regret for the action I had taken. I turned toward the entrance and walked through the room, gazing blankly beyond the walls and into the dusty street as I did so.

"How many is that?" I heard Grayson ask.

I tapped a cigarette from my pack, raised it to my mouth, and lit it.

As I watched the smoke slowly rise from the tip, I bit into the cotton filter and spoke through my teeth. "How many is *what*?"

"Kills. Cunningham said you killed a bunch of these sorry motherfuckers," he said.

I glared at him, capable of answering, but not necessarily feeling doing so was warranted – at least not to him.

He narrowed his eyes as he gazed into the street at the children playing. "God damned Muslims, we should drop a motherfuckin' bomb on this son-of-a-bitch if you ask me. Turn this sand to a fuckin' sheet of glass."

I closed my left eye, took a long drag from the cigarette, and studied him with my open eye. As I exhaled a cloud of smoke into the space between us, I responded in the only manner I saw fit.

"Well, *Private Grayson,* nobody asked you. And we're not fighting *Muslims*, dumb fuck. We're fighting terrorists." I paused and took a long pull from the cigarette.

I stared down at the toes of my boots and exhaled the smoke from my lungs. After a few long seconds of staring blankly at the dirt floor, I shifted my gaze upward and studied his eyes. A replacement for a Marine who had been killed by an IED, and all of eighteen years old, he would more than likely be dead in a matter of weeks if his attitude didn't change. As he looked back at me with the eyes of an over eager inexperienced Marine, I continued.

"I'm not here to condemn a man for his religious beliefs, but I'll send one straight to an early grave for his stance against the United States of America or one of my fellow Marines. You've got a lot to fucking learn, *Private*," I said, making sure he understood that I was not only aware of his military rank, but that he was as low and as inexperienced as a

Marine could possibly be.

His eyes went wide as if I had slapped him in the face.

He stared beyond me for a moment, shifted his eyes to me, and gave a slight acknowledgement of my condemnations.

"I'll do my best, Corporal Jacob," he said in an apologetic tone.

As I turned and walked out of the building, I considered Grayson's initial question, and wondered why I didn't accurately respond. I bent my knees and lowered myself into a squatted position beside the opening of the door and gazed into the street. The length of the deserted dirt road was littered with pieces of brick and chunks of concrete, a reminder of the many bombs dropped before our arrival. A young boy played with a soccer ball, bouncing it from his knees onto his chest and shoulders, oblivious as to what was going on around him. As I watched him balance the ball on his upper chest, I tried my best to recall the lives I had taken.

I wasn't ashamed, nor was I proud. Killing the enemy was something that had happened, and if given the same circumstances to do it all over again, I wouldn't change a thing. As far as I was concerned, there was only one thing that really mattered – if I didn't kill the men who were trying to kill me, my objective would never be reached.

My objective?

At the end of each tour of duty, I needed to make it home for one reason and one reason only.

To hold my wife in my arms.

I looked out into the dusty street. The boy was gone. The sound of small arms fire echoed in the air like distant music. I stood, raised my hands to my face, and rubbed my tired eyes. No matter how much I rationalized ending the lives of the men I had killed, the details of each of their deaths lingered in my mind, playing over and over like a slow-motion scene from a horror movie. It was the price I paid, I supposed, for doing something so contrary to man's religious, moral, and spiritual beliefs.

So far, I had killed thirteen men to reach my objective.

And holding her in my arms was all the justification I really needed.

CHAPTER TWO

Fall 2003, Wichita, Kansas, USA

I pushed my hand into my pocket and removed my wallet. As I thumbed through the bills the driver turned his head and glanced over his shoulder.

"Don't worry about it," he said. "Thanks for your service."

I shifted my eyes from the meter to my wallet, and removed a $10 and a $20 bill. "Meter says $18.80. Here's $30.00. Keep the change."

He shook his head. "I mean it. Keep your money. I'm not just saying it; I appreciate your service to the country. When they flew those planes into the towers, I wanted to have the guts…"

He paused as the car rolled to a stop. After shifting the gear selector into park, he turned toward the back seat. He was roughly my age, but his shoulder-length hair and full beard made him appear slightly older at first glance.

"Not all of us have the courage to do what you're doing. Me? I get to drive this cab and make an honest living because people like you are willing to fight to keep this country free. Keep your money. I mean it," he said.

"I appreciate it," I said as I folded the money and pushed it between the back of his seat and the bottom cushion.

He would find it at some point in time, probably the next time he cleaned his car. I'd never been one to accept charity, and felt I was required to pay for everything I obtained in life, one way or another.

"Going back?" he asked as I opened the door.

I got out of the car and adjusted my pack as I responded through the open window. "Until they tell me I can't, or it ends."

"Good luck," he said.

I nodded my head in appreciation.

Luck.

Some called me lucky. Others described me as gifted. Personally, I felt that I had a sixth sense; one that allowed me to see things as they truly were, and that wasn't always the way other people perceived them. Knowing what I believed to be the truth allowed me a second or so to react without contemplation or thought, which was often all it took to survive.

I folded a piece of gum and poked it into my mouth. As I chewed it and shoved the wrapper into the pocket of my trousers, she opened the front door. Her strawberry blonde hair was well past her shoulders, several inches longer than the last time we had seen each other.

"Oh my God. You didn't say…" she gasped.

Short of writing letters, I hadn't spoken to her in seven months, and hadn't told her specifically when I would arrive. Although many of the Marines used the calling centers or *morale calls* on SAT phones to call home, I felt the distraction on both ends was too much if we were to attempt to communicate by telephone. An old fashioned letter delivered in the mail, however, was something nice to read, and it could be read over and over, providing much more than a few moments of pleasure.

My eyes fell to her feet, and slowly inched their way up her body until stopping at her face. I stood in awe, recognizing her natural beauty, but trying the entire time to hide the excitement of seeing her again. She looked every bit as gorgeous as she did on any other day, which was more beautiful than any other woman who had ever graced the earth with her presence.

"I wanted it to be a surprise," I said, twisting my mouth into a smirk.

Unlike many of my Marine brethren, I was devoted to Suzanne wholly. Cheating or even lusting over another woman was completely out of the question. I was hers, and only hers, and she knew it. It was a large part of what allowed me to travel to another country and devote myself to a war while leaving her at home without her worrying about my commitment or loyalty – or me questioning hers for that matter. I knew, no matter when I showed up, she would be alone and waiting for me.

"God it's good to see you," she said as she ran down the steps.

"Come here, Babe," I said as I dropped my pack to the sidewalk and opened my arms.

I extended my arms and gazed into her green eyes. They were the most inviting eyes I had ever seen, and they were attached to the most beautiful woman to ever exist. Seeing her cry – even if they were tears of joy – was heartbreaking.

"No need to cry, Babe," I said as I wiped the tears from her cheeks with my thumb. "I'll be home for a while. I've got some leave before I have to go back."

"But you're going back?" she said, half asking, half stating.

I pulled her into me and held her tight to my chest. "Until the war is over, or they find me unfit to fight, I'll keep going back. I don't have a choice."

As she nodded her head in acknowledgement, I pressed my nose into her hair and inhaled a slow breath. I viewed my time at war as an opportunity to serve my country, and never really felt sorry for myself for what I was required to forfeit to do so. Each time I returned home, I was reminded of the things I missed, and although seeing Suzanne proved to me that God existed, inhaling a hint of her scent was much more satisfying.

It reassured me that *she* existed.

After swallowing my gum, I reached down, lifted her chin slightly, and kissed her. The kiss wasn't aggressive, extremely long, or close to what most Marine wives received upon their husband's return to the states, but it was appropriate, respectful, and provided all the support she needed to understand where it was I had placed her.

On a pedestal above anything and everything on the earth.

Most men, upon returning home from the war, more than likely greeted their wives or girlfriends with the tip of their dick. I believed there was a time and a place for sex, and was actually quite fond of fucking the woman I loved, but for the next hour or so I needed to simply hold her in my arms, inhale her scent, and talk to her. She'd been through this routine enough times that she knew what to expect from me. Sitting down, eating a meal together, and talking allowed my mind to return back to civilization, and at least for the amount of time I was home, feel like things were different.

"God, I love kissing you," she said as our lips parted.

She leaned back and shifted her eyes up and down my frame. "You look like you've lost weight. Come on, let me make you something to eat. Are you hungry?"

I reached for my pack, lifted it to my shoulder, and nodded my head. "I could eat."

"Come on," she said. "Let's eat, and then we'll curl up in a ball on the couch."

She turned away, walked up the steps and held the door open.

I paused at the first step and glanced at the front of the house before allowing my eyes to openly gaze around the yard. Leaves had filled the gutters, and the yard was littered with the various colors of fall.

Most men would perceive a yard full of leaves as a pain in the ass. Work. Time that could be spent watching a football game.

Me?

I saw it as exactly what it was.

Beautiful.

I grinned, exhaled, and followed her into the house.

God, it feels good to be home.

CHAPTER THREE

Early Spring 2004, Fallujah, Iraq
  The First Battle of Fallujah.

I grew up the only son of high school sweethearts who fell in love, married, and remained true to each other until my mother passed away. My father never remarried after her death, claiming his only love to be my mother, and further explaining that allowing another woman into his life, at any level, would be disrespectful to his deceased wife and only love.

I respected him for his position on love, relationships, and as a father. As a child, my friends often claimed their hero to be a television character, someone in a movie, or even a superhero from a comic book.

Me?

My father was my only hero.

He took me deer hunting for the first time when I was twelve. Although I was young, I had spent my short life around weapons, learning to respect them, understand their inner workings, and how to properly handle them safely. My father described me as *a natural*, claiming one day I would be in the Olympics as a marksman, but I knew otherwise.

I wanted to be like my uncle, who was a former Marine and a Vietnam war veteran. My father's brother, and a man who didn't demand respect

– but received it from those who understood him. He was less apt to speak than any other of my relatives, but when he did, his advice was always well thought out and easy to apply to life.

As we sat in the tree stand waiting for a deer to cross the trail a hundred yards ahead, my father questioned whether or not I was ready, and, ultimately, if I *was* ready, would I be able to make a shot at such a distance?

I later learned after they were shot, most deer ran through the woods for a hundred yards or more before finally bleeding so much that they expired from blood loss. A perfectly placed shot – straight up from the back side of the front leg, half way between the bottom of the chest and the back – was the only thing that would drop a deer in its tracks.

Filled with confidence, and hoping to make my father proud, I waited for a deer to cross the path in front of us. As the morning sun began to rise above the base of the trees, a buck stepped into the clearing, raised his head, and sniffed the air as if something was wrong.

As his shoulder twitched from either fear or an inner knowledge of impending threat, I squeezed the trigger.

The deer fell where it stood.

Two days later, as we sat and ate a meal of venison steaks, potatoes, and an apple pie my mother had prepared, I began to understand the permanency of death. My father, while describing the *impossible shot* I had made to my mother, was filled with pride.

As I listened to him speak, I didn't necessarily feel proud, but I was far from ashamed. I felt powerful, large, and almost invincible. The taking of a life wasn't something every man was able to do, but I understood death as the completion of the cycle of life, and something completely necessary for all living things to endure at some point.

Making the choice to end the cycle of life wasn't something I took lightly as a child, or as an adult. As I grew older, I eventually stopped hunting. My belief at the time was that it wasn't *necessary*. For me at least, hunting was a sport; and killing – for sport – was something I decided was wrong.

***

"We need to get off this roof before he shoots all of us," the young Marine complained.

In searching the building for insurgents, we had encountered a Marine Scout Sniper and his spotter. The sniper had been shot, was close to death, and the spotter appeared to be in slight shock. There was no doubt he had received considerable training to be a spotter for a Scout Sniper and to be a combat ready Marine, but nothing could ever replace the experience from actually being in combat, which was something he obviously hadn't had the luxury of experiencing.

"First tour?" I asked as I crawled toward the abandoned sniper rifle.

"Yes, Sir. We got here two days ago for this operation," he responded nervously. "We really need to get down from here. We're sitting ducks."

"Well, that's not going to fucking happen. Your sniper has a hole in his shoulder the size of a baseball, and I intend to kill the motherfucker who shot him before he shoots someone else. Now, take a breath, remember your training, and give me an accurate fucking distance to my target," I barked as I leaned my M4 against the parapet of the roof.

I flattened myself into a prone position and placed my cheek against the buttstock of the sniper's rifle. After pulling off my helmet, wiping the sweat from my brow, and closing my left eye, I peered through the scope toward the target. The man on the rooftop who had been taking pot shots at an approaching convoy was taking a new position at the corner of the roof and lowering his rifle to what appeared to be a sandbag rest.

I'm guessing eight hundred plus.

The mid-day sun provided aggravating temperatures, but also made finding my target rather easy. With half of a mile between us, the bullet from the .308 caliber rifle would reach him in roughly one second. In that same second, he could take a shot, change his position, or take cover behind the upper roof line.

If his intention was to shoot Marines, I knew I didn't have a second to waste.

I compared the four story building across the street to the building half a mile away and decided the distance based on the reduced appearance in size. After I studied the blowing dust for a moment, I reached up, and began to adjust the scope for an 800 yard shot. The wind was from my right to my left at what I guessed to be 6 miles an hour, which would carry the bullet from the right to the left slightly in the 2,600 feet it had to travel to get to the target.

As Cunningham and Grayson sat in wait and Whitmire tended to the wounded sniper, the spotter peered nervously through his spotting scope toward the target. I inhaled a deep breath and paused.

"Eight hundred and twenty meters. Wind from your immediate right to your left. Push right point two," the spotter said.

Point two is too much, kid. We'll do this my way.

I exhaled all of the breath from my lungs.

Sorry, motherfucker. I've got to make it home to see my wife, and to do so, I need to make sure you don't make it home to yours.

I gave no acknowledgement of the stats provided by the spotter.

After squeezing the trigger, I waited for him to acknowledge the kill.

"Holy fucking shit. Target down. Enemy KIA," he said excitedly.

I inhaled a shallow breath, turned toward the spotter, and nodded my head. The sound of small arms fire continued from every direction as the report of mortars thumped in the distance every few seconds. All but immune to the sounds and sight of death, I turned toward the three Marines I was in charge of.

"Whitmire, we need to get him to our fucking Corpsman. Hell, I don't give a fuck if you've got to find one of the 82nd's medics, we need to get him off this fucking roof," I said.

As I raised myself to a crouched position, hiding behind the cover of the parapet, the spotter moved his scope to the side and shifted his eyes toward me. "Nice shot," he said as he scanned my blouse for my name. "Sergeant Jacob. Nice fucking shot, *Jacob*."

"We can swap spit later. I need to get your sniper to a medic," I said.

"Roger that," he said as he stood from his bench.

What the fuck are you doing?

I waved my hand from side to side and pointed toward his feet. "Stay down, god damn it! You don't know if..."

The *thwack* of the bullet hitting his chest was sickening. His eyes widened with concern as he stumbled back, eventually falling onto the roof between where I was crouched and where Cunningham was positioned.

"God fucking damn it," I shouted as I gazed down at his body.

I shook my head and stared off in the distance, wondering how much longer the sniper would be able to last with the fist-sized cavity in his shoulder.

After securing my weapon, I bent down to pick up the fallen spotter.

As I peered into his eyes, I realized I didn't need to check for vitals, he wasn't WIA, he was KIA.

Son-of-a-fucking-bitch.

I reached between his legs with one arm and grabbed his wrist with the other, raising him over my shoulder. I clenched my jaw at the thought of one more dead Marine and one soon to be dead Marine, and thanked God the three men under my command were still alive.

"Cunningham, lead the way. Take the rear staircase. Whitmire, behind me. Grayson, secure the M40, the spotter scope, and the rest of their gear, and take the rear," I said as I tossed my head toward the staircase at the rear corner of the roof.

Upon reaching the street, we were met by a First Lieutenant, obviously new to combat, half-lost, and out of his element.

As the driver sat nervously and waited, the Lieutenant stepped from the Humvee and waved his arm toward the adjacent buildings.

"We've got a sniper on the roof six hundred meters east, and…"

"Sir, the enemy sniper has been eliminated. I've got one Marine KIA and one Marine WIA, soon to be KIA. We either need a Corpsman or to get this man to a hospital," I said as I lowered the dead spotter from my shoulder.

"That sniper KIA, is it confirmed?" he asked.

It was as confirmed as I needed it to be.

"Yes, Sir," I responded.

He nodded his head eagerly. "Who are you with?"

"We're with the two-seven," I responded. "I'm the Fire Team leader, and we were separated from our squad. We're searching…"

"Sergeant Jacob, two-seven. Got it. Load those men in the back," he said as he waved his hand toward the rear of the Humvee.

Apparently he didn't give a shit who we were with or what our objectives were. I motioned toward the rear of the Humvee, helped load the two Marines, and turned away. As I watched them speed away, I realized for us, nothing had changed. We had been separated from our squad, and the entire city was a chaotic mess of gunfire, RPG's, and mortar fire.

We'd be lucky if we lived through the night.

The Marines, no different than any other branch of the military, had a command structure. The structure was in place for a reason, and was necessary in the eyes of every Marine. It never ceased to amaze me, however, that while in combat and taking heavy fire, things seemed to go to hell in a handbasket at every level of the command.

I shifted my eyes back and forth between each of the men, "We've got no radio, no support from our squad, and no NCO other than me."

I flinched as a mortar impacted the building directly beside us. I gazed up and down the street for any signs of the enemy, relieved to see nothing or no one. Buildings were smoldering, half of the structures were collapsed from bombs we had dropped, and what remained was being searched by the Army's special forces and Marines, none of which I immediately recognized. The enemy, as always, was hiding in wait.

Our trip onto the roof had eliminated a sniper and potentially saved the lives of many, but left us with very little support or immediate hope of finding the remainder of our squad.

"We're going to try to make it back to our squad, and if you listen to me and follow my command, I can't make any promises, but I haven't lost a man on my team yet," I paused and surveyed the area for anyone I recognized.

To describe the scene as lawless would be to grossly understate the truth. In every direction, men were firing weapons. Marines and the Army's 82nd Airborne fired M16's, M4's, M203 grenade launchers, and SAW's at buildings, noises, who they perceived as a threat, and down the alleys between buildings. Fire was returned sporadically, but not from an identifiable location.

As I mentally found a path for my fire team to take to safety, I felt tremendous pressure in my thigh, and then my upper chest.

"Fuck," I said as I glanced down at my thigh. "We need to double time it toward that mosque."

"Jacob, you're hit," Cunningham said.

"I'll be fine," I assured him with a nod of my head. "Head for the mosque."

I wiped my left hand along my upper chest and returned a hand full of blood. I did my best to take a step to lead my men to safety, and everything around me slowly became small.

As the silence encompassed me, I wondered if upon arriving at the gates of heaven if it was truly guarded by US Marines.

I had no idea if the stories of Marines guarding the gates of heaven were true, but as I felt like I was slowly being lowered into a pit with no bottom that was filled with the essence of Suzanne's perfume, I was sure I was going to find out.

Everything around me faded from a blur into complete darkness and my body went numb.

But her scent remained.

CHAPTER FOUR

Fall 2004, Wichita, Kansas, USA

I gripped the sides of the weight bench and pressed the extensions to their limit. After holding my legs straight until my muscles began to fatigue, I bent my knees and lowered the weight to the machine's stops.

I sat up, wiped the sweat from my face, and stood from the bench. My leg was in as good of shape as it was before I was shot, and there was no doubt in my mind I had recovered 100 percent. Shot twice and determined to be still fit for duty, I felt fortunate to be able to return to a war I was convinced couldn't be won by either side. As I felt Suzanne's presence in the room, I turned toward the doorway.

As our eyes met, she spoke. "You're really going back?"

I stood and buried my face in the towel I held. I couldn't expect her to believe she was as important to me as she was and also understand my overwhelming need to return, at least not without some kind of an explanation. I pulled the towel away from my face and did my best to reassure her I was doing what was best for everyone, her included.

"Babe, I'm sorry. But until this damned thing is over, I'll go back. I've got to. I don't have a choice," I said.

"You *do* have a choice," she murmured.

I shook my head. "I *don't*. My men need me. I can't let them down. I took an oath and gave my word, you can't expect me to go back on that,

27

you just can't. The man who never gives up, is always there for those in need, and provides what others can only dream of is the man you fell in love with. For you to ask me to stay here would be to ask me to change who I am. To change who you fell in love with."

"I can't change that maple tree out in the yard into an apple tree, and I sure can't turn myself into a man unwilling to fight and willing to break his word." I flipped the towel over my shoulder and pointed both of my index fingers toward my chest.

"You fell in love with *this* man. The man that's going back to fight against the very terrorists who attacked our country and killed innocent civilians. And I'm going back to do my part in making sure they don't do it again to our children," I said.

"*Our children?*" she asked, her voice faltering as she spoke. "God, I love you, Alec."

I nodded my head. "Yes. Our children."

She smiled and wiped her eyes. "I can't argue with you. You're right. I fell in love with the man who never gives up. The man who wouldn't take *no* for an answer when he asked me out on that first date."

She paused and dropped her eyes to the floor.

"But I'm scared to death they're going to kill you," she said as she shifted her eyes to meet mine.

"My promotion to Sergeant was already in for this spring, so it was a given. After killing that sniper and being shot, I received a meritorious combat promotion, Suzanne. They kicked me up to a Staff Sergeant. I'll be in charge of over forty men. I won't really even be fighting any more, just commanding infantry troops. And there's never going to be anything worse than that fucking mess in Fallujah, so there's nothing to worry about," I said, doing my best to not only convince her, but to assure myself there would be far less risk of me being killed in my new position.

"Not even fighting, huh? Nothing to worry about, alright. I'll keep telling myself that. So, when do you think the war is going to end?" she asked.

I shrugged my shoulders. "Maybe one more tour?"

Her eyes widened slightly. "Really?"

I nodded my head, hoping to convince myself the war was nearly over.

Her mouth curled into a smile. She fought against it for a moment, and eventually shifted her eyes down at the floor. After a few seconds, she lowered her head slightly. Her blonde hair fell beside her face, hanging from her head like strands of straw-colored silk. She raised her hand and flipped her hair over her shoulder, lifting her head – and her gaze – until it met mine.

"You think this will be your last?" she asked as our eyes locked.

"I hope so," I said.

It wasn't much of a reassurance, but I really hoped it would end soon. I didn't see that there could ever be a clear winner in the war we were fighting, but if nothing else we were making a statement. The people we were fighting weren't the people who mattered, and the people who mattered weren't anywhere to be found. Continuing at the pace we were would prove nothing and gain very little.

"I just...I can't imagine...I can't imagine losing you," she said.

I shook my head. "Don't. Don't imagine it. Imagine me coming home one day for good, and you and I having a family. Imagine that."

She grinned and nodded her head. "I will."

The thought of losing Suzanne wasn't something I was prepared to digest. My only desire, short of making it out of the war alive and in one piece, was to have a family with her and live a new life to the limit of my mental, physical, and spiritual abilities.

I stood and gazed at her, and as I did, realized my desire to have a family with her was deeply etched into my being.

As she began to walk in my direction, no doubt to hold me in her arms, it saddened me slightly to know that my commitment to protect my fellow Marines was etched just a little deeper.

CHAPTER FIVE

Early Winter 2004, Fallujah, Iraq
The Second Battle of Fallujah

I stood and listened to my orders, not wanting to believe we were going back into the very depths of hell that I had barely made it out of alive. Fallujah was not only occupied by insurgents, but had been taken over completely. *Operation Phantom Fury* was being spearheaded by the United States Marine Corps, with the assistance of a handful of Navy SEALS, and a light offering from the United States Army.

"Sixty-five hundred Marines?" I asked, attempting to understand the complexity of the operation.

"That is correct, Staff Sergeant," he responded.

"And fifteen hundred from the Army?" I asked.

He nodded his head and continued in a stern tone. "Affirmative. Three six-man SEAL teams, a thousand Iraqi troops, and roughly five thousand British troops. You have reservations about going back into that shit storm, I need to know it now."

I straightened my stance and barked out my response like the devil dog I was. "No, Sir, I'm ready, willing, and capable."

"Well, Staff Sergeant Jacob, be advised," he paused and lifted his chin slightly.

"You are one tough son-of-a-bitch, that's a given. You command

31

your troops well, and make split-second decisions like no other Marine under my command. But. And this is a big but, son. This battle? I can't guarantee you much, but I can god damned guarantee you this. This son-of-a-bitch will go down in history as *one* of the, if not *the*, worst battle of urban combat in the history of my beloved Marine Corps," he said.

"Oorah," I grunted.

He slapped his hand against my shoulder. "Drinking gas and shittin' fire. You're one gung ho son-of-a-bitch, Jacob. Wish I had a dozen more just like you."

Considering the living hell we were going into, I wished he did too.

***

Two days into the operation, and it was already described as the bloodiest battle of the three-year war. Marine commanders were calling it the heaviest urban combat in Marine Corps history. All I cared about was that the forty men under my command were returned home alive and in one piece.

Our convoy was approaching an unoccupied intersection in the southern region of the city. The eerily quiet section of street had concerned me, but as we were almost to our destination, I was preparing to exhale a sigh of relief.

The earth beneath us exploded.

The bomb blast sent the Humvee in front of us ten feet straight into the air. The vehicle I was in, the third vehicle, drove into the void of earth the bomb had left, and the airborne vehicle landed on the hood of ours, crushing it completely.

Deafened by the explosion, I was able to feel the sounds and voices around me, but not quite capable of hearing or comprehending them fully. Realizing if I didn't make quick decisions and maintain my composure as a non-commissioned officer that I would lose every Marine in my command, I swung the door of the Humvee open and surveyed the damage.

The four men in the damaged Humvee were all alive, but wounded. The blast appeared to be remotely set, and not detonated by pressure, which – at least in this circumstance – was good. As fate would have it, the person with the remote switch detonated the bomb a fraction of a second too late, hitting the rear of the vehicle with the brunt of the blast, dislodging the rear axle, but causing minimal damage to the occupants. If it would have been a pressure device, the front tires would have caused the explosion.

Someone was watching us.

A quick head count assured me that although all of the Marines in the bombed vehicle were wounded, they would live if provided medical attention.

"Blast was late, it was remote. They can see us," I shouted. "Take cover beside the vehicles"

The intersection had rubble from bombed-out buildings on our right side, and still erect but heavily damaged buildings on our left. There was no doubt the buildings to our left were where the enemy was watching us from, and to protect ourselves, we needed to take cover behind our vehicles.

As the wounded Marines were dragged to cover, we began to riddle the buildings with machine gun fire and grenades.

"Todelli! Take your team across the street and see if you can get a visual," I shouted as I turned and glanced toward him.

He was covered in blood, but appeared to be willing to follow the commands I had given. As he turned to command his men, I shouted at him again.

"Todelli, are you hit?" I asked.

"Everyone's hit, Jacob. Shit, you're hit," he shouted in return as he waved his free hand toward me.

My head was throbbing, my ears ringing, and my heart was beating at a rapid rate. My hearing was slowly returning, and the dull drone between my ears was almost as deafening as the bomb blast. I shifted my eyes down along the front of my blouse, only to see that I was covered in blood from head to toe.

Filled with adrenaline, and numb to whatever pain I may have felt in its absence, I waved my hand to the other side of the street. Todelli and his fire team ran across the street and began to patrol along the side of the damaged buildings.

As I watched them work their way toward the corner of the intersection, a second bomb blast shook the ground beneath my feet with so much force it dropped me to my knees.

God fucking damn it, I'm not ready to die.

Not yet.

As I attempted to stand, I glanced over each shoulder. It appeared that my entire platoon of Marines was almost all injured by shrapnel, and all of the vehicles in the convoy were damaged to the point of being useless. Our only way out of the mess we were in was to fight, and I would be damned to hell if they were going to continue to detonate bombs at will without one hell of a fight from me and my platoon.

Still on my knees, I stared down at the ground. Incapable of standing on my feet, but confused as to why, a short study of my uniform provided the answer. My left leg was crimson colored and my hip had a piece of steel in it the size of a deck of cards. The exposed piece of steel burned into my fingers and the palm of my hand as I gripped it between them and pulled against it. As the pain reached a peak, I released my grip and stared down at the piece of shrapnel.

Half way there, Jacob.

I gritted my teeth and gripped it in my hand again. The smell of burning flesh rose into my nostrils as I clenched my jaw and pulled with all my might. As it finally came free from my trousers, I released my grip, exhaled, and collapsed onto the ground.

I peered up into the morning sky, realizing my left leg was incapable of functioning. I shifted my eyes toward the abandoned civilian vehicles on the other side of the street and gripped my M4 tightly in my right hand.

I don't ask for much, but I'm asking for a little assistance right now. I'm crawling across the street, and I'm protecting my Marines. Any help you can give me would be appreciated.

"Call in a medevac, and get these men treated by our Corpsman. I'm going to find these sons-a-bitches," I shouted toward Cunningham.

I turned toward the burned-out Toyota truck and began to crawl across the open street, dragging my damaged leg behind me. Using my elbows and one knee, I crawled the thirty feet against the pain, leaving a trail of blood behind me. As I reached the corner of the truck, movement in the open window of a bomb-blasted building across the intersection caught my eye. The building, facing the intersection, was at a ninety-degree angle of the convoy, and almost completely out of sight of the Marines taking cover behind the Humvees.

Excited to have found the insurgents, but not so foolish to let them know I had done so, I signaled to the Marines of second squad to come across the street and assist in taking out the enemy.

As soon as the first Marine stepped from behind the cover of the Humvee, he was shot. I watched in horror as the second Marine, directly behind the first, was shot as he tried to pull his fallen comrade to safety.

You motherfuckers.

I gave the signal to hold tight and turned toward the building. I had a straight line of sight to the window, but apparently the enemy had been focused on what he was able to see of our vehicles and hadn't seen me crawl across the street. I watched as three men with rifles sat and waited for another opportunity to shoot at my men. So far, they hadn't noticed me.

Realizing I could probably get one or possibly two shots off before giving away my position, I crawled toward the front of the vehicle, hiding the majority of my torso underneath the front of the truck.

With my chest, shoulders, and head exposed, I flattened myself into a prone position and took aim at the man on the far right.

Going home in a wheelchair is better than going home in a box. You can do this, Jacob.

One shot, one kill.

I squeezed the trigger.

The man slumped out of sight, obviously killed instantly by the impact of the bullet.

Two more, but you better be quick.

As I took aim at the second man, he and the third began looking frantically to determine where the first shot had come from. Now shooting toward the convoy, but causing damage to nothing but the vehicles, their silhouettes were clear in the open window of the building.

Squeeze, Jacob. Don't pull, squeeze.

I squeezed the trigger.

The second man fell out of sight.

The Marines taking cover behind the convoy began to cheer and scream. Out of my peripheral I saw one of them point in my direction.

And I wasn't the only one who saw it.

Fuck.

While the sniper in the window began to take aim at me, the sound of approaching Humvees shook the ground beneath me. As the approaching convoy came to a halt, the whizzing sound of a bullet and a puff of dust bursting from the street beside me told me the shot he had taken was off by no more than a few inches.

There was no doubt he was choosing to shoot me over shooting the arriving Marines.

As I heard them loading the wounded Marines into the convoy, I took aim at the one remaining threat.

"Jacob, hold tight. I'm sending two men to get you," I heard a voice shout.

I lifted my left hand in the air and clenched my fist.

If they tried to cross the street, he'd cut them down one by one.

"Do *not* approach. That is a fucking order," I shouted as I closed my left eye and attempted to gain sight of my target.

The shrill impact of the bullet into the hood of the truck I was using for cover startled me, and the following pressure in my left leg assured me that although the steel hood may have slowed the path of the bullet, I had been hit.

Son-of-a-fucking-bitch.

As the bullet burned into my flesh, I knew I had to act fast if I was going to kill him before he killed me. I tightened my jaw and steadied my rifle.

"Tandy, Rickman, get him out of there before he gets himself killed," I heard someone shout from the direction of the convoy.

"I gave a fucking order, and I'll see to it that you are god damned court-martialed if you cross that fucking street," I shouted over my shoulder.

"Get my fucking Marines medevac'd. You can drag my corpse out of here after I shoot this prick," I said through my teeth.

The impact of another bullet into my upper back pressed me into the ground, but I could tell it wasn't a through shot, probably either a ricochet or a deep surface wound.

You. Mother. Fucker.

I felt like a piece of Swiss cheese. I could no longer hear anything. Either from the massive amount of adrenaline I was producing, from being shot repeatedly, or from the loss of blood, I had gone completely deaf, but the warmth of my own blood pooling beneath me made my loss of hearing seem inconsequential. As I saw a few of the vehicles pull away out of my peripheral, I exhaled the remaining breath in my lungs. It didn't matter if he shot me again or not, I fully realized I had only a few minutes to live either way.

You either put me here to die, or to administer your will.

I don't know which it is, but all I need is one more shot.

A bullet slammed against the heel of my boot. It felt like I had been hit in the foot by a sledgehammer. Out of time, completely out of energy, and almost out of blood, I regained my line of sight, exhaled, and squeezed the trigger just as he was preparing to take another shot at me.

As I watched his body collapse over the edge of the window opening, everything around me slowly disappeared.

And the sweet smell of Suzanne's perfume engulfed me.

CHAPTER SIX

Late Winter 2004, Landstuhl regional Medical Center, Landstuhl, Germany

Incapable of moving anything but my head, I shifted my eyes around the room. Everywhere I looked, white. White walls, white floors, white curtains, and white medical equipment surrounded me. I had been in and out of consciousness for days, and was well aware a reasonable amount of time had passed since sustaining my injuries.

Somewhat convinced I was paralyzed, but sedated to a point of near delirium, I tilted my head from left to right and gazed down along the edge of the bed. After blinking my eyes a few times and allowing them to come into focus, I realized my arms and legs were secured to the bed with restraints.

What the fuck is going on?

I pulled against the restraints, but my movement was something the medical staff was obviously trying to prevent. Shifting my body from side to side caused tremendous pain in my hip and lower back, and twisting my unrestrained torso was all I was really capable of doing.

I pressed my tongue against the roof of my dry mouth and pried my chapped lips apart.

"Nurse?" I murmured.

The distant sounds of monitors and an occasional muffled moan were all I could hear. I attempted to swallow and tilted my head back slightly.

"Nurse! Nurse! I need a fucking nurse!" I weakly shouted as I fought against the restraints.

Within a few seconds several members of the medical staff were in front of me, all speaking at once.

"Stop. Everybody stop. I can't fucking understand a word you're saying. Who's the senior…" I paused, realizing they weren't Marines, but Army doctors and nurses.

"Who's in charge?" I asked.

A doctor and what appeared to be two nurses stood at the foot of the bed and returned stares of disbelief.

"I'm Doctor Nguyen. I'm the doctor assigned to you," the doctor said.

"Alright. Why am I restrained? I'm not a prisoner, am I?" I asked.

He crossed his arms in front of his chest, inhaled a shallow breath, and shifted his eyes toward the nurse on his left. She returned a glance of uncertainty.

The tone of my voice changed to one of concern.

"Am I?" I asked.

The thought of being charged with crimes against the Geneva Convention began to run through my mind, but as close as I was able to recall, everything I did was according to policy, procedure, my standing orders, and the Uniform Code of Military Justice.

"What the fuck is going on?" I asked at the same time the doctor raised his hand to speak.

"No," he responded. "You are not a prisoner, and that is not why you have been restrained."

The two nurses that flanked him looked at me with concerned eyes as he continued.

"You sustained multiple severe injuries," he said with a nod of his head. "A concussion, lacerations, puncture wounds, a broken jaw, and four gunshot wounds were the most severe wounds."

"You had been treated at the Combat Support Hospital in Baghdad, Iraq, and flown here for..."

"Where's *here*?" Where the fuck am I? Where are my men?" I asked, interrupting him as he spoke.

I gazed into the corridor and watched as two doctors rushed a bloody body down the hallway. As I shifted my focus back to the doctor, I knew one thing, and one thing only. If I wasn't being charged with a crime, I needed to get the fuck out of there and get back to my Marines. As I pulled against the restraints I noticed the audible signal of my heart rate increase on the monitor. I alternated glances between the nurses and the doctor as I waited for a response.

"Mr. Jacob, I'm trying to explain, please settle down and listen..."

"*Staff Sergeant*. I'm Staff Sergeant Jacob. *Mr*. Jacob is my father, and where are my Marines?" I asked.

"Staff Sergeant Jacob. I will have you sedated if you don't settle down," the doctor said.

I relaxed onto the bed and did my best to remain calm. "I'm calm. I have questions, and I expect fucking answers. Where am I, and where are my men? Are any of them here?"

"You are in Landstuhl, Germany at the Landstuhl Regional Medical Center. I have no information regarding your men, Marines, their whereabouts, or their medical condition," he said.

Confused, groggy, weak, and not wanting, but *needing* to find out about my Marines, having them remove my restraints, and allowing me to return to combat was my priority. As my mind fumbled with ideas of ways to coerce them to release me, the doctor continued.

"You attacked your nurse on several occasions. That was our reason behind the restraints. Now that you're conscious and coherent, if you'll promise to comply with our medical recommendations and requirements, I will have the restraints removed," he said.

As I did my best to nod my head, two Marines in dress blues, both officers, walked past the partition. A few seconds later, they stepped into the opening and stared. The silver and gold oak leaves on their uniforms informed me that they were a Lieutenant Colonel and Major.

And I needed to stand at attention when they entered the room.

"Staff Sergeant Jacob," the Lieutenant Colonel said as he entered the makeshift room.

"Sir," I responded with authority. "If you can give the order to have these restraints removed, I'll stand at attention, Sir."

"As you were, Staff Sergeant," he said, relieving me of the requirement to stand at attention.

Personally being visited in the hospital by a Lieutenant Colonel and a Marine Major was something only a handful of Marines could claim. Knowing for certain that something was wrong – and terribly wrong – to prompt them to fly halfway around the world to pay me a visit, I silently waited for them to advise me of their reason for the visit.

"How are you feeling," the Lieutenant Colonel asked as he approached the foot of the bed.

"Rested and ready to return to combat, Sir," I barked in response.

He glanced at the Major and coughed a light laugh.

"Quite a mess your platoon stepped into in Fallujah," he said.

"Yes, Sir. I was only protecting my Marines, Sir. That's all it was," I responded.

He reached toward the Major with an open hand, and the Major handed him a piece of paper. As he unfolded it, my heart raced at the thought of what crimes they were going to charge me with.

"I'm not going to bore you with all of this, Staff Sergeant Jacob, but I'll hit the highlights," he paused and inhaled a shallow breath.

"Without hesitation and with complete disregard for his own safety, Staff Sergeant Jacob, while acting as a Platoon Sergeant during the Second Battle of Fallujah, exposed himself to enemy fire while commanding his fellow Marines to maintain a position of safety. After giving the order to provide medical attention to Marines in his command, he advised First Squad Leader Todelli to carry out a flanking maneuver, distracting the enemy as he crawled across an open street further exposing himself to enemy fire. After sustaining life threatening injuries in the deadly blast of an IED which completely disabled his convoy, Staff Sergeant Jacob positioned himself behind the cover of an abandoned vehicle and single handedly eliminated the three snipers who had been accredited with the death of no less than nine US Marines prior to his platoon's arrival. In doing so, Staff Sergeant Jacob sustained four gunshot wounds, a broken jaw, multiple lacerations, and shrapnel wounds. His actions, however, preserved the lives of his entire platoon. By his undaunted courage, bold fighting spirit, and unwavering devotion to duty in the face of almost certain death, Staff Sergeant Jacob reflected great credit upon himself and upheld the highest traditions of the United States Marine Corps." He paused and lowered the sheet of paper.

"Son, you've been put in for the Bronze Star with Combat 'V'. You're an official war hero," he said with a smile.

Feeling elated to a point of almost shedding tears, and incapable of doing much more, I returned a blank stare.

"I envy your courage," he said as he nodded his head in my direction.

Tied to the bed, filled with emotion, and now with a mouth much drier than it was prior to his speech, I couldn't speak. I glanced toward the side of the bed at the pitcher of water sitting on the table.

"Get these restraints off of my Marine," he bellowed over his shoulder as he reached for the pitcher of water.

The two nurses immediately came to the side of the bed and removed the restraints from my arms and legs. After pouring glass of water and handing me the cup, I took a slow drink, realizing as I did so, it would take time for me to fully recover from my wounds. Aching from head to toe, but unwilling to admit it, I shifted my eyes to the Lieutenant Colonel and cleared my throat.

"My Marines. They're all accounted for? No KIA?" I asked.

"That is affirmative. Your actions saved the entire platoon," he said with a nod.

Thank God.

I exhaled what little breath remained in my lungs and tried to sit up, only to learn the pain in my hip was much greater than I realized.

"Permission to speak freely, Sir?" I asked.

"Granted," he said, his mouth curling into a slight smirk as he spoke.

"With all due respect, I don't want – nor do I need – a medal of valor, Sir. I *need* someone to get me out of here. I don't belong here. I need to get a ride on a transport back to Fallujah and command my men through that operation," I said.

He chuckled and glanced at the Major. As he shifted his eyes in my direction, he continued. "Your commanding officer advised me of your gung-ho hard-charging attitude, and I, we, hell the United States Marine Corps appreciates your willingness and desire to fight, but you're going to be given a medical discharge after what you've been through. They'll be shipping you stateside."

Stateside?

Home?

You're shipping me home?

Emotionally, I collapsed. I felt like he had plunged a knife into my chest. Going home would mean no longer being a Marine, and I couldn't fathom the idea. My heart sank. The mere thought of leaving, especially after seeing the level of fighting we were exposed to in Fallujah made me feel useless, weak, and as if I was letting down the men I had risked my very life to defend. There wasn't another man on earth who would give the level of devotion to my platoon that I had. Under anyone else's command, there would certainly be lives lost, and I couldn't allow that to happen. Going home was not an option.

Not if I was alive and able to fight.

I fought against the pain and did my best to sit upright. I fixed my eyes on the Lieutenant Colonel. "I need to get back to my platoon. I don't want discharged, Sir. I can't be. The two-seven needs combat experienced Marines who have proven themselves. I've never been one to beg for anything, but I'm begging you, Sir. Send me back into combat."

His mouth formed into a full-blown grin as he broke my gaze and turned toward the Major. "Three years into this war, and Staff Sergeant Jacob's got two Purple Hearts, a Bronze Star with Combat 'V', and a ride home on a bird. And all he can think about is the welfare of his Marines and how to get back into battle."

He cleared his throat. "You remind me of someone, Staff Sergeant. My grandfather, who fought for our beloved Corps in the Battle of Bataan in World War II. Crazy bastard begged to be sent back into battle twice after having being wounded, just like you. Marines like you aren't trained, Jacob, they're born. Born and raised by men who I can't help but admire. I tell you what. You get yourself cleared medically and mentally, and I'll get you back to your war."

As much as it wasn't what I should have done from a medical standpoint, and as contrary as I was sure it would be to the doctor's best wishes, I gritted my teeth, moved my legs to the side of the bed, and allowed them to fall to the floor.

As the doctor began to protest, I pulled against the hoses of the I.V., giving myself a little more room.

The Major raised his hands toward the doctor.

"Let him be," he said sternly.

As I stood on my rubbery legs, I cupped my hands and pressed them to the outside center of my thighs, and stood erect.

Marines differed from the other branches of the armed forces, with the exception of the Navy. Marines did not salute officers indoors while not under arms or 'on duty'. As I wasn't wearing my uniform or on duty, a salute wasn't proper protocol.

But standing at attention was.

I fully realized he had no expectation of me standing at attention and acknowledging his order. I didn't do it for me, or to show off, prove anything, or gain his approval. I did it as a matter of respect, and because as a Marine, I felt I had to.

"Make myself mentally fit and physically capable. Aye-aye, Sir," I said as I clenched my jaw muscles and fought back the tears.

Both he and the Major stood erect.

"As you were, Staff Sergeant," he said.

I exhaled, did my best to perform an about face maneuver, and collapsed onto the bed.

That afternoon as I slept out of sheer exhaustion, I dreamt of raising a child.

A son.

One with the same moral values that were instilled in me by my father.

And I slept more peacefully than I had in longer than I cared to try and remember.

CHAPTER SEVEN

Early Winter 2005, Wichita, Kansas, USA

She asked, and because she did, I had to tell her the truth. One thing I had never done – and never would do – was tell a lie. My concerns were whether or not she would be able to accept the truth as being what was in our best interest as a couple.

"You can't. They've got to let you out. Alec, you've been shot to pieces. You have pieces of metal inside of you. You were…" She paused and began to cry.

I reached for her shoulder and pulled her against me. "Babe, don't cry."

She sobbed for a moment, caught her breath, and leaned away from me. With her face filled with a combination of concern and fear, and her eyes still dripping droplets of hope down her cheeks, she continued.

"You were in the hospital for two months, Alec. Two months. You've been…you've been shot over and over. I asked Steve. And I've looked on the internet. *I know*. You *can* get discharged. Have they offered you a release?" she asked as she wiped the tears from her cheeks.

Steve, my best friend since childhood, was a trauma surgeon at the local hospital, and an excellent source of information and support for her. Since my first deployment, she had used him as a sounding board for her concerns, always receiving well thought out replies and opinions.

A wealth of knowledge and a very sensible man in general, I trusted him with not only my life, but Suzanne's. Truthfully, if it wasn't for him, I suspected Suzanne may have given up on me many years in the past.

"Let's have a seat," I said.

She raised her hands to her face and nodded her head as she rubbed her fingertips against her eyes. I realized she probably felt embarrassed for crying, as it was something she never did, but I didn't view her as weak for doing so. As easy as it was for me to want to return to the war, it was impossible for me to fully understand why I had the desire to continue to fight. My beliefs on the matter were mine and mine alone, and came from nothing other than a self-performed diagnosis of myself.

"You can barely walk," she said as she sat down on the couch.

I sat down in the chair across from her. "I ran three back to back six minute miles this morning."

"You have a limp," she said.

I chuckled. "Marine Corps swagger."

"Alec..." she said sarcastically, her voice trailing off as she shook her head.

I nodded my head in acknowledgement of her sarcastic tone. "My hip hurts a little, but it's much better than it was. And my heel is tender, but it's getting better too."

"So you're justifying it? Going back? Can you get out? Have you asked?" she asked.

I pressed the palms of my hands together and held them in front of my chest for a moment as I studied her. She was a beautiful woman, and not only in her appearance. She had remained by my side through four years of me fighting in the war, and she had done so, for the most part, alone.

Suzanne was one of the strongest people I had ever met. Her ability to accept what most would be incapable of even considering was instrumental to our success as a military couple. I realized I had to tell her the truth, but explaining how I felt would be difficult – if even possible. I folded my cupped hands open, lowered my face into my hands, and sat for a moment, breathing into the palms of my hands. After a moment's thought, I slid my hands from my face, and gazed across the room at her.

"Let me try to explain," I said.

She wiped what little remnants of tears remained on her cheeks. "I'm listening."

"While I was in Germany, two officers came to let me know I was going to be pinned with a medal for valor in the Second Battle of Fallujah. They told me I could get a medical discharge…"

"Take it," she blurted excitedly.

I raised my hand as I cleared my throat. "Hear me out."

With wide eyes, she nodded her head eagerly.

Damn, I hate to do this to you.

"I begged them to let me stay. I talked to the doctors, and I lied to the psychiatrist to get a clean psych-eval. He granted it, declared me fit for service, and I denied the discharge. I'm sorry, Suzanne, but I'm going back," I said.

She sat, far less emotional than I expected her to be, and glared at me. After what seemed to be an hour, but was probably a matter of thirty seconds, she stood, turned away, and began to cry.

I stood from my seat. With her back facing me, she raised her right hand and held it in the air between us. "Just give me a minute."

"Suzanne…"

"Give me a minute, Alec," she said, her voice filled with emotion.

I sat down in the chair and waited, wondering how many other men in my position would have taken the offered discharge and walked away. There was no doubt in my mind that the war had changed me, but as I sat waiting for her to gather herself, I wondered just how much I had actually changed. I raised my hands to my face, pressed my palms to my cheeks, and covered my eyes with the tips of my fingers. I had always been able to think more clearly with my eyes closed, and sat hoping some newfound clarity would wash over me.

My mind immediately went to thoughts of my Marines, and I filled with guilt for sitting in the living room with Suzanne while they were dodging bullets and returning fire under someone else's command.

Someone far less capable of protecting them than me.

"You know," I said as I lifted my head. "Most of the men think I'm lucky or something."

She turned toward me and wiped her eyes. "And you think you have some sixth sense about danger or whatever."

I nodded my head. "Men are going to die in this war, Suzanne. I can't change that. But what I can do is do my best to protect the men in my command. In my platoon. And in doing so, we rid this earth of what is evil, one bad guy at a time."

"You know what's sad? I can't argue with you. I want to, but I can't, because you won't listen. You think you're a superhero or something. It's been almost five years, Alec. *Five years.* Five years of me sitting here crying myself to sleep, waiting on the next letter, and hoping each time I go to the mailbox I'm not going to be met by two Marines in dress blues who are here to tell me the man I love is coming home in a god damned flag covered box."

Apparently I wasn't the only one worried about me coming home in a casket.

I stood from my seat. "I can't sit here and let my men die."

She stomped her foot on the floor so hard she shook the pictures hanging on the wall. "You're not *obligated* to protect them. Your *obligation* is to be my husband."

I pressed my cupped hands to the outside of my thighs and stood erect. After clearing my throat, I recited the oath I had taken upon entry to the Marine Corps.

"I, Alec James Jacob, do solemnly swear that I will support and defend the Constitution of the United States against all enemies, foreign and domestic; that I will bear true faith and allegiance to the same; and that I will obey the orders of the President of the United States and the orders of the officers appointed over me, according to regulations and the Uniform Code of Military Justice. So help me God," I said, pronouncing each and every word clearly and precisely.

She blinked her eyes and stared.

"I took an oath before God, before the flag, and in the presence of an officer of the United States Marine Corps; and, I took an oath to be your husband. You took one as well, Suzanne. For better or for worse. In sickness and in health. Well, this is the *worse* and the *sickness*. I'm upholding my end of the two oaths I took. I'm still your husband. And, until this god forsaken war is over, I'm going to be a Marine," I said.

"You're always right, aren't you?" she asked.

I cocked my head to the side, shrugged my shoulders, and smirked.

"Go find Osama or Saddam or whoever it is you're trying to find, kill that son-of-a-bitch, and come home, okay?" she said as she slowly walked in my direction.

"So, we're good on this?" I asked as I spread my arms wide.

"As good as we're going to be," she said as we embraced.

And that was all I could have asked for, because even when Suzanne and I were at our worst, we were better than any other married couple on earth.

And I loved her for it.

CHAPTER EIGHT

Summer 2005, Haditha, Iraq

In a briefing with my commander, I learned a six-man Marine sniper unit had been overrun outside the city of Haditha, and all six men were eventually killed. Five of the Marines died relatively quickly, possibly executed as soon as they were identified as US Marines. The one Marine who lived – while covered in blood and stripped of his uniform – was paraded through the city with the five dead members of his unit, and the event was videotaped and played on Iraqi television. Later, the sixth Marine's throat was cut by his captors.

Two days later, *Operation Quick Strike* began, and 1,000 Marines were sent into the city – not as a retaliatory action – but in an attempt to identify and capture the insurgents who had overtaken the city. At the onset of the operation, an amphibious assault vehicle carrying 16 Marines hit a roadside bomb, and 15 of the 16 Marines were immediately killed in the blast. The one living occupant was burned over most of his body, and wasn't expected to live. The crater left in the earth by the bomb was large enough to fit a four-bedroom home inside of it.

On the second day of Operation Quick Strike, it was determined the US Marines were outnumbered, and command likened the city to Fallujah, only worse. House to house searches, close quarters combat, and gun battles in an area the size of a living room were a common occurrence. In short, savage extremists had taken over the city, and were going to any length to kill the US Marines or the civilian population who opposed them.

Every Marine being sent into the city wanted revenge for the deaths of their brethren. The 115-degree daytime temperatures, severe wind, and blowing sand only added to the tension. Our convoy arrived at 0800, and the sun pressed down on us like a heavy weight.

As we approached the city, smoke bellowed from the tops of half of the homes and buildings. Bombs exploded every few seconds, and the earth beneath our Humvee shook repeatedly as we slowly rolled into the city.

"We're going to fucking die in this one, Staff Sergeant Jacob," Parsons complained as we hit the outskirts of town.

I shifted my eyes toward him for a split second. He looked no different than anyone else in my platoon. He was scared, and his eyes clearly showed it. Given the amount of insurgents in the city, and the temperament of the group who had executed the Marines, we were likely to be in for one hell of a fight and everyone realized it.

Price tilted his helmet up slightly and shook his head. "Jacob is immortal. Only motherfucker that can kill Jacob, is Jacob."

"Enough about dying. Nobody's fucking dying. We're going to stomp in this motherfucker, capture insurgents, and send their asses to Al Asad Airbase for interrogation," I said. "And then we're going to finish that fucking football game."

"Oorah!" Price grunted.

I didn't think I was immortal, but I was beginning to believe I was *something*. After five solid years of fighting, I had sustained many injuries, but no one had killed me. The eerie vision of the C-130 filled with caskets still haunted my dreams, and I suspected it always would. Be it luck or the gracious hand of God that kept me from it, however, my body had yet to be shipped home in a casket.

And I was grateful.

"First and second squad take the far side, and third squad will go house to house, just like we discussed. If you *think* they're insurgents, they're insurgents, is that understood?" I asked as we assembled alongside the edge of the street.

"Oorah!" the squad leaders barked.

"We need to capture as many of these motherfuckers as we can. If you're threatened, don't think, just kill. Understood?" I asked.

Another *Oorah* rang out from the squad leaders and the Marines in the accompanying squads. The sound of small weapons fire in the background filled the air. With my eyes filled with sand, and my uniform soaked from sweat, I gave the signal to begin the house to house search.

Fifteen minutes into the search and we had captured four insurgents and found two weapons caches, one large enough to supply a battalion of men. Both weapons caches were in the homes of civilians, making it immediately apparent not only that we were in the right place, but that the city had been overrun by insurgents who were taking over the homes of civilians in their attempt to blend in.

As the Marines of third squad searched another home, an argument broke out between the occupants of the small house and the squad leader. In an effort to keep things as peaceful as possible, and to prevent tempers from flaring even higher than they already were, I stepped into the home to evaluate the situation.

"This motherfucker ain't sayin' shit, Staff Sergeant. Got twenty fucking AK's hid behind that shitty fucking bed over there, and he just grunts when we try to ask him anything. Vingelli's got a woman and a little girl in the back, and they're both fucking screaming," he said excitedly as I stepped into the small home.

The homes in Iraq, at least the ones I had been inside of, were far different than the homes in the United States. I was aware that the country also had mansions, and homes similar to Beverly Hill's offerings, but the typical civilian home consisted of one large room where the family stayed, and a place to cook; and that was it. Some, but not all, had bathrooms. To the typical civilian in Iraq, having a rug thrown on the floor was a luxury.

As I stepped into the rear room of the house, I found a woman and a girl who was no more than twelve-years-old being detained by two of my Marines. The woman remained quiet until the girl began to scream, then the woman would begin to plead with the girl, obviously telling her to remain calm. The scene was far from calm, and I realized as soon as I entered the room if I didn't take charge of the situation I would have two dead civilian women in my daily report.

"Settle the fuck down. I assume no one speaks English?" I asked of the two Marines.

"Fuck yeah they do, but they ain't sayin' shit. Cocksuckers got AK's in the front room. They're fucking al-Qaeda," one of the Marines responded.

I turned to face the woman. "English. Do you speak English?"

Both she and the girl responded in Arabic, shaking their heads as they spoke. The woman seemed nothing but concerned for her family's welfare, but the girl seemed to have something she wanted to say, and wasn't interested in being quiet.

Although it wasn't a common occurrence, women and children

had opposed Marines in previous battles, shooting small arms, using grenades, and detonating roadside bombs. As sickening as it was to do so, on occasion, women and children had to be killed. In determining whether or not the person was a threat to my men, I couldn't let gender come into play. Every person must be assumed a threat until it was determined they were *not* a threat. That determination came by no other than me, and was based on nothing other than my gut instinct.

To date I had yet to be wrong.

"Vingelli, go get the Terp. I think we've got a situation here, but this woman and her daughter aren't al-Qaeda," I said as I studied the eyes of the girl.

Her eyes told me she was scared, but not of my men. Her fear was deeper. In my opinion, she feared the men who had left the weapons in her home. Unintimidated by my uniform and weapon, she made eye contact with me, opened her brown eyes wide, and pressed her tanned hands against the hips of her red cotton pants. She began to babble so quickly even if I spoke Arabic I wouldn't have been able to keep up. Calmly, I reached over and brushed the dust from the floral pattern shirt she wore, and earned a grin as I did so.

"They might not be, but the old man is. He isn't responding to a god damned thing we ask him. He's keeping fucking secrets. Ship his ass to Al Asad and let the CIA water board him for an hour and he'll give it up," Vingelli said as he turned away.

With two of my Marines guarding the front door of the residence, and the entire family in the kitchen, I studied each of the people we detained. An entire family incapable of speaking with nothing other than their eyes, they needed to say no more as far as I was concerned. They feared the same men we were searching for and wanted to simply be left alone.

They were one of the reasons I was fighting this war.

To provide them with the freedom to live a life free of fear and the threat of harm would satisfy me to no end, but after five long years of fighting and seeing no progress, I had my doubts if it could or would ever happen.

"Who's got candy?" I asked as I reached into my pocket.

I found one sand covered peppermint in the pocket of my trousers.

"Fuck these motherfuckers. I say we load up the weapons and kill these cocksuckers; that little girl included," PFC Mann said.

I clenched my jaw, inhaled through my nose, and turned to face him. "And it's a good god damned thing you're not in fucking charge, PFC Mann. I've been fighting in his god forsaken war longer than you've been in the Corps, and I'm the NCO of this platoon. One more suggestion like that out of you, and I'll bring charges against your sorry ass, is that understood?"

He lowered his chin and shifted his eyes to the floor. "Yes, Staff Sergeant."

"God fucking damn. We're here to protect people like this, not kill them," I said as I turned toward the sound of someone entering the home.

The platoon interpreter came into the small room, making it far more crowded than I was comfortable with.

"Everyone out except the Terp and me," I said as I waved my left hand toward the front room.

"Ask the little girl who's weapons they are," I said as I handed the girl my peppermint.

She accepted the candy, unwrapped it, and poked it in her mouth. As her eyes changed from worry to what I expected was the surprise of the candy's sweetness, the interpreter began to question her.

He questioned her in Arabic, and she immediately responded, tossing her dirty black hair from side-to-side as she spoke.

"She says men brought them here over a month ago. They've been forcing the residents to provide them shelter, food, and weapons storage," he said.

I turned toward the girl, smiled, and nodded my head.

"Ask her why her father isn't speaking," I said.

Another line of questioning in Arabic by the interpreter, and the girl, clearly frustrated, began to cry. After a moment, she turned to her father, who shook his head from side to side.

I pursed my lips and studied the father. As he shifted his eyes to meet my gaze, I spoke to the interpreter.

"Tell her, hell, tell them all. Tell them if they don't tell me why he isn't responding, I'll assume he's al-Qaeda and take him to Al Asad and lock his ass up. Between you and me, I know he's not, but he's keeping something a secret and I want to know what it is," I said, my eyes still locked on his.

He alternated glances between them all as he spoke. Calmly, as he explained everything in Arabic, the girl began to scream her response.

"Holy shit," the interpreter said as he raised his hand and covered his mouth.

"What?" I asked as I shifted my eyes from the elderly man to the interpreter.

As he shook his head from side to side and lowered his hand the girl and the woman began to cry.

"What?" I asked again.

"The men who came here were Saddam Hussein supporters. She

said they demanded they be allowed to keep weapons here. Her father opposed them." He paused and shook his head.

As he turned toward the elderly man and nodded his head, he continued. "The father told the men when they came that Saddam Hussein was a coward and a murderer. He went on to tell them the US Marines were going to capture and kill Saddam, and that they should surrender."

He tilted his head toward the father. "They held him down and cut out his tongue for opposing Saddam."

I released my weapon and crossed my arms in front of my chest. "Motherfucker. Do they know where these cocksuckers are hiding? Ask the little girl."

"I think she does," he responded.

"Well god damn it, ask her," I said as I shifted my eyes to the girl.

A lengthy exchange followed, and the interpreter sighed heavily.

"She does. She said she's been following them nightly. She wanted to get revenge for what they did to her father, but she said she's too small," he said.

"Tell her I'm big enough. And how many of them?" I asked. "How many of these motherfuckers can she lead us to?"

After a quick series of questions, he sighed heavily. "Twenty. And get this. She said they're the ones who cut the Marines throat in the street the other day."

I shifted my eyes toward the girl. "Is she sure?"

"Don't need to ask, she already answered. She's sure," he said.

"Vingelli!" I shouted.

Vingelli rushed into the room. "Yes, Staff Sergeant."

I lowered myself into a crouched position and reached for the girl's hand. After a few seconds, she reached out and gripped my hand in hers. Her eyes lowered to my free hand, studied it, and slowly shifted back to meet mine.

"Get on the radio and find the LT. I need him in here immediately. And get first and second squad's leaders in here. I want the entire first squad guarding the front of this house, and the second squad at an oblique to the rear, by the alley. Anyone tries to get in, and I mean *anyone*, I want them detained. If they oppose, kill 'em. And no one gets to this girl, is that understood?" I said, attempting to refrain from sounding excited.

"Yes, Staff Sergeant," he responded.

"And get me as much candy in here as you can," I said as he turned away.

"Candy. Roger that," he said.

It sickened me to think of what was currently going on in the country, and what atrocities had been happening for years before our arrival. The ethnic cleansing of families in the north, mass graves filled with women and children, and the torture of civilians for opposing the ideas or actions of savage leaders was common.

The attacks on the United States soil started the war and brought me to Iraq, but as the war progressed and I was exposed to more and more locals, the thought of making the country a better place for people like the three before me was what kept me there. I was quite sure my ideas, beliefs, and mental support system was different than most of the other Marines, but for me, it kept me fighting for something I truly believed in.

***

"With all due respect Lieutenant, I've been in this motherfucker since it started. If we don't get them out of here and protect them, they'll be killed five minutes after we pull out," I said.

"We don't have the ability to protect them," he said flatly.

"We *do* have the ability," I said, raising the tone of my voice slightly. "It appears one of us doesn't have the *desire*."

He shifted his eyes from me to the girl and back. "How do you know she's telling the truth? She's what? Ten years old for Christ's sake?"

"Kids and drunks are the two most truthful motherfuckers on earth, *Sir*," I said.

He pursed his lips and shook his head. "Not a good enough reason."

I fixed my eyes on his and glared my best *don't fuck with me* glare. "I've been shot six times. Six, Sir. I've survived two bomb blasts, killed four snipers, and fifteen other insurgents who were trying to kill either me or my Marines, while you, Sir, were humping your desk. The only fucking reason I'm standing here alive right now is because I know things other Marines don't, you included. The girl is telling the god damned truth."

As he narrowed his eyes the muscles on his jaw flared. "Humping my desk, Staff Sergeant?"

I tightened my jaw and shifted my eyes to meet his.

"That is correct, Sir. Humping your desk. I understand rear echelon Marines are needed, but it's the front line Marines, Sir, who are required to live and breathe this shit. And no one who's spent the last five years sitting behind a desk with their cock in their respective hand is going to tell me right from wrong on the front lines," I said through my teeth.

"War hero or not, Staff Sergeant, I could have you demoted for speaking to me in that manner. I am an officer, and need I remind you, although you are a *non-commissioned* officer, you are an enlisted Marine, not an officer. You will address me with respect, and you will…"

"How many times have you been shot? How many battles have you fought in? How many Marines did you hold in your arms while you waited one motherfucking minute too long for a Corpsman or a medevac? How many of your *officer* brothers died, Sir, in your god damned arms? Shit, Sir, how many times have you even fired your fucking weapon?" I interrupted.

The muscles in his jaw loosened, and he stared back at me blankly, remaining silent.

That's what I thought.

"I'm not sure I can trust an Iraqi girl to…" he began.

I shook my head from side to side. "*My* reputation is on the line, Sir, not yours. Radio the Battalion Commander, *Sir*. Advise him this girl can lead us to the men who murdered the Marine sniper unit. See what *he* says. If you don't want to radio him, don't. We'll pull out. But be advised, *Sir*. My daily report will be accurate, truthful, and detailed. And in it, *Sir*, I will not only detail the girl's message to the Terp, but mine to you – including your denial of my request to find the men who murdered the six Marine snipers, *Sir*."

He inhaled a long slow breath through his nose, studied me, and eventually exhaled through his mouth. My *fuck off* glare didn't change one bit.

"Get me a radio in here," he shouted to the Corporal guarding the door.

He left the room and spoke on the radio in private. Five minutes later, he returned with a whole new attitude. I stood in the corner of the room facing the door, holding the girl's hand in mine. With her mouth full of candy, and her mother and father waiting for a response from the Battalion Commander, I shifted my eyes to meet the Lieutenant's.

His face stern and his eyes fierce, he shifted his gaze toward each Marine in the room. "Be advised, we are to protect this family at any and all costs. Staff Sergeant Jacob, advise the family they will not return to these quarters. Search the premises thoroughly and secure the weapons. After the family gathers their personal effects, escort them out the rear of the residence and to the vehicles. Any effort to detain this family is to be met with deadly force. Staff Sergeant Jacob, that little girl is *your* responsibility."

"Aye-aye, Sir," I said.

I turned toward the interpreter. "Tell them what he said. Tell them we'll protect them, and they'll more than likely be given a new life in the United States. And tell the father I'm sorry for what he's gone through, but tell him I'm personally going to make sure I make the men who did this to him pay for what they did."

As the interpreter began to speak, I gazed down at the girl. Her mouth filled with candy and her eyes filled with hope, she listened intently as he explained what we were going to do.

"Tell them that I appreciate their courage," I said.

As he explained what I said, the little girl squeezed my hand and smiled. I didn't speak her language, but I didn't need to. Her eyes told me all I needed to know. She trusted me.

She trusted me because I placed trust in her.

Two days later, using a map we prepared based on the information we received from the little girl, we captured the insurgents responsible for killing the Marines in a raid of their hideout. Two of the insurgents were killed in the mission, one of which was killed for resisting, but only after he admitted to cutting the tongue out of the mouth of the girl's father. The remainder of the men were detained, interrogated, and eventually sent to a P.O.W. camp.

No Marines were injured and I was offered a promotion based on my intuitive nature, stellar performance in the field, and quick thinking. The promotion would have all but assured me free passage through the remainder of the war without being harmed.

I denied the promotion.

Because real Marines don't hump desks.

CHAPTER NINE

Fall 2012, Wichita, Kansas, USA

Twelve years after the war started, and only after the last infantry Marines were shipped out of Afghanistan, I returned to the United States. With a chest full of medals and a soul full of pride, I landed at an airport and was met by no one other than a man trying to sell me cell phone service.

There was no celebration, no parade, and no welcome home banners. The aisles in the airport were not lined with appreciative citizens. No one shook my hand for playing a large part in keeping the country free of terrorists. Not one person patted me on the back for the pieces of shrapnel I would carry with me for the rest of my life, or for the bullet holes my body was riddled with.

After giving my country and the residents in it all I had to give and watching so many of my Marines die attempting to do the same, I felt as if the country wanted to believe the war didn't even happen.

I knew better.

I lived with the recollection of it every moment of every day.

I did my best to put the war behind me and focus my attention on the one woman who supported me unconditionally throughout the war, my wife. My escape from the day to day difficulties associated with civilian life was riding my motorcycle, and I soon found comfort in riding in a motorcycle club with a few old friends and some men I never met, but quickly grew to trust.

Teddy reached up, wiped the bottom of his beard with a napkin, and turned toward Erik and then to face me. As he placed what was left of his hamburger onto his plate, he cocked one eyebrow and leaned into the edge of the table.

"This fuckin' hamburger's the biggest son-of-a-bitch I ever seen. I fuckin' swear, how in the hell can an establishment sell a burger like this for five fucking bucks and make money?" he asked, shifting his eyes back and forth between Erik and me.

Teddy was six foot two at least, and weighed probably 260 pounds. His beard was full and an easy four inches long, covering his entire face. His club name for years fit him well, *Bear.* In a recent drunken stupor, he had wrecked into a long line of bikes in front of a bar, and knocked all of them over, earning the new club name of *Crash.* He was a practical joker, uneducated, and as funny as any comedian. He was also trustworthy, and I gave him the same trust I gave my Marine brothers.

I nodded my head toward his mug of beer. "What'd that mug of beer cost?"

He gripped the handle and raised the glass into the air. "This big fucker? Six bucks. But god damn, look at this monster."

I swallowed the bite of burger I was chewing on and chuckled as I studied the glass mug. The walls of it were an inch thick, and the bottom of it was two inches thick. The interior of the mug, if filled to the top, might have held twelve ounces of beer. On the outside it appeared to be filled with much more beer than it was.

"So, they make money by charging fools like you six bucks for twelve ounces of beer, but they deliver it in a cool mug," I said, laughing as I spoke.

"Bein' over there in that sand pit for the last ten years fucked up your sense of measure, Brother. You're probably thinking in centimeters and meters instead of inches and feet," he said with a nod of his head. "This fucker's twice the size of that bottle."

I glanced at Erik. Although something seemed to be bothering him, he forced a smile and leaned back into his seat. The most sensible of the group of men I was riding with, and the president of the motorcycle club, he was a psychiatrist by education, but lived off of his wealth and didn't practice medicine. Considering his education, it came as no surprise his club name was *Doc*.

"Whether he's measuring it in inches or centimeters doesn't matter, Crash. The fucking mug is thick glass and holds very little liquid," Erik stated.

Teddy narrowed his eyes and stared in disbelief. "What do you know about beer? Shit, Doc, you don't even drink."

Erik leaned forward and rested his tattooed forearm on the edge of the table. "I know if I took the radius of the interior of that mug in inches, squared the number, and then multiplied by 3.14, and then multiplied by the depth in inches, I'd have the volume. Then, smart ass, if I divided that by 2, I'd have the amount of ounces that cup held. Roughly speaking, that is."

"Well, I ain't a fuckin' rocket scientist or a fuckin' doctor, Brother. I'm a biker, a fighter, and I know a good burger and a cold god damned beer when I see 'em. But I also know you two fuckers are full of shit," Teddy said as he drank the remaining beer in his mug.

The waitress walked up to the side of the table and grinned as she pressed her hands into the sides of her hips. "Big burger, huh?"

Teddy nodded his head. "Sure as fuck is. Good son-of-a-bitch, too."

"Can I get another beer?" I asked.

"Sure," she responded. "Anything else?"

"Bring me another frosty mug," Teddy said as he raised his empty mug in the air.

"Bring him a new mug, would you?" I asked.

She nodded her head and grinned. "Sure."

"So, Doc and I was talkin'," Teddy said as he reached for his burger. "You been gone for a bit…"

I shrugged my shoulders and stared.

"You and Doc decided I've been gone for a bit? And I thought you said you weren't a rocket scientist," I said sarcastically.

"No, god damn it, just listen. I wasn't fuckin' done talkin'. So Doc and me was talkin', and we kinda decided we needed to have a talk, you know, like just bring you up to speed on…" He paused and leaned to the side, shifting his focus to Erik.

Seated beside Erik, I turned to face him. Still maintaining eye contact on Teddy, he narrowed his gaze and relaxed into his seat.

"What?" Teddy snapped as he tossed his hands in the air. "I don't know what to tell him."

The waitress slid a mug and a bottle of beer onto the table. "Anything else?"

"The check," I said as I raised my index finger.

She nodded her head. "Be right back."

"First things first," I said as I poured my beer into Teddy's empty mug.

The mug held the twelve ounces of beer, and had an inch to spare. It looked identical to the mug of beer he was delivered.

He stared at the mug, shifted his eyes to his new mug, and slid the new mug beside the one I had just filled. They were identical. He narrowed his eyes and stared at the two mugs.

"How big of bottle is that?" he asked.

I pointed at the label and held it between us. "Twelve ounces."

"No wonder this fucker's got cheap burgers," he murmured.

As the waitress placed the check on the table, a guy seated three booths down from where we were seated raised his hand in the air and whistled a loud shrill whistle to get her attention. Still standing at the end of our table, she glanced in his direction and turned to face our table again, rolling her eyes as she faced us.

He whistled again, this time louder.

I pushed myself out of the booth and turned toward the whistler. As his eyes met mine, he slumped into his seat.

I nodded my head toward Teddy. "You can finish your story when I get back."

"Stay here," I told the waitress as I stood.

"Oh shit," I heard Teddy say as I walked away.

I walked to the table, glanced at the two men who were seated across from each other, and fixed my eyes on the one who was whistling. Both were in their mid-twenties, looked like former high school jocks, and were dressed in hockey jerseys.

"You lose your dog?" I asked as I folded my arms in front of my chest.

"I was just, I was trying to just…" he stammered.

I raised my hand in the air to stop him from continuing. I wasn't interested in hearing whatever he had to say.

"She's a woman, not a dog. Do you understand me?" I asked.

He nodded his head.

"Do you fucking understand me?" I asked through my teeth.

"Yes, Sir," he responded with a nod of his head.

I uncrossed my arms and flexed my chest. "That's better. Now, when she comes to help you, *if* she comes to help you, apologize. And don't do it again. It's rude, and it makes you look like an asshole. In the future, if you want the waitress, wave at her and smile. Understood?"

"Yes, Sir," he said.

I turned, walked back to the table where we were seated, and sat down.

As I shifted my eyes toward the waitress, I tilted my head toward the whistler. "He wants to apologize."

"Thank you," she said with a grin.

As she walked away, I glanced at Teddy. "You were saying?"

Teddy lifted his mug of beer and spoke over the top of the glass. "Doc?"

"What the fuck is going on?" I asked, shifting my eyes back and forth between them.

"I'm going to cut right to it," Erik said. "Your wife. She's been spending a lot of time with that friend of yours, Steve."

I shrugged my shoulders. "He's a friend. Hell, he's my best friend. I'm sure he was just comforting her while I was gone."

Teddy lowered his mug, fixed his eyes on mine, and raised his eyebrows. I turned toward Erik. He shifted his eyes to the table, stared for a moment, and met my gaze.

"You need to have a talk with her," he said.

As much as I didn't want it to, my heart hurt. Regardless of what comfort she had found in Steve while I was away, I was sure we could get through it with a little conversation. What most men would perceive as inappropriate I would probably accept. I was away for a little more than a decade, and to think my wife wouldn't seek comfort from someone would be foolish.

"I'll do that," I said as I reached for my wallet.

I opened the bill folder only to find the ticket had been paid. A cash receipt sat in the folder.

"I was going to pay for this," I said.

Teddy nodded his head toward me. "Half a dozen bullet holes and a pound of steel in your ass? I think you already did."

"I appreciate it," I said with a nod.

"Appreciate what you done," he said. "Just have that talk with your wife."

I lifted my beer and held it between us. He lifted his half-empty mug and clanked the glass against mine.

"As soon as we're done here," I said.

I wanted their opinions to be wrong, but if the war taught me one thing, it taught me to expect the unexpected.

But in this particular circumstance, I wasn't prepared for the unexpected.

CHAPTER TEN

Fall 2012, Wichita, Kansas, USA

I sat across the street from the coffee shop and watched as Suzanne pulled in, walked inside, and met Steve with a hug. After a few minutes of sitting and drinking coffee, they stood, hugged again, and went their separate ways.

Certainly nothing that would have alarmed me in the past, but considering the input from my brothers in the MC, I decided their meeting warranted a slightly more in-depth investigation. Still sitting in the adjacent parking lot on my motorcycle, I pulled my cell phone out and dialed Suzanne's number.

"Hey, Babe, where are you?" I asked.

"On my way home," she responded.

"I just stopped at the gas station. Want to get a coffee?" I asked.

"Actually, I'm pulling into the drive now, I'd have to turn around," she said.

That's a lie, you're two miles from the house.

"Alright, I'll be there in a bit. What's for dinner?" I asked.

"I was going to make burgers," she said.

"Sounds good, see you in a bit," I said.

"Okay, love you," she said.

"Love you, too," I said.

I hung up the phone, pushed it into my pocket, and sat on the seat of my bike staring blankly toward the western sky. As the late fall sun came to a rest along the horizon, I started my bike and took the short ride home.

They were the longest two miles of my life.

CHAPTER ELEVEN

Fall 2012, Wichita, Kansas, USA

I wiped my hands on my napkin, reached for my glass of tea, and took a slow drink as I studied her. I didn't want to believe anything had changed while I was away, and I still hoped it had not, but I was prepared to find out. I needed to have her full attention when I spoke to her, so my manner of questioning her needed to be more formal than informal.

"Suzanne, we need to talk," I said.

"Okay," she said as she looked up from her plate.

I pressed my elbows onto the table and rested my chin in my hands. "So, while I was gone, did you and Steve ever become more than friends?"

Her eyes shifted downward slightly. "No."

Bad question. Lead her into it Jacob, just like an interrogation.

"Explain your most intimate encounter with Steve," I said.

"What? Why?" she asked.

"Some of the guys I ride with said they've been seeing you two together a lot," I said flatly.

"We're friends," she responded.

I nodded my head. "I realize that. Entertain me. Explain your most intimate encounter with him."

"I can't believe you're asking me this," she said.

"Well, I am," I responded.

"Our most intimate encounter," she said.

"Well, you know, we met for coffee, and we met for dinner, just to talk while you were gone. He comforted me, Alec. He's a great friend to us both. Uhhm, I'd say," she paused, and her eyes immediately darted to my left side and slightly upward.

"Well, we hugged on several occasions, and he kissed me several times, but not kissed me, kissed me. You know, on the cheek," she said.

She's lying.

"What did he typically wear?" I asked.

"Wear?" she asked.

"Yes. What did he wear? You know, typically." I asked.

"That's a weird question," she said.

Her eyes shifted to my right and upward. "Normally he wore his scrubs, but sometimes he wore jeans and a tee shirt. Mostly his boots. I can't believe you're asking me this."

Well, that was truthful, at least.

I didn't know to what degree they had been intimate, or if they even had, but I did know she was lying about their intimacy. To what degree she was lying would be hard to tell. As I sat and studied the woman I absolutely adored, my blood pressure increased with each tick of the second hand on my watch.

"He ever stick his cock in your mouth?" I asked.

She glared at me and her mouth went agape. "I can't believe you asked me that."

"And I'm not surprised you didn't answer," I said as I stood.

"What's that supposed to mean?" she asked as she stood and crossed her arms in front of her chest.

"You lied to me," I said.

"What? Lied to you? I can't believe…" she began.

"Suzanne, you know that I've been trained to interrogate people, right? You realize I can tell when you lie? When I asked what was your most intimate encounter, you made up everything you said. You lied. Now, I'll ask you one more time, have you ever had his fucking cock in your mouth?" I asked in what she had always described as my *mean voice*.

And she began to cry.

"Please don't do anything to him," she said as she began to sob.

"God fucking damn. Did you fuck him?" I asked.

Her eyes fell to the floor. "Please, don't do anything to him."

I couldn't believe it. I could almost dismiss it if she had fucked some random stranger one night in a hotel while I was gone. But to fuck my best friend, and while I was fighting for the same freedoms that let her be the independent woman that she was…

As my head began to spin and my mind immediately went to violence as a means of resolve, I mentally admitted I had been gone for twelve years on and off, and I fully understood the time I was away had to be extremely tough on her. I needed to be understanding of the difficulties she went through, not quick to condemn or react.

"Alright, listen. Whatever happened, happened. It's over. Never again. We can get through this. We can," I said, more in an effort to reassure myself than to reassure her.

I folded my arms in front of my chest and gazed down at the floor. As she continued to cry, I provided no comfort, only serious thought on the matter before us. As I shifted my eyes up toward her face, I had very little sympathy for how she felt. I was sure I felt worse, for many reasons.

"Do you love me?" I asked.

"With all my heart," she blubbered.

"Well, that's all we need. We'll make this work. I'll talk to him…"

"Don't hurt him," she begged.

"I'll talk to him, that's all. But you are *done* seeing him, meeting with him, everything," I said sternly.

"Do you understand me?" I asked.

She nodded her head.

I inhaled a deep breath and cocked one eyebrow.

She continued to sob. "Yes…Yes, I…I understand."

"No dinner, no coffee, no secret meetings, no *nothing*," I said.

"Okay," she murmured.

That night, as I stared up at the ceiling of our bedroom, I wondered just how separated from me she had become in the twelve years I was at war. Regardless, I convinced myself we could get through it. Because in the end, I still loved her.

And love was the most powerful thing in my arsenal.

CHAPTER TWELVE

Fall 2012, Wichita, Kansas, USA

Two weeks after my discussion with Suzanne, she called me stating she was going to be late from work, and explained that she was on her way to get something to eat. As we spoke on the phone, I recognized the music in the background as being Steve's favorite indie rock artist, *The Weeks*. Knowing Suzanne's car didn't have satellite radio, and that local stations didn't play that particular artist, I questioned her as to whether or not she was with Steve at the time.

An *oh my God, he knows we're together* whisper followed, and that was all it took.

I regretted being as considerate as I had been regarding her relationship with Steve. I felt used, cheated, betrayed, and alone. After completely losing my composure in the telephone conversation, I warned her to never come back to the house we had lived in.

After gathering my weapon, sat loading the magazines with bullets. With each round of ammunition, my mind went to thoughts of each of them, and what I felt they had taken from me.

I pressed another round into the half-filled magazine.

This one is for the day I carried you from the treehouse with the broken arm.

With my jaw clenched and my mind wandering to thoughts of what

I perceived to be justice, I pressed another round into the magazine.

This one is for believing you were the woman I could spend the rest of my life with.

I grabbed another bullet from the box.

For allowing you to call me a true brother. You're no brother of mine.

And another.

Teaching you something I truly loved, how to ride a motorcycle. I'll make sure you'll never ride another.

And another.

For sharing something as sacred to me as sex with you.

I grabbed another round and pressed against the bullet in the top of the magazine. Incapable of pressing the bullet into the device, I stared down at the rifle magazine. It was clearly completely full.

But I had many more reasons for detesting each of them for deceiving me.

Armed with my rifle, ammunition, knife, and a carton of cigarettes, I drove to his home and parked in the street across from his residence. I sat and blankly stared at her car as my level of anger slowly rose to a point of being unhealthy.

No one is worth your sanity, Jacob. Just walk away.

I had sent a text message to her and to him, and left them both voicemail messages. In the texts messages and in the voicemail, I explained that if I saw either of them through an open window, I would kill them. I further warned if any police arrived, I would kill them, and that the blood of the officers would be on Steve's hands, as calling the police would be his choice.

Now in the middle of a waiting game, I recalled a lifetime of friendship Steve and I shared, and not only how we used to do everything together, but how he considered joining the Marine Corps with me.

I tossed my cigarette butt out the window and onto the pavement, alongside the other two dozen just like it. I checked the rearview mirror as a car drove past, and blew the smoke out the window and into the night air.

Our friendship, even as children, seemed to be a lie. Everything we had learned, experienced, and shared led to the event that had me sitting at his home with a rifle, ready to kill him at first sight.

I lit another cigarette and studied the home. All of the windows in the front of the house were in my view, and were dark. The interior lights were now off, and had been for some time, but I had my doubts the two occupants were sleeping. After having sat and quietly waited for either of them to show their faces in a window for over eight hours, I was tired of the aggravation that was building inside of me.

I chuckled to myself, knowing I had not only the knowledge – but the ability – to enter the home, kill them both, and leave without so much as a trace. I took a long drag from my cigarette and considered why I had chosen not to.

I exhaled the smoke, tossed the butt out the window, and stared down at the pile of cigarette butts. It was apparent I had no intention of killing them. I had a habit, not unlike many combat Marines, of policing my cigarette butts, leaving no trace of my existence and no DNA.

The littered street was proof that subconsciously I had not only let go of Suzanne, but that I had not intended to harm them, only to express my inner anger and disappointment in what I felt they had done to me.

Controlling a person's love, I decided, was impossible. If a woman could fall in love with me, who was to say she couldn't fall in love with someone else? It was quite possible she had actually fallen in love with Steve, and if that was the case, for me to stand between them would be selfish, shallow, and no better of an act than what they had done to me and my marriage.

I reached over, picked up my phone, and sent a text message to them both.

I'm filing for divorce in the morning. Enjoy your lives together. I will not harm you as long as you never intentionally cross my path.

I pressed send, lit another cigarette, and gazed down at the proof of my existence. As I laughed to myself as to what they must have been feeling, I pulled away, knowing my future life would be an interesting one. At least, I decided, I would have the ability to move about the earth freely.

I realized I would always have to return to Wichita to see my father, but I had serious doubts I would be able to stay, considering all things. As large as the city was in population, it was still reminiscent of a small town, and I knew myself all too well.

Killing my former best friend and ex-wife wasn't something I really wanted to do.

At least not unless I had to.

CHAPTER THIRTEEN

Spring 2014, Austin, Texas, USA

Eighteen months had passed since my divorce from Suzanne. Thoughts of the war still lingered in my mind, stuck there permanently like an ugly stain on the cloth of my life. My once clean mind was now littered with bits and pieces of recollections of the war, screaming Marines as they took their last breath, and the eyes of the men I had killed as they held on to the hope of being able to be saved from the permanency of the very death they hoped to cast upon each of the Marines they fought with.

I had no regrets over what I had done, but the constant replaying of events in my head told me my subconscious mind viewed things much differently. My time had been spent, entirely, riding my motorcycle and being as *free* as I believed any citizen of the United States could be. Tied to no one, bound to nothing, and living off of my military retirement and combat pay, I rode with my newfound brethren, my MC brothers.

Although I made no effort to contact Suzanne or Steve in the time that had passed, from time to time I would catch sight of them at their favorite coffee shop. Each time I did, my temper flared slightly, fueling my desire to get out of town. A club ride to Austin, Texas had been scheduled for a few months, and as the date approached, I found myself itching to make the ten-hour trip by motorcycle.

The motorcycle club I rode in decided to look into starting a new chapter in Austin, Texas, and while we were in the area, planned on looking for a clubhouse. As we rode north on Interstate 35 on our way back to the hotel at the end of the weekend, it wasn't a potential clubhouse that caught my attention, it was a billboard at a local gym advertising a fundraiser for amateur fighters. The same gym was advertised in a flyer for the bike rally we planned on attending the following weekend, and after noticing the sign, I decided to I wanted to see if the gym was open.

Riding in the front of the group right beside the president, Erik, I raised my hand and motioned toward the sign. He nodded his head and signaled for the group to slow and then motioned for everyone to exit the highway. As twenty of us pulled into the parking lot of the small gym, the sound from our exhaust was deafening.

After parking under a light pole I got off the bike, stretched my legs, and gazed at the gym. A Harley sat in the parking lot beside the front door and at least some the lights seemed to be on in the front of the building, although the entire side of the building facing us had no windows, we decided to see if they were open for business. I glanced at Teddy, tilted my head toward the door, and walked up to it. After checking the handle and finding it unlocked, I pulled it open.

In the summer, I typically rode with my leather vest and no shirt. In as good of physical shape as I was when I was at war – or maybe even better – I would have described myself as an intimidating man. The man who stood on the other side of the door when I yanked it open however, was an absolute monster.

Wearing a pair of sneakers, cargo shorts, and boxing gloves, he stood beside a petite woman and glared in my direction. His upper body and arms were covered in tattoos, which certainly wasn't anything new to me, but his presence told me he was no amateur to boxing or fighting.

"What can I do for ya, Brother? We're closed, we were just locking up," he said as he cocked his cleanly shaved head slightly to one side.

To make sure he fully understood I wasn't intimidated by his size, I stepped inside the door a few feet and cleared my throat lightly as I flexed my chest. "Well, we rode into town for the ROT rally coming up. The flyers for the rally said you were having fights next week. I boxed in the Marines, and while we were at the bar I made a bet with the president of our motorcycle club. He's boxed a little, and we'd like to see if there's two spots open."

He glanced over his shoulder at the woman who stood beside him, nodded his head slightly, but didn't respond.

"To tell you the truth, we didn't think anyone would be here. We were just going to see if we could find the place and saw the scoot in the lot. You ride?" I asked.

He nodded his head once. "Yep."

Man of few words, huh?

I folded my arms in front of my chest and grinned as Teddy stepped up beside me. "So, have any spots left?"

"Yeah, we got some paperwork to fill out in the office, but it's locked. Can you come back in the morning?" he asked.

I nodded my head and lowered my arms. "We'll be back in the morning. Can you save me two spots? One of the other fellas said he'll fight if there's another spot. Kind of an inside bet with the club. Bragging rights. Hell, if you ride, you know how it is."

He nodded his big bald head. "I'll tell the boss. His name's Kelsey. There's at least two left for sure, ain't had much traffic on it yet. What's your name?"

I extended my hand. "My name's Alec Jacob, but I don't really go by that. You ride, so you call me either Train or A-Train."

He reached toward me, realized he was wearing boxing gloves, and chuckled a light laugh. "I'm Mike Ripton, you can call me Ripp. Pleasure to meet you, A-Train."

I glanced around the gym and nodded my head. It was small, but it was extremely tidy. It reminded me of the gyms at the Marine Corps base in Camp Pendleton. "Alright. Well, it's a nice place you have here, Ripp. We'll leave you to it. Appreciate the help."

I turned around and pulled the door closed behind me.

"So, you and Doc going to do some boxin', huh? Hell I'd get in that little ring and fight, but I ain't the kind of fucker that follows rules. Probably get my big dumb ass tossed out on my ear if I tried it," he said.

I glanced over my shoulder toward Teddy. There was no doubt in my mind that he was a tough man. Hell, I'd seen him in a few fights. But he had no finesse, no style, and no formal training. He was just a big brawler who did his best to protect those he cared for and what he believed in.

I, on the other hand, needed to get into a fight just to keep my sanity. Being in a good fight was similar to being at war. It kept my adrenaline level up, gave me a little excitement, and allowed me to appreciate the mundane pace of my day-to-day post-war activities a little more. With absolutely no excitement in my life, I yearned for something to keep me on edge.

The violence of a fight was miniscule compared to the violence of war, but the same principles applied. The adrenaline, excitement, and uncertainty of a fight allowed me to believe – if even for a short period of time – that I hadn't stepped so far away from the war I desperately missed.

"So what did they say?" Doc asked as I climbed onto the seat of my bike.

"Said to come back tomorrow. Seems they've got a few spots left, but there's still time to back out," I said with a laugh.

Erik was a massive man, but built like a natural athlete, not a bodybuilder. He was big, muscular, and physically fit, but he didn't look like a gym rat. I'd never seen Erik in a fight, and had only heard stories about his quick fists and keen eye. He boxed his way through college, and fought in the golden gloves arenas, but it wasn't something he yearned for.

He rolled his shoulders and flexed his chest. "Back out? That's not going to happen, Train."

I flipped the switch on my hand controls and started the bike. As the engine came to a roar, I tossed my head toward his bike.

"Well, we better get the fuck out of here, then. You're going to need some sleep, Old Man," I said.

He shook his head and coughed a laugh. "Saddle up!"

As we rode to the hotel I wondered if there would be a chance I could fight the big fucker at the gym.

Ripp.

Fighting that guy would put me in a damned good mood.

One that just might last for the rest of the summer.

CHAPTER FOURTEEN

Spring 2014, Austin, Texas, USA

We went back to the gym to fight in the boxing matches we had signed up for, only to find out Ripp had been arrested and was being detained for murdering a man. The stories around the gym varied, and his best friend, the man who was scheduled to fight for the Heavyweight Championship of the World, Shane Dekkar, shared a little information which I suspected was the only real truth we would hear on the matter.

It was still unclear exactly what prompted it, but someone did something to Ripp's little sister, and when he went to question the man who did what he did, the man pulled a gun. He reacted the way I probably would have by fighting the man, and somehow, in the fight, broke the man's neck. Now in jail facing murder, his girlfriend, an attorney, was preparing his defense.

Although I really didn't know Ripp, I felt compelled to talk to him about the challenges not of going to trial, but of living with the horror of taking another man's life. There weren't many people a man could talk to regarding such matters, and I felt I could offer him a little advice, possibly helping him accept what happened as being God's will, and further allowing him to focus on the upcoming trial.

We proceeded with our fights as scheduled, with me feeling uneasy the entire time, knowing Ripp was being forced to deal with so much emotion. I recalled the first time I killed someone, and how difficult it was to accept it as being what was just, proper, and acceptable in the eyes of God. At the time, I had other Marines to talk to, men who had experienced the same things as I. Ripp had no one, or at least I expected he didn't. Mentally, as we prepared to begin the fights, I considered staying in Texas for a while, hoping to provide Ripp a little support.

The small gym was crowded with people hoping to catch a glimpse of the local hero, Shane Dekkar. Erik knocked his opponent out in a matter of seconds, but his challenger was some kid with a big mouth and a jaw made of glass. As soon as Erik hit him once, the kid wadded up in a ball like a crab.

My opponent was a local who was about as big as Ripp, and twice as pretty. As the crowd cheered in anticipation of me losing my respective ass against the guy, we stepped to the center of the ring and touched gloves.

An extremely informal match, and really for nothing but fun, I had hopes of not only lasting the entire match against the guy, but giving the crowd one hell of a show. It was my understanding the money was going to a good cause, so I felt giving the crowd a good show would allow them to feel they got more than what they paid for.

As the bell rang, I shuffled to the center of the ring and studied my opponent. An apparent right-hander, or at least fighting right-handed, he was in for a surprise. I was ambidextrous, and could fight southpaw or right-handed. I stepped to him right-handed and waited to see what he had planned.

He swung an immediate right hand directly in front of my face.

I don't know if that was for show or you intended to land it, but you were off a mile, Big Boy.

96

I leaned back, and as the punch passed my face, I swung an uppercut that landed against the bottom of his chin. A quick left hand to his ribs was rewarded with a shallow cough of breath from his lungs.

As I mentally prepared a left cross, he leaned into me and tried to hug me.

A three round bout for charity and you're going to try and dance?

I shoved him off, and as our bodies separated, swung a left jab and a right hook, the first connecting with his lower chest, and the second with his mid-section. His wild punch that followed was countered by my left jab – again landing against his chest.

I thought they said you were a pro? I'm nothing but a retired Marine, let's see what you've got.

I stepped away from him and waved my gloved hands toward my chest, indicating I was ready for a fight and he wasn't bringing it. The small crowd began to cheer, and I heard Teddy begin to talk shit to my opponent. In an actual boxing match what I chose to do would have been considered extremely disrespectful. In the match we were fighting, it was enough to rile the crowd into a wild cheering session. He clenched his already tight jaw even tighter, and came to me like a madman.

It was just what I was after.

He swung a well-telegraphed uppercut, and I leaned back and let it fly by my face. As he stumbled from the shock of missing the punch completely, I leaned toward him and unleashed a five or six shot combination of punches to his face, connecting all of the punches solid.

The small crowd was in an uproar.

As he again began to stumble, trying to keep his footingI continued with my advance, pummeling him with a series of punches, each one unanswered.

It was exactly what I needed. I felt alive. Every ounce of my frustrations that had built up over the years was being exerted with each punch. As I leaned forward for what I expected to be the punch to end the fight, the bell rang, signaling the end of the round.

Shit.

I went to the corner for a short breather, and was met by Erik and Teddy.

"Holy shit, A-Train, you're fuckin' that dude up somethin' fierce. This fuckin' crowd is lovin' it," Teddy said.

With a mouthpiece in my mouth and no trainer to remove, it, I simply nodded my head in agreement.

"You're not even breathing hard," Erik said with a laugh.

I did my best to grin and shrugged my shoulders.

I ran almost every day, and did strength and weight training on a daily basis. There weren't many men at any age that were in better physical shape than I was, and I attributed it to my Marine training, and still living the life of a disciplined Marine.

As I mentally prepared to step back into the center of the ring and give the crowd what they seemed to enjoy, an elderly man ducked under the ropes and waved his hands.

"Ladies and Gentlemen, this fight is over," he said.

I widened my eyes and shrugged my shoulders. With his eyes fixed on mine, he shook his head from side to side and walked to the corner of my opponent.

Well, fuck.

After Erik unlaced my gloves and removed them, I pulled my mouthpiece. A few seconds later, and the old man in charge of the gym was outside the corner of the ring beside Teddy and Erik.

Standing beside Erik in sweats, a silk jacket with the gym's logo on the back, and *Kelsey* stitched on the front, he pressed his hands into his hips and shook his head. "Jesus Christ. Ripper said you were some Army guy that fought on a military base. You were beating the hell out of my boxer. Just who the hell are you?"

I grinned at his question and did my best not to sound arrogant in my response. "I'm a Marine, I wasn't in the Army, Sir. And I've fought a little."

"You've fought *a lot*," he growled, his voice old and gruff. "That guy you were educating on the sport is a local who was undefeated and we'd like to keep him that way. His trainer stopped him from a serious old fashioned ass whipping, that's for sure. You ever think about considering boxing as more than a hobby?"

I shrugged my shoulders. "I might."

"Let me know," he said with a nod. "And that's a mean left hook you've got."

I nodded my head toward him as he turned away. "Appreciate it."

"But you need work, a lot of work," he growled over his shoulder as he walked away.

As I stepped away from the ring and toward the locker room, I considered what he asked. I had planned on leaving Kansas, coming to Texas for seven to ten days, and going back to Kansas. Considering Ripp's situation and my need to find an outlet for my frustrations associated with the war, maybe making a few changes would be in my benefit.

As Erik and I changed clothes, I made up my mind. I didn't say anything to him just yet, but I decided to stay in Austin.

At least for a while.

I knew one thing for sure – the more space there was between my ex-wife and me, the better off I would be.

CHAPTER FIFTEEN

Summer 2014, Austin, Texas, USA

The MC rode back to Kansas, leaving me in Texas. It was understood when the time came to start a chapter in Austin, I would be the president of the chapter. After a few trips back to Wichita to get my truck and most of my belongings, I was happily living in a rental house in the sunny state of Texas.

I found the people of Texas to be quite different than the residents of Kansas, primarily due to their hospitality. While riding my motorcycle down less traveled county roads, off of the highways and interstates, everyone waved at me as if they knew me. While walking past someone in the grocery store I was generally met with a *howdy* or *how are you doing?* At first, I dismissed it to the people I was encountering being intimidated by me and their hospitality, at least in person, was done in an effort to comfort themselves. After multiple daily trips to the store to buy fresh fruit and vegetables, and seeing nothing change, I realized it wasn't done out of intimidation or fear, but simply out of kindness.

I quickly developed a friendship with Ripp, finding him to be someone who caused me to feel comfortable in his presence. His offered friendship was genuine, and although I would have guessed no one could be, he was funnier than Teddy. It was our common bond of dealing with the taking of life, however, that immediately brought us together.

I found another friend in Shane Dekkar, and the old man that managed the gym but claimed to be nothing more than a trainer, Kelsey. Kelsey was gruff, unwilling to smile, and had an *all business* attitude, but as difficult as he probably was for most people to understand, I felt I knew exactly how he felt.

His stern attitude was a front. He cared deeply about the men he trained, and he took their success or defeat as his own, leaving him no room for an outward friendship. Personally, I admired the man greatly. I found it entertaining that every time he saw me in the gym training, he asked what I was doing there. He fully realized what I was doing there, but his opinion was that I wasn't going to stay in town for long, leading him to antagonize me about it.

I felt a slight guilt, at least initially, about being away from Kansas, which I had always considered to be home. As time passed, I realized as an adult, I had spent all of my time at war, and if I had to claim a place as home, it would be in the war-torn country of Iraq. For the time being, I accepted Texas as my home, and did so without reservation.

My mind seemed to quickly clear itself not of the images of war, but of thoughts of Suzanne. After considerable thought, the love I had always believed I felt for her was dismissed as comfort. I met Suzanne when I was young, and although I wouldn't consider myself as ever being a foolish man, I came to believe I attached myself to her to replace what I was missing in my mother's absence.

Suzanne supported me. She comforted me when I came home from the war after each deployment, cooking me meals, holding me in her arms, and providing me an ear willing to listen and a mind hoping to understand, rarely challenging me or my thought processes.

In short, she was a motherly figure to me.

In the days leading up to and including Ripp's trial, I felt different. I would never be able to change who I was or what I had done, but my mind, soul, and spirit felt as if they had opened up, revealing a new me. A person who had, in the almost two years since I had left Suzanne, become willing to allow myself to once again feel emotion and become more human and less mechanical.

I knew I would always remain methodical, and slightly OCD in my behaviors, but I hoped the way I was feeling would remain for a lifetime, allowing me to be at peace with myself, the war, and the decisions I had made.

I learned in the time I had spent with Shane that he met a woman who was in an abusive relationship, and that she eventually left, but only after her partner of ten years decided to beat her unconscious. At the time, Shane and the woman were simply good friends, and Ripp, as any true friend would, refused to let Shane react to the situation.

He insisted on handling it himself, for fear if Shane tried to resolve it, it may tarnish his career as boxer, and more than likely would land him in jail. A true friend, doing what he felt needed to be done to protect his friend and brother.

In dealing with Shane's girlfriend's abuser, Josh, Ripp lost his temper and hit the man in the face with a hammer, knocking out almost all of his teeth. He followed up by cutting off the man's index finger with a pair of shears, and took the finger home as a prize.

Hearing the story, I couldn't help but laugh, because it sounded exactly like something I would have done. Now, however, with Ripp seemingly winning his trial against the charge of murder, the prosecution was calling the former lover of Shane's girlfriend, the man with the missing finger, to the witness stand.

It appeared the prosecutor felt the fingerless fool's testimony would convince the jurors of Ripp's desire to resort to violence in an effort to solve problems. The problem, in my mind, was not Ripp. It was the two men who had abused the women. One Ripp's sister, and the other Shane's girlfriend.

The comparison between Ripp and me came easily, me protecting my Marines, and him protecting his sister and best friend. He was willing to go to any length, including taking a life to protect the people he loved.

And so was I.

Very few men shared our opinions, ability, and willingness to act. Although I had no experience in losing my freedom, I likened being in prison to being dead, and believed if someone like Ripp was going to spend a lifetime in prison for protecting his sister, the sentence should just as well be death.

Watching a friend die wasn't something I could ever do.

I sat in a park south of the South Congress Bridge and waited for sunset. 750,000 pregnant female bats showed up every spring, each giving birth to one offspring. For the entire summer, 1.5 million bats lived under the bridge, coming out on a nightly basis to hunt for their food. The sight of the bats leaving the bridge was peaceful for me, horrifying to some, and a ritual for others.

There was no doubt people's perception of the nightly event was different. Each night, the bats flying out from underneath the bridge by the hundreds of thousands at the same time darkened the still sunlit sky to black, providing a perfect comparison between dark and light. Many considered the bats evil, carriers of disease and transmitters of rabies. I found them to be far from it – a necessary evil of this earth – ridding the planet of bugs that were a greater nuisance than the bats themselves.

As the sun lowered itself over the tops of the downtown buildings, a wave of bats blackened the sky as they flew in formation off in the distance to find their meal of a few flies or other flying bugs. I thought of the bat population doubling, and that for each adult bat, there was an offspring. Each year, from what I had learned, the mother bats returned, but the offspring did not; leaving the parent and the child separated for a lifetime.

As much as I distanced myself from some, distancing myself from my true friends or family for a lifetime seemed like an impossible task, and as I watched the last of the bats flying out over the river, I realized I had, although not necessarily intentionally, separated myself from my father since the end of the war.

Be it from embarrassment or from a desire to keep to myself regarding the events of the war, I differed very little from the bats. I sat, staring at the bridge, realizing the bats would soon return to their home – but wondered when, or if, I ever would. After a few more minutes, the sun went down completely, and the sky darkened into blackness.

I stood, walked to my motorcycle, and once again felt as if I was right where I needed to be.

In the home I had created for myself.

CHAPTER SIXTEEN

Summer 2014, Austin, Texas, USA

I parked a considerable distance from the home and walked up the block. As I approached the driveway, I verified the address, walked to the garage, and removed the length of wire from my pocket. After fishing it through the upper trim on the garage door, I released the security latch, raised the door, and walked inside.

The entire process took no more than a few seconds. Breaking into someone's garage took a matter of seconds, and as long as they left their door from the garage to the house open, getting in the home took no more than turning a door handle. It amazed me how people never forgot to lock their front or rear door to the home, but historically left the door leading to the garage unlocked.

I walked to the door leading into the home, turned the handle, and grinned as it opened.

Based on my study of Josh, he should have been arriving in roughly thirty minutes. I calmly walked into the home, sat down on the living room couch, and waited for him to come home.

As I heard the key in the front door, I slumped in the seat and waited for him to come. After confirming he was alone, I stood from the couch and began to walk in his direction.

"What the fuck? I'll give you whatever you want," he said, no doubt confusing me for a burglar.

Holding my pistol in my right hand to help convince him I was serious, I spoke calmly, but with a convincing tone.

"I'm not here for your belongings. I'm here to make sure your testimony tomorrow doesn't land my friend in prison," I said as I walked toward him.

"I uhhm, I…" he stammered as his eyes shifted to my pistol.

"Listen, I'm going to make this simple," I said as I placed my pistol on the kitchen counter.

"I won't testify," he murmured.

I gazed over the counter and nodded my head. "Yes, you will."

"And," I paused and shook my head from side to side as I studied him. "Unless I ask you to speak, do not speak again, or I will cut off one of your ears."

His eyes went wide as he raised his right hand to the side of his face, touching the bottom of his ear as I continued.

"That, Sir, is not an idle threat. It is a promise. I'll add it to the collection I already have. Make note that I do not like you or those like you. People like you make me feel sick, is that understood?" I said.

I sighed as I pulled my knife from the sheath.

I glared at him, wanting acknowledgement of my question.

"Nod your head," I said.

It wasn't my intention to try and intimidate him by how I acted, or how I appeared, only make him aware of his options. The more I looked at him, however, the more I grew to dislike him.

He nodded as I placed the knife on the counter beside the pistol.

"I'm sure you still have nightmares about our mutual friend visiting you and relieving you of a finger and a few teeth. Smile and hold up your hand," I said as I lifted my chin slightly.

I had yet to see Ripp's handiwork, and had only heard stories. Josh was obviously scared to death, but did his best to fight against the urge to cower and piss his pants as he forced himself to smile, revealing snow white teeth. As I admired his porcelain replacements, he held up his right hand, which was missing seventy-five percent of the index finger.

A small, almost unnoticeable stub remained.

As I studied his missing finger, I nodded my head. "That cleaned up quite nicely. And those teeth look remarkable. They're nice, really nice. Well, for what it may be worth, Josh, I'm not at all a pleasant person."

His eyes remained fixed on me, filled with uncertainty and fear.

I'm not like Ripp, "I continued. "You were given an opportunity by our mutual friend to keep your mouth shut. You made a poor decision, and chose to speak. I do not know, nor do I fucking care to know the circumstances surrounding your involvement with the authorities. I will say this. I hate most cops about as much as I hate you."

As I pressed my palms against the edge of the countertop and flexed my biceps his eyes fell to my chest and quickly raised to meet mine as I began to speak again.

"Now, your testimony. You spoke to police, and I suspect you told them of the removal of your finger, the ass whipping, and the fact your teeth were knocked out. They now expect you to testify tomorrow regarding what happened and why. That, Sir, will not happen. I will not allow it. It will not. Do you understand me?" I asked.

He remained silent.

"Speak."

"Yes, I understand," he responded.

"Did you ever file a police report on your loss of teeth or finger?" I asked.

"Speak," I said after a few seconds of silence.

He shook his head. "No."

"Until this particular case, did you or have you ever discussed with authorities your loss of teeth or the finger?" I asked as I ran my finger down the edge of the knife.

"Speak."

"No, not until now."

I nodded my head as I studied the blade of the knife. "Alright. You will testify tomorrow. I will make clear what you will say. Phrase it how you prefer, but you will say this; you will state, when asked, that your association with Mr. Ripton is through your former girlfriend. You will further state that you chose to concoct an utter lie regarding the loss of your finger to attempt to get back at her, because she is friends with him. That, in effect, is all you will say."

He stood and stared as if confused.

"Is that understood?" I asked as I rotated my wrist and twisted the blade of the knife back and forth.

He nodded his head.

"I need to hear it. Speak," I sighed.

"Yes. Understood."

The more I looked at him the more I wanted the world to be rid of him. My problem with eliminating him prematurely, as much as I wanted to, was that I historically gave everyone a chance to correct a mistake, my ex-wife included.

It was a weakness of mine.

I glared at him and continued. "You see. I find the entire process disappointing. You being smacked with a hammer and having a finger cut off has nothing to do with *this* case. Not one damned thing. One has nothing to do with the other. But, if the jury hears what you have to say, they'll assume Ripp is a violent man and they'll certainly side with the state. They'll find him guilty. If you *don't* testify, they may find him innocent. In all honesty, they should give him a good Samaritan medal for doing what he's done. It irritates me to have to be here. People like you disgust me. You need to understand that."

He nodded his head. At least he was willing to entertain me.

"Now. I will close with this. I like killing people. I really do. It's the only fucking way I can make that God forsaken war make sense in my head. If I stop killing people, it means all the killing I did for years over there was wrong. And, killing people that wreak havoc on others must be God's will for me, because the government paid me for over a decade to do it. I like to think it was justified, killing all of those people." I paused and considered what I was saying. It seemed as I was speaking, I was not only convincing him of how I felt, but convincing myself.

I was raised to understand killing was wrong. After all, it was one of the Ten Commandments.

The Marines, at a time of war, took every adult male that was willing and capable and taught them how to kill. They didn't teach Marines how to obtain a home loan or balance a checkbook. Upon my returning to the states, they didn't encourage me to make any changes to my mental process regarding killing. They merely expected me to flip a switch and become human again. A lesson or class in how to un-do what they had spent so much time doing was necessary.

"You know, the only way I can convince myself it was justified, all of the killing, that is, is to continue killing people that take from society. You're a taker. And I administer justice by attempting to balance the

111

scales. I do, however, believe people can change. I hope you're one of them. I'm assuming Ripp's previous visit left a little doubt in your mind. I want to remove that doubt. I want clarity," I said with a nod of my head.

I was convinced my speech was not only informative to him, but cleansing to me.

"Are we clear?" I asked as I looked up from the blade of the knife.

As he stood and silently stared, I felt as if I was playing *Simon Says* on the schoolyard as a child. "Jesus fucking Christ. Speak."

"Yes, Sir. I understand."

"Now, I will not be in court tomorrow. Would you like to know where I'll be?" I asked as I picked up the pistol.

He shook his head.

"Humor me. Say you want to know," I said with a laugh.

He swallowed heavily and stared.

"Speak," I said.

"I want to know where you'll be tomorrow," he said, his voice quaking as he spoke.

"Josh, I'll be where ever you go. But you won't see me. You'll never see me. If you testify as to any other facts than what we discussed here, I will find you. And, I can assure you of two things after I find you. One, I will torture you. And two, when I get bored with torturing you I will kill you. I will promise you those two things."

I placed the pistol into the holster and nodded my head sharply.

"Oh, and one more thing," I said as I slid the knife into the sheath.

His eyes widened as I watched his Adam's apple raise and lower.

"Never, regardless of the circumstances, come in contact in any way with Kace again. Are we clear?" I asked as I stepped in his direction.

He nodded his head.

I tilted my head to the side and rolled my eyes. "Say it."

"I, uhhm. Yeah. It's crystal clear. Never again," he responded.

I turned and walked toward the front door.

"I'll let myself out," I laughed as I walked to the door.

As I reached for the door handle, I looked over my shoulder toward the kitchen. Josh remained standing by the countertop, staring down at his feet with his hands at his sides.

"You see, Josh, the entire world can be separated into two groups; those that give, and those that take. Those that give provide *something* to the rest of the people on the earth. Something useful." I paused and opened the door partially.

"The takers? Well, their only concern is themselves. They take from society, providing little, if anything, to others. In the future, start asking yourself what you've done lately for society. For other people. If the answer is nothing, you're doing something wrong."

Ripp didn't ask for my assistance, but he didn't have to. I was able to help him out, and I did. It was the least I could do for a friend.

Hopefully my visit to Josh would persuade him to do what was right.

In doing so, maybe I could help save a life instead of taking one.

CHAPTER SEVENTEEN

Summer 2014, Austin, Texas, USA

Disappointed I wasn't there to witness it, Ripp was found not guilty. I was invited to a celebration dinner at his parent's home, and I eagerly accepted. Upon arriving, I found his mother, father, two sisters, girlfriend, Shane Dekkar, Shane's wife, Kace, and a friend from the gym, Austin, were all in attendance to celebrate.

I had heard the phrase *everything is big in Texas* many times. The table, the meal, and the crowd held true to the statement. The table had ten people seated at it and had room for four more. The home-cooked meal of chicken, countless side dishes, bread and iced tea was plentiful and reminded me of meals at home before my mother died.

Mr. Ripton turned toward me and lowered the fork that dangled from the tips of his fingers. "It's a shame your friends couldn't make it, Alec."

My friends from Wichita had all come to Austin to support Ripp throughout the three-day trail, and watched intently as the procedure unfolded. Ripp's parents were appreciative of the support, and expressed it throughout the trial.

"They just came down to support Mike, Sir. As soon as the trial was over, they had to get back to Kansas. As early as it ended, they were able to get back tonight," I said, making certain to use the name *Mike* instead of Ripp.

I had been warned by Shane about Ripp's parents, and their rules regarding the use of nicknames or cussing at the dinner table.

"I knew it was all over as soon as Vee said *Boom! Too late, you made the wrong decision* and blew on her finger. That sent chills down my spine. I like you, Vee," Kace said.

Ripp's girlfriend and attorney throughout the trial, Vee, chuckled. "Pretty dramatic, I know. And I like you too, Kace."

The story I had heard regarding the end of the trial, was that Vee had provided an exceptional closing argument. In her close, she asked the jurors what they would have done if the man in question, the deceased, would have pulled a gun on them in a drunken stupor. As the jurors sat and shrugged their shoulders, trying to decide how they'd react, she shouted, "*Boom! Too late. You made the* wrong *decision. You should have reacted differently.*" Leaving them all sitting with open mouths, realizing during such a situation, the person on the receiving end of the gun has only seconds to react.

In the end, she made her point and won the case.

"Ma'am, the chicken is fantastic," I said as I shifted my eyes toward Ripp's mother.

Ripp's younger sister, Katie, interrupted. "I cooked it, thank you. Have some more."

She made eye contact as she lifted the platter of chicken and held it in the air. She was beautiful, blonde, and I would have guessed her age at mid-twenties.

I raised my hand and waved it toward the platter. "I want to make sure everyone gets enough. No, thank you."

"No, really. There's plenty, have some more," she insisted.

I grinned and nodded my head. "Alright, just one more."

Ripp's father looked up from a chicken bone he was gnawing on. "Called Bug and told her the news. Told her to get to cookin' 'cause we was comin' home. Glad that mess is over."

"No nicknames at the table," Ripp interrupted.

His father reached for his fork, pointed it at Ripp, and waved it as he made his point. "It ain't a nickname, and you know it. We been callin' her Bug since she was a baby. Katie Bug. It's her god damned name, Mike."

"No cussing at the dinner table," Mrs. Ripton said without so much as looking up from her meal.

It was apparent she was used to the shenanigans of her son and husband.

"It ain't her name, Pop. Her name's Katie. It's funny. If I say a nickname, you and Mom get all over me. But you guys say *Bug* all the time like it's her name; and it ain't her god damned name," Ripp complained.

"No cussing at the dinner table, Michael," his mother said.

Sitting at their dinner table was like being a part of a television sitcom. My eyes, for the entire meal, darted back and forth across the table, listening to the playful banter between Ripp and his father, often wondering just how much of it was intentional on Ripp's part. His father wasn't much better, constantly teasing and taunting Ripp.

"Her name's Bug, and that's the end of it. I ain't got to be nice to you, Mike, the trial's over," his father said as he pulled the fork from his mouth and pointed it at Ripp.

Ripp finished his piece of chicken, licked his fingers, and glanced around the table.

"After we eat, Dekk, Shorty, Vee, A-Train, The Kid and I are going to go out for a drink," he said.

His mother, without looking up from her plate, condemned Ripp for his use of nicknames. "No nicknames at the table, Michael."

"I don't like it when you call me Kid," Austin said.

Ripp shifted his eyes toward Austin and glared. "Shut up, Austin. Feel lucky you're even invited. You're still proving your worth."

Without looking up from her plate, Ripp's mother once again chastised him. "Don't say that word Michael, it's a bad word."

"Yes, Ma'am," he responded.

"I want to go," Ripp's sister said.

Mr. Ripton glanced up from his meal. "Go where?"

Katie turned toward Ripp and smiled. "I want to go with you guys tonight."

"Bug, we're going out drinking and acting like fools. It ain't a place for you," Ripp responded.

I shifted my eyes toward Katie. She was the sister who had been abused by the man Ripp later confronted – and subsequently killed – and although I didn't know the extent of what was done to her, it was apparent the assault was nothing short of savage. As I sat and admired her beautiful looks and calm demeanor, I wondered what type of person would ever be able to do anything to such a woman, or any woman for that matter.

She shrugged her shoulders and widened her eyes. "Well, Vivian and Kace are going. So girls can go, and I want to go."

Ripp shook his head. "Bug, you're just a kid, you can't…"

She shook her head and narrowed her eyes. "I'm not a kid. I'm old enough to drink. I'm four years younger than Kace, basically. So kiss my ass, Ripp. I want to go."

"No cussing, Bug," Ripp's mother said flatly.

Katie glanced toward her mother, grinned, and as she shifted her eyes toward Ripp, locked her eyes on mine for a moment. I had been blankly staring, but not out of anything but slight admiration and wonder. I grinned as our eyes locked, and she quickly broke my gaze.

"Let her go, Ripp," Austin said.

I wanted her to look at me again, and felt slightly guilty for desiring it so deeply. Her eyes were a translucent blue and not only complimented her well, but were rather difficult not to become fixated on.

"Bug, Austin, no nicknames at the table," Mrs. Ripton said.

"Sorry, Ma'am," Austin said apologetically as he turned to Mrs. Ripton. He turned toward Ripp's father and nodded his head. "And, sorry, Sir."

"Ain't nobody asked your opinion Austin, shut up and eat," Ripp complained.

Kace grinned and turned toward Ripp, undoubtedly recognizing his use of the word *shut up*. Shane, who hadn't said a word all night, also shifted his eyes toward Ripp.

"Michael," Kace said playfully.

"Michael, that's enough," Ripp's mother said, reminding him of the *bad word* he had used.

I shifted my eyes from Ripp's mother toward Ripp, and met Katie's gaze half-way across the table, stopping me from looking any further.

Damn, your eyes are beautiful.

"So, you were a Marine?" she asked.

I had every intention of looking away when I responded, but failed to do so.

I nodded my head as my mouth went dry. "Once and always."

She continued to stare into my eyes, all but hypnotizing me to return her stare. "What's that mean?"

With my eyes still locked on her, I grinned at her curious nature. "Well, it means once you're a Marine, you'll always be a Marine. What is instilled into you lasts a lifetime. *Once a Marine always a Marine.*"

"He's teaching me hand-to-hand combat and self-defense," Austin said.

Katie broke my gaze, turned toward Austin, glared at him, and quickly shifted her eyes to meet mine.

"So, you were in the war?" she asked.

"Bug, don't be rude," I heard Ripp's father say.

I turned toward Mr. Ripton. "It's alright, Sir. No offense taken."

"I was over there for roughly ten years, yes," I said.

With her eyes still locked on mine, she blinked a few times. "Did you kill anyone?"

"Bug!" Ripp's father complained.

His mother repeated the complaint. "Bug!"

"It's quite alright, Ma'am," I said as I nodded my head toward Mrs. Ripton. "And, Sir," I said as I shifted my eyes toward Mr. Ripton.

"I'm not ashamed. Yes, I killed people. It was my job. In a perfect world, a Marine mission is complete without anyone dying. My battalion was reconnaissance, like Navy SEALS on land. We gathered intelligence through interrogation. In *that* war? Well, it was different. There was nothing to gather and no one wanted to talk. So, we killed most of the people we encountered before they killed us," I explained.

"How many?" Katie promptly asked.

The sound of Mr. Ripton clearing his throat was followed by his complaint of what I expected was his opinion of her inconsiderate

120

nature. "Bug. Damn it,"

"Again, Sir, no concerns here. I have no shame," I said over my shoulder.

It seemed I had become incapable of prying my eyes from Ripp's sister. I told myself as I sat and admired her throughout the conversation that I had no business doing so, as she was not only the sister of a friend, but young, and, above all things, a woman.

My eyes and mind, however, argued.

She was a beautiful woman, there was no doubt about that.

"I don't know how many. I never counted. More than most, I'd guess. I was either in the right place at the right time, or the wrong place at the right time. I was wounded several times, and each time it seems death followed. I don't know," I said, although I did know exactly how many.

"We had to rescue some trapped Army Rangers on hill 571 in late 2005. I remember on that night there were eight. I didn't think it would ever end. I got shot as soon as my boots hit the dirt. Took a round in the thigh. I knew it happened, I just don't really think I cared. I'd been shot in the leg twice already, and I knew immediately this was superficial. I had a job to do, and there were Rangers that were pinned down. We were all they had. Well, it was us and a hand full of SEALS. We got them out of there. That, I suppose, is what was important. But a count? Like a total number? It'd be a guess," I said.

I broke her stare. As I glanced around the table, everyone sat quietly and stared.

I shifted my eyes back to Katie and continued. "But every one of them? Every one? They had one thing in common. They were trying to kill me, I just got to them before they got to me."

Still staring directly into my eyes Katie grinned and batted her eyelashes. "I like Marines."

"You don't know any fuckin' Marines, Bug. Leave the man alone," Ripp growled.

"Michael Allen Ripton!" Mrs. Ripton snapped.

Mr. Ripton scowled at Ripp, turned his head in my direction, and nodded his head. "I like 'em, too, Bug. Thanks for your service, Son."

"Shut up, Ripp. I do too know Marines. Well, I *did*."

"Bug," Mrs. Ripton said.

"Just stop, Bug. You don't know any Marines. Leave it alone. I'm sorry Alec," Ripp said.

"He was a senior when I was a freshman. I'll never forget him," Katie explained. "You knew him too, Ripp. He came here for dinner once. He joined the Marines and went to Iraq. He was some special Marine. Like Special Forces. He got killed, I remember reading it in the paper and they talked about it in church and at school. If you ever went to church, you'd remember."

"I have no idea who you're talking about," Ripp said.

A Marine dying in the line of service was something I was compassionate about, and I was willing to listen to whatever she had to say about it.

She shifted her eyes away from Ripp and once again met my gaze. "I went to that house party, the one I got in trouble for. And Greg Shook was grabbing me. He said I *filled out* young. He was being a dick. And Billy pushed him and told him to stop. But he didn't stop - he kept saying stuff - suggestive stuff about me. Billy took him outside and beat him up, and then came in and apologized for Greg being a jerk. I remember his knuckles were all bloody. And he came here for dinner a few weeks later."

I shifted my eyes toward Ripp.

He shrugged his shoulders.

"And he got married. And his wife had a kid while he was gone. And he never came back," Katie said.

"Cunningham," Mr. Ripton said.

A chill ran down my spine. There was no way.

Lance Corporal Cunningham.

Longhorns.

He was from Texas.

Mr. Ripton nodded his head. "I remember him. Big kid. Tall. Bug made a big deal of him kickin' that Greg's ass. Billy Cunningham. Yep. He was a nice kid."

My body went numb. I stood from the table and stared at Mr. Ripton. "Billy Cunningham? Billy *Ray* Cunningham?"

"Yeah. That's him. Billy Ray Cunningham," Katie blurted.

"You went to school with *Billy Ray Cunningham*?" I asked.

The man had saved my life on a rooftop one day, killing an insurgent who would have shot me had he not stepped in between us.

"You alright, Bro?" Ripp asked.

I stared at Katie, recalling the events of the day on the rooftop. "Billy Ray Cunningham saved my life."

I turned toward Ripp. I shared the story with him while his trial was preparing to start. I felt if he could understand the process I went through in dealing with death, he could deal with the death of the man who pulled the gun on him.

"I told you about him, on the roof. Remember?" I asked.

He nodded his head and stared.

"Hold on," Katie said as she jumped from her chair.

"Excuse me," she said as she ran from the room.

"What's going on?" Ripp's other sister asked.

Ripp's mother shook her head as she glanced toward Manda. "Leave your sister alone, Manda, she's been through a lot."

Katie walked back into the room, holding a book in her hands. As she flipped through the pages, she glanced upward. "Here. Come here, Alec. Look at this."

I walked around the table. As I stepped to Katie's side, I inhaled the soft fragrance of her perfume. As my eyes focused on the page, goosebumps rose along my arms. Staring back at me, was Billy Ray Cunningham, the man who saved my life.

I swallowed heavily as I stared blankly at the page.

"That's him. That's Lance Corporal Cunningham," I said with a nod.

"What happened? You said he saved you," Katie asked.

Ripp's father interrupted. "Bug!"

"I'm squared away, Sir. It's all right," I said.

I reached for the yearbook, accepted it as she handed it to me, and held it gingerly in my hands as I looked down at his photo and recalled the day he died. I felt my lower lip begin to quiver as I considered where I would be in his absence.

Although I had no intention of doing so, I began to speak.

"We followed two of them onto the roof of a building. They'd shot one of the Marines on my team as soon as we'd entered the building. It was Cunningham and I who followed them. I had a feeling. You know that deep down in your gut feeling?"

For some reason I paused and turned toward Mr. Ripton. He nodded his head once as if giving me permission to continue. With glazed over eyes I continue to stare down at the page and recite the events of that awful day.

"Well, I was right," I said. "One of them stepped out from behind a structure on the roof they were using for cover, I missed him. Didn't see a thing. Billy Ray stepped in front of me and…"

"Lance Corporal Cunningham was struck by enemy fire, and I returned…"

I paused, realizing I was reciting the words that had been written on the daily report. Words that had stuck in my head for years. I took another slow breath, regained my composure, and continued. I needed to tell the story. I owed it to him.

"He acted like it didn't faze him. I imagine it was adrenaline. Either that or desire. You know, in hindsight, it was probably courage."

I paused and inhaled a shaky breath. "He returned fire. Hit the guy in the hand, chest, and torso. I returned fire, killing the second gunman. Cunningham died right there on the roof. He uhhm. He had a daughter."

I glanced up from the yearbook and fixed my eyes on Katie.

"She's uhhm. She's probably," Katie said, pausing as she counted on her fingers.

"She's probably six or seven now," she nodded.

"I'd like to meet Cunningham's wife," I said as I handed her the yearbook.

"I know where she used to live. I bet I can find her," Katie grinned as she accepted the yearbook.

I nodded my head, walked to my seat, and sat down. Most people, if given an opportunity to truly know me, know my inner workings, and know just exactly who I was, would be of the opinion that I was not a man who was close to God. The truth would be quite the contrary.

God was my only true guidance in life, and although I often did things people would perceive as evil, I believed I was always acting as a man who administered God's will. Sitting in the chair gazing blankly across the table at Katie, hoping I may be able to find the wife of the man who saved my life, I began to understand I was exactly where I needed to be when I needed to be there.

Sitting silently, still in somewhat of a trance, Ripp broke the silence.

"If we aren't focused on living life to the best of our ability, we're slowly dying a death that's of our own choosing. The odd thing is we get to pick the course we take. Why would someone choose not to live life at full capacity?" he said.

Kace chuckled. "Wow. I like that. Who said *that*? I know it's not a Ripp original."

"*My* father. Jack Ripton," Mr. Ripton responded.

"Come on everybody. Let's get out of here," Ripp said as he stood from his seat.

"Where we going, Ripp? Huh?" Austin asked.

"We're all gonna go pound down some beers, see if we can get in a fight, and then I'm going to take Vee home and fuck her until she passes out," Ripp responded.

I waited for the axe to fall, alternating glances between Mr. and Mrs. Ripton. Although they said nothing regarding his comment about fucking Vee, Vee slapped her hand against Ripp's shoulder and gave him the stink eye.

"Michael, we don't like it when you get in bar fights," his mother said softly.

"Damn it, Mike," his father said as he dropped his fork onto his plate.

Ripp shook his head and pressed the web of his hands into his hips. "Pop. Just hold on a minute. Here's the deal. I can't change who I am. I like fuckin' and I like fightin'. Today's a victory for me. A big one. I'm going to celebrate. Doing the two things I love. Come on, let's get out of here. Bug, Manda, this includes you."

As Katie jumped excitedly from her seat, we once again made eye contact. I was pleased that she was going to be included in our evening out on the town.

I was damned sure there wasn't going to be any fucking on my part, but I wouldn't have made any promises on the fighting.

I had a sinking feeling two professional boxers, a boxer in training, and a Marine were sure to get into some kind of trouble.

I just hoped I had a few minutes to get to know Katie a little bit better before it happened.

CHAPTER EIGHTEEN

Summer 2014, Austin, Texas, USA

We hadn't been at the bar for half an hour, and Ripp stood true to his word. He and a half-drunken Austin began running their mouths to a table full of drunken college football players, and within a few minutes, we were in the parking lot.

In the middle of the dark parking lot, between the parked cars and under a lamp pole, Shane and I stood back and watched as Ripp beat the one who had been arguing with him in three punches. The entire time, I was eager to see if my hand-to-hand combat lessons with Austin had been doing him any good.

The arguing match Austin was in eventually turned into what looked like might be a fight, and as it did, I cheered Austin on. The man he was arguing with was an absolute asshole, calling Austin every name in the book, including insinuating he was gay. As Austin reached his limit, he finally raised his hands and warned the guy to prepare to fight.

"Come on, Austin, remember what I taught you," I said.

"Get him, Steve!" his friend screamed.

Great name, asshole.

Austin raised his hands and circled his opponent. If for no other reason than the man shared the name of my former best friend, I wanted Austin to pound the guy into the ground.

"Kick his fucking ass, Steve," the other friend yelled.

Katie stood by my side, almost touching me as Austin spread his feet apart and took a fighting stance. As the man swung a punch at Austin, he stepped into him, blocked his arm, and punched him in the base of the neck.

And just like that, Steve collapsed in the parking lot.

"Good damned job, Kid," I said.

"Who the fuck are you? Their coach? Y'all just come here to beat the shit out of people?" one of the peanut gallery from the idiot corner asked.

"Come on," I said to Katie as I turned to the side. "Just walk away."

"I heard you. You better walk away," he grunted.

There was no doubt in my mind I could beat the guy in a matter of seconds, but I had nothing to prove. Although we had only been at the bar for 30 minutes, I was having a great time talking to Katie, and I wasn't about to ruin her night.

As we were walking away, I noticed the idiot running up behind us. I tilted my head to the side and waited for him to get close enough to strike him if need be. As I prepared to spin around, he shoved his hands into my back.

Big mistake, asshole.

"Stand to the side," I said to Katie as I reached down and tugged against the thighs of my jeans.

I spread my feet to a fighting stance and fixed my eyes on his. "You're going to want to turn around and walk away from this, and I'm going to let you."

It was his opportunity to correct his mistake. The same one I gave everyone.

"Fuck you," he said. "You guys beat the shit out of Steve. I'm gonna whip your ass."

My mouth curled into a smirk at the thought of him even challenging me. I felt it my duty to talk him out of it if there was any way I could.

"That pretty fucker standing beside you whipped Steve's ass, all by himself," I said as I nodded my head toward Austin. "And, to tell you the truth, Steve needed it. You see, he has an alligator mouth and a hummingbird ass. He needs to learn when to keep his mouth shut. Now my best advice to you is to go home. This is over."

"It ain't over till I kick the shit out of one of you for what you did to Steve," he said as he doubled his fists.

I coughed a laugh. "You see, that's where things are getting kind of cloudy for you. You're obviously confused. You're not going to win this fight. Not even if you get all your friends to join in. You see, I don't *think* I can whip you. I *know* I can. Just go home. It's probably best for us all."

"My pappy always told me the guy that's a runnin' his mouth is the one that can't fight a lick," he said with a laugh.

I hated to bring the guy's father into it, but I felt I had to.

"Well, I'm afraid to tell you that *this* time your father is sadly mistaken," I said,

"You calling my pappy a liar?"

"Here we go again with the cloudy judgment. I said he was *mistaken*. I didn't call him a liar. Go home. Save yourself being disgraced in front of your friends," I said as I tossed my head toward his friends.

"I'm fixin' to disgrace *you*," he said.

Katie stepped behind me.

"Kick his ass," she whispered.

131

"Probably be a good idea if you and those big titties of yours get back away from him so you don't get hurt, little girl," the asshole said as she whispered in my ear.

Disrespectful prick.

I stepped forward and swung the heel of my palm into his chest. As he bent over, coughing for breath, I pulled my right hand back, grabbed the back of his neck with my left, and struck him in the base of the neck with my right hand. As he stumbled, I struck him on each side of the neck with the outside of my flattened hand.

As he collapsed, I caught him and prevented him from falling to the asphalt.

Shane Dekkar, who had been quiet all night, shouted. "Holy fuck!"

"It's gonna be tough, but try and stand up. So you can apologize," I said.

"Come here, Bug. He won't hurt you," I said over my shoulder.

I had struck him pretty violently with what was described by Marines as a knife hand strike, hitting him in the mastoid muscles of the neck. The strike, if properly executed, paralyzes a man for several seconds.

Katie stepped beside me and stared down at the man.

"Now, I know you can hear me," I said. "This isn't the first time I've done this. Apologize to the girl."

He returned a glassy-eyed stare.

"I'm going to count to three," I said. "And you better apologize."

"One…Two…Three," I counted.

"That's a bad decision on your part, really. Like I said, I know you can hear me. If you try to, you'll be able to talk," I explained.

Nothing.

I shook my head. "Austin, come here. Hold him while I light a

132

cigarette."

Austin stood and stared at me as if I was crazy.

"Dude, you fucked Randy up bad, let him go," Steve said.

"Steve, you'll need to back the fuck up, right now," I said as if I was giving a command to a Marine.

Steve stopped in his tracks.

I widened my eyes. "Austin?"

"Hold this prick up. I need a cigarette," I said.

Austin walked up behind who I now understood was Randy, and took him from my grasp, holding him upright. Most of what he was doing was a show, I was sure. I had performed the strike on many a Marine as a joke, and the paralysis lasted all of a few seconds.

I lit a cigarette and took a slow drag. As I held it in my teeth, I explained my concerns to Randy. "You see. This is always the problem with certain people."

I bit into the filter of the cigarette and drove both hands into his neck again.

"Dude, what the fuck? He wasn't doing anything!" Steve screamed.

"You're correct, Steve," I said sarcastically.

I exhaled a large cloud of smoke. "I gave him an opportunity to apologize. He'll have another chance here in a minute."

As Austin stood and stared at me as if I had killed Randy, I reached for his arms.

"I've got him," I assured Austin.

"Randy, you need to apologize to the girl. I will count to three again. Tell her you're sorry for being an inconsiderate asshole," I said.

"One…Two…"

"I'm…" he murmured.

"Sorry," he said.

"Tell her why you're sorry," I said.

"I uhhm. I'm sorry. I was. I'm sorry I was disrespectful," he said.

"Will it ever happen again?" I asked.

"No, it won't happen again," he said.

"Bug?" I asked over my shoulder.

She walked up behind me and rested her chin on my shoulder as she pressed her chest against my back. "Yes?"

"Satisfied?" I asked.

"Very," she whispered into my ear.

I released my grip. Randy stumbled, almost fell to the asphalt, and was helped up by his humiliated friends.

"You'll feel funny for a minute or two, but you'll be fine," I said jokingly as his friends helped him walk away.

With her chest still pressed into my back, Katie breathed into my ear. "That was so awesome. What did you do to his neck?"

"Knife hands," I said with a laugh.

"Knife what?" she asked, grazing her hand over my cheek as she spoke.

I glanced toward Ripp, fully enjoying Katie's playful nature, but concerned he might not feel comfortable with her acting the way she was.

He returned a smile.

"I'll show you some time. It's a good way to gain control of a situation," I replied to her.

"Vee's got a stomach ache. We need to get the hell out of here. It's been a long day," Ripp said.

"You're full of it, Ripp," Kace said. "We know what you're going to do."

"Well, you guys do whatever it is you want to. It's still early. But we're leaving. I need to make up for some lost time. Austin?" Ripp said.

"Yeah, Boss?" Austin responded.

"Look after Manda until the night's over," Ripp said.

"Got it, Boss," Austin responded.

Katie continued to hang on my shoulders.

Ripp shifted his eyes from Austin to me. Vee hung on his shoulders, clearly imitating Katie.

"A-Train..."

"Semper fi," I responded with a wave.

And I meant it.

Regardless of what Katie asked, did, or attempted to do, I would stay faithful to my friend Ripp.

I was just worried how long I would be able to keep it up if my interest in her continued to grow at the rate it had been for the entire night.

Only time would tell, I supposed.

CHAPTER NINETEEN

Summer 2014, Austin, Texas, USA

We sat and shared a pizza at an all-night pizza joint. Not my favorite food by any means, and definitely not something I would have chosen to eat so late at night; but considering the circumstances, it was a pleasant change.

"I wish the world was full of people like you," she said.

I held the folded slice of pizza in my hand and watched as the grease from the pepperoni ran down my arm to my elbow. "Believe me, you don't."

I reached for a napkin and wiped my forearm clean of the grease, shaking my head and laughing as I did so.

"Why?" she asked. "You're one of the good guys."

In the middle of taking a bite of pizza, I shook my head. "I've got good intentions, but it doesn't make me one of the *good guys*."

"You and Ripp are a lot alike. He acts all mean, but he's a big softie. He likes to fight, but he doesn't beat people up for no reason. Dad says he fights to keep his day-to-day anger at a manageable level. I think he's right. But when people are mean to other people or do things that aren't right, Ripp steps in and beats them up. He thinks he's teaching them a lesson. He's done it since he was little," she said.

I had never considered fighting as a means of anger management,

137

but it made perfect sense. Katie's explanation of Ripp's stepping in when he felt he needed to teach someone a lesson sounded exactly like me. I often felt the need to place myself in a situation most men would perceive as none of their business, only to attempt to teach someone my perception of what was right.

I was quite sure, however, that my general means of resolution, however, might differ from his considerably.

"Well, it does sound like we're a lot alike, but I don't think the world needs to be full of people like me," I said as I took another bite of pizza.

I did my best to stay focused on the food, and not spend as much time staring at her as I did at the dinner we had earlier in the night. Not admiring her was more difficult than I would have imagined, and I attributed my fascination with Katie to my lack of exposure to females in general since my having divorced Suzanne.

"I do," she said.

She gazed beyond me and appeared to be in deep thought. As she sat there obviously focused on something, I admired everything from her hands to her choice of clothes. Wearing a baseball tee with the word *baseball* across the front, a pair of jeans, and sneakers, she looked not only comfortable, but adorable.

After a moment, she shifted her eyes toward mine, and caught me in the middle of my admiration. As I shifted my embarrassed eyes to my lap, she began to speak.

"You know, how God puts everything on this earth for a reason. Not everyone sees the reason, but I don't think most people take the time to really think about it. A centipede, for instance. Most people are repulsed by them. They think they're gross and wonder why they're even here. The same with spiders. But God has everything on earth for a reason. So, the spider is here for many reasons, one of which is to feed the centipede. And, the centipede? It's a staple in the diet of many lizards. The centipede relies on the spider, and the lizard is dependent on the centipede. And, at some point, a hawk, incapable of finding another source of food, swoops down and eats the lizard. At some point, a bobcat catches and eats the hawk, only to be later killed and eaten by a wolf."

She sounded like a biology professor explaining a theory, but it made perfect sense. I shifted my eyes upward. "The food chain."

She nodded her head and smiled. "You're here for a reason. You're necessary in God's eyes. Some people on this earth are like the spider or the centipede. And they need eaten. And you're the wolf. You're necessary," she said with a smile.

She had an odd way of putting things into perspective, but so far, I liked what she was saying. She reminded me all too much of myself, and her way of thinking about things was almost identical to mine. I didn't like being compared to the lizard, but for the time being, I decided it was okay. I did wonder, if her analogy was accurate, who ate the wolf?

"So, what eats me? Who eats Alec Jacob? Where does it end for me?" I asked.

Life, I guess.

She took a bite of crust, shrugged her shoulders, and chewed it for a moment as she thought. I took another bite of the pizza and waited for her to think about my question while I did the same.

Her personality was, at least for me, very inviting. She was beautiful, but seeing her without the distraction of her family present made her much more attractive than her looks alone. Watching her eat, drink, and even talk was fascinating to me, and as I sat and watched her think while she ate her crust, I tried desperately to determine why I was so interested in her.

"Life, I guess," she said.

Perfect answer.

I nodded my head and swallowed the bite of pizza. "I was thinking the same thing."

"I guess if the world was full of people like you, we'd have no bad guys. And I suppose we'll always need to have a few bad guys," she said.

I laughed out loud and dropped my pizza to my plate. "Why would we need bad guys?"

"To justify having guys like you around," she said with a grin.

"Vicious cycle," I said as I reached for my pizza.

I felt like I was in high school again. Not because of her age, but because of the innocence I felt sitting with her. I felt no pressure, no need to act in any way in particular, and extremely comfortable – with the exception of being overly excited about being there with her.

Sitting there with her made me feel as if I was preparing to gather the courage to ask a date to the prom. Crossing my legs repeatedly, only to find no real comfort in doing so, and rubbing my hands together repeatedly were tell-tale signs of my excitement. I didn't once try to hide my feelings or the signs of them, only smiled each time I noticed I was doing something contrary to my norm.

It was a nice change.

"So, are you...you're single, right?" she asked.

"As single as they come," I said with a nod.

She smiled and her eyes fell to my chest. After a second or two she lifted them to meet my gaze. "How?"

"My choice, I suppose," I said flatly. "I went through a divorce after

I got back from the war. My wife wasn't quite faithful. I tried to fix it, and thought I could fix it, but in the end, she wasn't willing to stay faithful, so I left."

"And you were faithful?" she asked.

"Absolutely. I don't take things like commitment lightly. It's a promise, or at least it is to me. That's the way I see it," I said.

She narrowed her eyes. "She cheated on you?"

"She sure did," I responded.

"Wow," she said. After a second or two of silence, she shrugged her shoulders. "Sorry."

"Glad it's over now, and glad we didn't have kids, I guess. Not that I don't want any, just glad I didn't have any with her," I said.

Her mouth formed a smile large enough to expose her extremely white teeth. "You like kids?"

I nodded my head. "Love 'em."

She focused on me for a minute, dropped her eyes to the table, and after a few seconds, cleared her throat. "But. I mean. You're like. You're just. Well, you're not the typical single guy."

I chuckled. "What's the typical single guy?"

"A douchebag," she said with a laugh.

"Well, I'm not one of those," I responded.

She coughed a laugh and reached for her glass of tea. "No, you're sure not."

"And you. You're single?" I asked.

I was pretty sure she was, but not positive. Thinking of a girl like her being single was almost impossible to imagine.

She lowered her glass. Her eyes went wide as her mouth curled into a smile. Almost as if she realized she was outwardly expressing her excitement, she tried to shake off the smile, but didn't quite succeed.

She wiped her mouth and nodded her head. "Sure am."

I grinned and nodded my head, expecting she'd expand on her answer.

After a few minutes of fidgeting in her seat, she gazed down at the table and once again seemed to fade off into deep thought. In an effort to not get caught again, I shifted my eyes from my remaining pizza to her and back repeatedly, finding something about her with each glance that I enjoyed.

"I don't know what Ripp told you about the guy he was in court about," she said as she glanced upward. "The guy he uhhm. You know, the guy he killed."

I shook my head as I wiped my hands on my napkin. "Nothing, really. I just know he did something to you, and then when Ripp confronted him, he pulled a gun."

"Well, it was a long time ago, really, but the guy and I were hanging out, you know. And, after a while, it got serious. So, as far as sex went, he knew I was saving myself for the right man, and I didn't know if he was that man. So, uhhm, we never had sex."

I admire you even more.

"That's admirable," I said.

"It *was*," she said.

No, don't tell me...

"I have no idea why I'm telling you this, but..." she paused and shifted her eyes up from her plate and gazed beyond me.

I was afraid I didn't want to hear what she had to say.

"We were seeing each other, and he knew...he knew that I was... you know, that I was a virgin. I told him *no*, but...he uhhm...he forced himself on me..."

She paused and shifted her eyes to meet mine. I raised my hand and shook my head, she didn't need to continue.

But she did.

"He uhhm...he raped me," she said.

I filled with rage. The thought of anyone raping a woman infuriated me. I felt like digging up his grave and beating his corpse to an absolute pulp. It was a good thing Ripp had broken his neck, because if he hadn't, no jury would have found me *not guilty* of anything. I fought against my inner self and tried to be calm.

I whispered a raw apology. "I'm sorry."

She pursed her lips and gazed past me as she nodded her head. "Me too. It happened almost a year ago. I've gone to a ton of therapy, and it helped me accept some things. I didn't tell anyone about it at first, and really never planned to. It really bothered me. So, I told Manda, and she told me to go to therapy. It helped a lot, but it still bothered me. Then one day at dinner, long after it happened, I just lost it."

I sat and stared at her blankly, not really knowing what to say, if anything.

"So I'm not a virgin anymore and it sucks. You know, having it taken from me like that," she said.

I didn't dispute that she was raped, but I didn't necessarily agree with her thoughts on the matter of her losing her virginity. I had previously considered the exact same scenario, when a friend's cousin was raped.

"As far as I'm concerned, you're still a virgin," I said.

She narrowed her eyes and stared. "How?"

"Well, it's just a theory, but hear me out," I said.

She nodded her head. "Okay."

"A person is with a guy who commits murder, but doesn't know going into it that he's going to do that, and has no knowledge it was going to happen. Does that make the bystander a murderer?" I asked.

"No," she said with a slight grin.

"Had he murdered?" I asked.

"The second guy?" she asked.

I nodded my head.

"No, I guess not," she said.

"If you go golfing with a friend, say just to watch him play a round, and he golfs, but you don't participate, you're just there riding in the cart, when the round is over, have you ever golfed?" I asked.

She smiled even more. "No."

"He may have raped you. But you haven't had sex. Does that make sense?" I asked.

She stood from her seat.

I wiped my hands and stood. With her blue eyes fixed on mine, and mine clearly glued to hers, she walked around the edge of the table. Without speaking, she opened her arms. As odd as it seemed to be hugging her, for whatever reason, it felt more right than anything I had done in a long, long time. As she wrapped her arms around me and held me against her, she rested her chin against my shoulder.

Once again, I inhaled a hint of her soft perfume. I closed my eyes, pleased I could help her see things slightly differently.

"Thank you," was all she said.

And it was all I needed to hear.

CHAPTER TWENTY

Summer 2014, Austin, Texas, USA

I quickly found myself in a place I hadn't expected to be, feeling in a way I hadn't anticipated feeling, and confronted with a situation I was awkwardly excited about. For a man who planned everything from the exact moment I got up in the morning to what my meals were going to be a week in advance, and everything in between – including how many of my tee shirts were in each stack in my dresser – I felt a strange sense of comfort.

Katie talked to Ripp about her desire to have me take her on a date, and although I wish she would have let me be the first to talk to him, I accepted not everything in life would always be in my control. I did talk to Ripp at length following their discussion, and was relieved to find out he trusted me with his sister.

One more stop and I was home free to take her on an actual date.

I took a breath and knocked on the door twice. I had always looked at a doorbell as a lazy way of knocking, and I was far from being a lazy man. I waited nervously with my hands at my sides for the door to open.

He opened the door slightly, recognized me, and smiled. "Alec, how are you?"

"I am well, Sir, thank you," I responded.

"Come in," he said as he opened the door fully.

As I followed him into the house I realized this was something I had only done a few times in my life. As simple as a date may seem to most men, to me it was a tremendous commitment, and something I certainly didn't take lightly. For me to ask a woman on a date, I had to see the possibility of a future relationship with her. I realized a date was simply that – an event on a specific day where two people chose to spend time together – and that there were no assurances, but if I didn't feel the potential existed for a long-term relationship, I wouldn't even ask.

"So, what's the occasion," he said over his shoulder as he walked toward the living room.

"Well, Sir, I'd like to speak to you about your daughter," I responded as I followed him into the room.

"Have a seat," he said as he sat down in the recliner positioned in the corner of the room.

He wasn't as big of a man as Ripp, but he was close. It was easy to see that in his prime he would have been an intimidating figure. Although he wasn't attempting to terrorize me, he was doing a good job of making me nervous. As I chose the seat next to him, I placed my hands in my lap, turned to face him, and smiled.

Smiling was something that I did infrequently, and many people often assumed I was angry at all times. My face permanently etched with a stern look and my walk filled with Marine Corps attitude, it was easy to assume I was a man who was rarely happy.

Most of the time I was happy, just not happy enough to share my feelings with the outside world.

He fixed his eyes on mine and chuckled a light laugh. "I'm guessing when you all went out the other night you had fun. The girls said it was a pretty good time. Hell, you never know with girls, they'll tell you whatever you want to hear, won't they, Son?"

"Yes, Sir, I'm sure that's a true statement," I nodded.

He raised his hand to his chin and rubbed the slight growth of beard on his face. "So what's the problem? Did one of them act up the other night?"

I rubbed my palms along the thighs of my jeans and shook my head lightly. "No sir, certainly not. It's not anything like that. I wanted to ask your permission for something, Sir."

I'd walk into a firefight with a dozen insurgents without question, but talking to Katie's father made me a nervous wreck. Sitting there knowing I now needed to continue caused my throat to constrict and my palms to sweat. I swallowed the lump in my throat and forced a dry grin as he looked at me with a face filled with confusion.

"Permission? Hell you don't need my permission for anything, Son. What the hell you needin'?" he asked as he lowered his hand from his chin.

"Sir, we went out the other night, and I was able to spend a considerable amount of time with the entire group, your daughters included. We had a really nice time. In doing so, Sir, I was able to get to know Katie a little better…"

I paused, took a shallow breath, and allowed him to digest what I had said before I continued.

"In getting to understand her more, I realized a few things. One, she wants a man in her life. Two, she *needs* a man in her life. And three, I believe, Sir, I can be that man. I'd like to ask your permission, Sir, to take her on a date," I said.

His mouth curled into a smile. "You called and came here to ask my permission to take my daughter on a date? Bug?"

"Yes, Sir, that is correct," I responded with a nod of my head.

He coughed a light laugh and glanced beyond me for a moment. "Well, normally I suppose I'd have a lot of shit to say. You know, to be respectful. Or remind you that she's been through a lot lately, and she doesn't need a guy trying to get in her pants right now. Hell, maybe I'd offer a few choice words about wearing protection, birth control, and how there's plenty of kids in this country that don't have parents..."

"But with you, I don't think I need to say any of those things directly. Instead, I'll say this; Mike and I have talked about you. At length, I might add. He thinks the world of you. If Mike thinks the world of you, I believe him. He's a hard man to impress. I've formed my own opinions about you, and I'll admit you easily rise to the top of the pool of men that I'd choose for Katie. Suppose it brings me to this," he raised his hand in the air and extended his index finger.

"Two things. First one is this. You're not from here. And I ain't lookin' to have my daughter taken from me, Mr. Jacob. Not now or ever. As far as I'm concerned, she can leave Texas when I'm dead, but not before. Now, before I get to number two, what do you have to say about that?"

I suspected as close knit as the family was he may have such concerns, but I didn't expect him to express them prior to giving me permission to go on a date with Katie. I lowered my chin, shifted my eyes from his finger to face, and responded.

"Well, Sir. I have been offered a job at the gym. I intend to teach a women's self-defense course as well as a hand-to-hand combat course. Kelsey and Joe made the deal with Mike and me last week. I've already started scheduling people. Short of the men I ride with, I have nothing in Kansas, and I'll stay here as long as your daughter will have me," I responded.

"Does that job at the gym pay you enough money to survive?"

"I suppose not, Sir. The United States Government does. I get a check monthly. A very healthy one, I might add. Being shot half a dozen times pays pretty well, I suppose," I said with a grin.

He chuckled and nodded his head. "I suppose so."

He cleared his throat and raised his middle finger. "Alright, number two. Sunday dinners. We have 'em here, on Sundays. I realize there are times when you may not be able to come. Hell, things happen. But you'll never miss more than two weeks in a row, is that understood?" he asked as he slowly raised one eyebrow.

The thought of attending that fiasco on a regular basis was not only entertaining, but something I would look forward to. Since my mother's death, I missed the feeling of having a meal with family. My mouth broke into an immediate smile at his choice of *is that understood*, because it was exactly what I asked my Marines on a regular basis.

"Yes, Sir. I like to eat, and your wife is a great cook," I said with a nod.

It seemed, in some respects, that he felt as if I was asking his permission to marry Katie. I suppose it was possible he was merely doing his best to look out for what he believed was in her best interest. If the things that were important to him were not important to me, he probably saw no value in letting me take her on the first date. As he began to rub his chin again, I waited for his approval.

"Well, I lied," he said as he lowered his hand and leaned forward. "There's one more thing, and I'm afraid although I might discuss it, I won't bargain much."

I pressed my palms along my jeans from my upper thighs to my knees. "Yes, Sir."

"My understanding is you're a smoker, and you smoke a lot. I don't want my future son in law, who by the grace of God almighty has made it out of wars in Iraq and Afghanistan unscathed, to die of lung cancer. I'll need you to figure out a way to give up those cigarettes, Son. I'll need that to happen here real soon. No exceptions. We have a deal?" he asked as he stood from his chair and extended his hand.

I stood from my chair and proudly shook his hand. "Deal."

"Well, I must say, I couldn't be happier for you or for Bug. She's a damned fine girl. I like it that you came here like this, Son. It was downright respectful of you. I'm anxious to see how this thing pans out," he said, gripping my hand firmly in his.

"Can you excuse me, Sir? I have something on the bike I need to give you. I'll need to go get it," I said as I released his hand.

He widened his eyes, smiled, and tossed his hand toward the door. "Sure. Hell, whatever you need to do. And when you come back in, don't bother knocking. Family doesn't knock."

I walked back to the front porch and out of habit, almost knocked. I grinned at the thought of being *family*, as he said, and reached for the door handle. I walked toward the living room rather eagerly, and upon walking in, noticed he and Katie sitting across from each other talking.

I walked to his chair and extended my hand.

He furrowed his brow and looked at the pack of cigarettes.

"What are you doing, son?" he asked.

"Take them. If I ever want to smoke one, I'll ask you for it. Other than that, I'll never smoke another, Sir. Fair price to pay for what's on the port side of your living room, sir," I said as I motioned toward Katie.

He smiled and accepted the pack of cigarettes.

"Now, the last thing," I turned to face Katie.

"Katie, would you like to accompany me on a date this Saturday night?" I asked.

She crossed her legs, placed her hands on her knees, and smiled as she cocked her head to the side. "Possibly. At what time?"

"I expect, Ma'am, I would like to pick you up around six o'clock. And bring you back at let's say," I hesitated and turned to face her father.

He held one finger in the air.

"One o'clock in the morning," I said.

"I'd love to," she responded.

"Great. Well, I've got to get to work now, Sir," I said as I extended my hand toward her father.

He stood from his chair and shook my hand.

I nodded my head toward Katie and grinned. "Katie."

She smiled in return and rolled her eyes.

I turned toward her father and smiled. "I'll let myself out, Sir."

As I walked to the door, I grinned at the thought of starting over. Potentially developing a long term relationship and maybe even having a family. As I opened the door, I heard Katie's father yell.

"Alec?"

"Yes, Sir," I responded over my shoulder.

"Welcome to the family," he yelled.

Somewhat premature, Sir, but I'll accept it.

I opened the door and stepped onto the porch. As I pulled the door closed, I stuck my head into the opening between the door and the frame.

"Thank you, Sir," I responded.

I won't disappoint you.

CHAPTER TWENTY-ONE

Summer 2014, Austin, Texas, USA

People often described me as *different*, and I can't say that I would argue with them. I didn't march to the beat of a *different drummer*, I marched to the beat of my own drummer. Everything I did, I did for a reason; and if I was doing it, I was exceptional at it. I didn't attempt things I wasn't able to succeed at, and although I would consider myself to be an open-minded man, I wasn't open to new things without a reasonable amount of consideration in advance.

My madness had meaning.

Always.

"This is the coolest date ever," she said as she shouldered the water-powered rifle.

"You should just give up," I said with a laugh. "That stuffed cat is ugly anyway."

"That stuffed cat's name is Winky. Pardon my French, but that son-of-a-bitch is mine," she growled as she nodded her head toward the man in charge of the game.

In my travels on my motorcycle a few days prior, I had found a carnival a few miles south of the city, and decided it would be the first event of the night for our date. Once we were in the gate, our first stop wasn't a ride, but a carnival game; and we had been there for almost an hour. The BB gun she was shooting was powered by water, and to win the prize she had to shoot the red star out of the center of a sheet of paper.

This was her sixth attempt.

As she nodded her head the man flipped the switch on the timed water pump. As close as I was able to tell, the time allotted was 30 seconds.

The BB's spit from the barrel of the rifle toward the target like rounds from the USMC Squad Automatic Weapon. With great form, one hell of a cute pair of jeans, and a never-say-die attitude, she sprayed the target until the buzzer went off.

The man retrieved the target and handed it to her without looking as if he already knew she hadn't won the prize.

"Sorry," he said with a shrug of his shoulders. "Looks like this isn't your ball of wax."

She glanced at the target. A small corner of the red star remained on the paper, one shot away from being eliminated. She shook her head and tossed the target beside the others.

"According to who?" She snapped back. "The sights on this piece of shit are off. I've about got it figured out, let's go again."

"You want a different rifle?" he asked, waving toward the five other unoccupied stalls.

"No," she said sarcastically. "I already said I have this one figured out."

"Again," she said as she nodded her head toward the gallery.

He placed another target on the chain, secured it in place, and widened his eyes comically. "Ready?"

She nodded her head. "Yep."

He flipped the switch.

Again, she sprayed the target with B.B.s as fast as she was able. I stood and admired her choice of jeans, turquoise sneakers, and well-fitted top she wore, but above all, I admired her devotion. As the buzzer sounded, she slammed the rifle down on the edge of the counter and pointed at the target.

"Let's see *that* one," she said, wagging her finger toward the target as she spoke.

He reeled the target to the end of the chain and pulled it from the metal clip.

"Sorry," he said as he handed her the target.

She studied the target at length. "Sorry what? Sorry you've got to give me the cat?"

She handed him the target. "Have another look, Buddy."

I raised my hand to my mouth and tried to cover the grin on my face. It was apparent, even from where I was standing, that she had won the prize. As she stood on her tip-toes and eyed the prize, she glanced over her left shoulder and grinned a prideful grin.

In return, I lowered my hand and revealed my smile.

He glanced down at the target, raised it over his head, and held it under the dim overhead lights. After a few long seconds of staring at it, he sighed heavily and pinned the target to the *wall of fame*.

"Which one?" he asked.

"You *know* which one," she said as she nodded her head toward the stuffed cat.

He pulled the striped cat from the overhead hook and handed it to her. "One prize per group per night. Have a nice time, folks."

She turned to face me, grinned, and shoved the cat into her purse.

"That took longer than I expected."

"You could have given up an hour ago," I said as I glanced at my watch.

"Seriously? And give up? Uhhm, no. I would have stayed there until midnight if I had to," she said.

Good to know.

"Pretty nice shooting, though," I said.

"I'm from Texas. Everyone in Texas knows how to shoot," she said.

I nodded my head in agreement. Texas was without a doubt the most gun friendly state I had even been in, that was for sure.

"Your brother teach you?" I asked.

She shook her head. "No, dad did. Our house used to be on the outside of town when I was a kid. The city kind of grew around us. But yeah, dad taught me. He taught all of us."

"Pronto Pups. Holy crap. When was the last time you had a Pronto Pup?" she asked as she pointed to the hot dog stand on our right.

"Easy. Never," I said.

"You've *never* had a Pronto Pup?" she asked.

"Nope."

"It's a banquet on a stick," she said, quoting from memory what was painted on the wooden sign displayed over the wooden structure.

"Not a part of your diet?" she asked.

I chuckled. "Not exactly."

"Two Pronto Pups, please," she said to the attendant.

As he produced the two hot dogs on sticks, I reached for my wallet. She shook her head, reached in her purse, and paid for the hot dogs.

"My treat. Your first, and probably last, Pronto Pup," she said as she handed me one of the oversized corn dogs.

I held the stick in my hand and stared down at the glob of fried cornmeal batter.

"Mustard. You've got to put mustard on it," she said as she squirted mustard along the length of the dog.

I leaned to the side and did the same. In unison, we bit into our dogs, each widening our eyes toward the other as we attempted to fit the oversized Pup into our mouth. As I continued to eat the *World Famous Since 1947* carnival favorite, I was slightly disappointed.

Not in the Pronto Pup – because it was actually quite good – but because I knew that I was adamant in maintaining my diet, and realized this would likely be not only the first time – but the last time – I would ever eat one of the tasty treats. As I finished the snack and stared down at the stick – making sure there was no remaining fried batter to gnaw off – I paused and glanced up at Katie.

With the sides of her mouth covered in mustard and her mouth curled into a smile, she stood and stared at me.

"You've got mustard on your mouth," I said.

"And you've got nice teeth," she said.

I reached beside the condiments, grabbed a few napkins, and handed her one. "Thank you. I try to take care of myself, teeth included."

"Well, it shows. I'm guessing you liked it?" she asked as she tossed her stick and the mustard-covered napkin in the trash.

"It was actually pretty good," I admitted.

"Stick around," she said. "I'll change your mind on a lot of things."

As much as I hated the thought of change in my life, I hoped she was right.

"What's next?" she asked.

"Ferris wheel," I said.

She grabbed her stomach. "Oh God."

"What?" I asked as I walked to her side.

"Those things kind of make me queasy," she said.

"So…"

"No," she said. "I'll do it. We'll see how it goes. It's been a long time."

A few minutes later, we were atop the Ferris wheel, sitting stationary, gazing back into the city we had driven from earlier.

"I haven't seen the city from this perspective. It looks peaceful and small," she said.

"That's one of the reasons I like these things," I said.

She glanced over her shoulder. Although it was pitch black, and I was able to see very little, her blue eyes stood out in clear contrast to her tanned skin. After a few seconds of staring at each other silently, she grinned. "Why?"

I felt like I had been awoken from a dream, and couldn't immediately remember what we were talking about. I shook my head, feeling somewhat foolish for losing my train of thought.

"Why do you like them?" she asked.

I pried my eyes from hers and gazed out over the city as the wheel slowly began to turn, lowering us to our next stop. The city of almost 2,000,000 people seemed to be much smaller than the city of 400,000 I had recently moved from. The speeding traffic, busy highways, and overcrowded restaurants and bars were hidden by the distance, making the city seem rather unoccupied and peaceful.

"Perspective. It lets me see things from a different perspective," I said as I shifted my eyes to meet hers.

As she gazed in my direction, waiting for me to continue, she tossed her blonde hair over her shoulder. She was obviously more comfortable on the ride than she expected she would be. After gazing over her shoulder for a moment, she turned to face me again, and I continued.

"It's all too easy to be stuck in a certain mindset about something, and often we can't convince ourselves to maintain an open mind. This lets me see the exact same thing from a different vantage point. It doesn't change anything; it just provides a different point of view. It's a great reminder to maintain an open mind," I said.

"I like that. And, I like you. Let's do this again," she said.

"The Ferris wheel?" I asked.

She shook her head and grinned.

"No, *this*," she said as she waved her hand in a circle over her head. "Do something together."

And I couldn't have agreed with her more.

CHAPTER TWENTY-TWO

Summer 2014, Austin, Texas, USA

My Saturdays during the summer months had been spent doing whatever the weather permitted, but almost always it was something outside. Now, the only difference was that Katie was present. My time with her was something I enjoyed immensely, and it didn't seem to matter what it was we were doing, I found it to be pleasant.

I quickly realized not only was she different than Suzanne, but that I found pleasure in doing things with her I would have never considered with Suzanne. After considerable thought, it was clear to me that what little time I spent with Suzanne was done more out of a feeling of necessity than out of desire.

I spent time with her because she was my wife.

Being with Katie wasn't something that was expected of me, but it was exactly what I wanted.

"Did you see that movie with Josh Brolin? The one where he found the case full of money?" she asked.

We were hiking along the Colorado River northwest of the city, and the scenery was beautiful. The river had etched its way through the terrain hundreds of years before we arrived, through the solid rock formations, leaving a sheer rock cliff up one side of the river bank, and a shallow berm on the other. Both sides were lined with trees, rocks, and

161

crevices that made the river perfect for hiking.

I stepped over a large rock, stopped, and responded to what she had asked me.

"I haven't seen a lot of movies, except the recent ones. I've got about twelve years of catching up to do. When did it come out?" I asked.

She shrugged her shoulders. "I don't know, maybe like six years ago. Dad has it on DVD."

"What's it about?" I asked.

Dressed in canvas shorts, hiking boots, and a loose-fitting tee shirt, she sat down on a rock ten feet away from where I stood. I stepped back and sat down on the one I had just stepped over. As she situated herself on the rock, I pulled off my pack, set it to the side, and pulled out a bottle of water.

"Drink?" I asked.

"Sure," she said.

I tossed the bottle into the air, and wondered as it began to fall if she was going to catch it or drop it. As it fell in the space in front of her, she reached out and caught it one-handed.

"Impressive catch," I said.

"Thanks. It's brutal out here, and I wanted a drink," she said as she wiped her brow.

"That it is," I said.

It was late in the summer, but unseasonably warm. I had yet to spend an entire summer in Austin, but from what I could see it was considerably warmer than Wichita. I gazed over my left shoulder and toward the drop-off to the river, admiring the deep blue color of the water.

"Here," she said as she tossed the bottle of water in my direction.

Instead of tossing the bottle upward, she tossed it directly at me. Trying to catch it would have made a fool of me, so I rolled my shoulders back and let it slap against my chest. As it fell toward the ground, I reached down and caught it in my right hand.

"Yeah, that's not going to happen here," she said with a laugh as she stuck her chest out. "These things are like huge pillows."

Katie was tall, probably five-foot ten or a little more, thin, and had an extremely large chest for her size. In believing she was probably self-conscious about her breasts, I had yet to mention them one way or another, and did my utmost not to ever stare. Apparently, however, the size of them was a subject she didn't mind joking about.

"Probably not. You'll need to work on your hand-eye coordination. So what about the movie?" I asked as I unscrewed the lid from the bottle of water.

"Okay, Josh Brolin. He plays a guy that's maybe kind of like you. Maybe a little bit. The movie didn't say, but you get an idea that he's former military. It starts out, and he's out in the middle of nowhere hunting. He shoots an antelope, and while he's tracking it in the scope of his rifle, he scans across a bunch of abandoned trucks and SUVs. And there's dead guys all laying around," she paused and stretched her arms wide.

"So, he searches the vehicles and finds a ton of heroin. He leaves the dead men…wait…all but one is dead. So he leaves the dead men except for one who's alive, and goes home. The next day he goes back and the almost dead guy is under a tree right beside the place where they were shot. He walks up to the guy, and now he's dead, just like the others. And, he's clutching a case with two million bucks in it. So he takes the money and leaves him there."

"So, before I tell you the rest of the story, would you take the money?"

I didn't even need to think about it. "Nope."

She narrowed her eyes. "Really?"

"I live in a black and white world. It's either right or it's wrong. That's stealing. It's wrong. I guarantee you, that money was intended for someone, and they'd not only want it, but need it. Even if the reason behind it was dope, it's part of the cycle of life for that group of people. And for that group of people, the money would buy more dope, which would eventually get more bad guys killed, and the cycle would continue until the end. But no, I wouldn't take it," I explained.

"Wow," she said. "I ask everyone. And so far, everyone I've asked would take it."

I found it interesting she would ask everyone such a question. Now it was my turn.

"Would you?" I asked as I held the bottle of water up.

She shook her head. "Oh hell no."

"Hell no on the water or hell no on the money?" I asked.

"No on the water, and hell no on the money," she said.

"Why not?" I asked. "They're all dead. Dead men don't talk. It'd change your life."

She reached back with both hands and adjusted her ponytail as she glared at me. After shaking her head and satisfying herself it was as she wanted it to be, she responded.

"Damned right it'd change my life. For the worse. Karma. Or whatever you want to call it. If you do bad stuff, bad things happen to you. If you do good things, good things happen to you. I'm not interested in doing bad, being bad, however you want to look at it," she said.

"Good to know," I said.

"You know, in Baghdad there were several Marines who happened onto a lot of gold. I mean a lot. So, quite a few of them tried to ship it home in drums and boxes and however they could devise a way they thought would work. And every one of them got caught. Every damned one. And they were all sent to prison. Money makes people greedy. I'd much rather be poor and happy," I said.

"Same here," she said. "I'm glad you said you wouldn't take the money."

"I lead a simple life. You know what? As much as I've been through, and as much hatred and killing as I've seen, I still live every day happy. Some are tougher than others, but every day above ground is a good day," I said.

"I agree," she said as she stood. "Are you ready?"

I didn't have to convince myself I enjoyed my time with Katie. For once, I felt that I was truly where I should be, and I didn't have to worry about how I acted or reacted to situations. She seemed to accept me as I was, without explanations or excuses. It was refreshing to think a woman was interested enough in who I was to accept me without reservation.

I shoved the bottle of water in the pack, pulled it over my shoulder, and stood from my rather comfortable rock.

"You want to follow the river?" she asked as she pointed along the exposed edge of the cliff.

"Sure," I responded.

As she began to walk along the rock formation I adjusted my pack. A few more steps toward her, and she froze.

"Alec…" she whispered as she raised her hands in the air.

"What?"

"Rattlesnake," she whispered.

She no more than spoke, and I could hear the rattling of the snake's tail. As far as we were from the truck, and as long as it would take for us to get to a hospital, the possibility of dying was pretty probable if one of us were bitten.

Fuck.

Standing behind her and with the snake in front of her, I couldn't see it, but I could hear it, and it didn't seem to be interested in going away. It wasn't uncommon in the latter part of the summer when the days began to shorten and the nights became cooler for rattlesnakes to lie on rocks and absorb the warmth. When startled, they coiled, raised their heads, and prepared to strike at whatever they thought was a threat.

But in all actuality, the snake was just as scared as the human.

"How close?" I asked as I began to quietly make a large sweeping circle around where she stood.

"Five feet," she whispered.

"Don't move," I said as I walked around her.

"Alec…" she whispered.

"Don't worry," I said.

As I walked past her, I saw the snake. Easily four or more feet long, it was one of the largest rattlesnakes I had ever seen. Coiled and prepared to strike, there was no doubt if it felt threatened any more than it already did, it could bite her from its current position. I circled around her, stepped behind it, and stood still.

"Don't move," I whispered as I silently snapped a branch from the mesquite tree beside me.

She nodded her head.

One carefully placed step at a time, I approached the back of the snake, holding the stick in front of me for protection. When I was close enough to touch it, I lowered the tip of the branch onto the rock surface behind the snake's back.

I pressed the stick against the stone ledge, making a scraping sound with each stroke. The snake quickly turned toward me, coiled, and struck at the stick.

"Walk away," I said flatly as I continued to distract the snake.

She turned and walked away, toward the rock where I was seated earlier. After taunting the snake for a few more seconds, I dropped the stick and walked toward her.

Standing beside the rock staring down at the ground, it was obvious the encounter with the venomous snake had her rather upset. As I stepped in front of her, she reached out and wrapped her arms around me. I pulled her against me, held her tight, and I could feel her body trembling.

I leaned back and pulled my chest away from her. Her eyes were fixed on the ground between us. Slowly, I reached out, lifted her chin, and gazed into her eyes. They were filled with fear, and it was genuine. Although I couldn't always comfort those with fear-filled eyes I had seen in the past, there was something I could do for her.

It was something I wanted to do, but had not yet attempted. With our eyes locked on each other, I lowered my mouth to hers and kissed her.

Her soft lips pressed against mine, kissing me fully, passionately, and perfectly. As we embraced, our hands fumbled to find the perfect place to land, each of us positioning them in a location making the kiss even more flawless than it already was.

It was the first time I had kissed her, but it seemed to be my first kiss ever. Later, I decided it was. For that moment, it was the only kiss in my life that mattered, and I wanted it to never end. Throughout the embrace, she was slowly transforming me from a man with very little emotion into a man whose mind was opening into a sea of possibilities.

If a simple kiss had the ability to allow a person to see the compatibility of a prospective partner – and I did believe that to be the case – it was immediately apparent Katie and I were not only compatible, but placed on this earth to be kissing one another.

The kiss was long, passionate, and exactly what I felt I needed. When our lips eventually parted, she said two simple words. Simple, but more effective than anything else she could have said to convince me both of our lives were clearly in order.

"Don't stop," she breathed.

And I didn't.

CHAPTER TWENTY-THREE

Late summer 2014, Austin, Texas, USA

It had been a month since Katie and I started dating, and our time together was always enjoyable. Ripp and Shane shocked the family three-weeks prior, announcing simultaneously that their wives were pregnant. I couldn't have been happier for either of them, and was excited for the day to come when their children arrived. In my opinion, no one was more excited than Katie's father, who was having a hard time hiding not only his excitement, but his naturally protective nature of those he loved.

He pulled his fork from his mouth and wagged it toward Ripp. "You need to give that woman some space, Mike. You're crowding her. Inch over and give her some damned room."

I shifted my eyes toward Ripp. Sitting in his wife beater, covered in muscles, and littered from head to toe in tattoos, he probably didn't appear to be a soon-to-be father by all of those who saw him, but I knew where his devotion lied.

He lifted his head from the piece of chicken he was eating, glanced toward his father, and glared.

"The table ain't shrunk since we was all here last has it, Dckk?" Ripp asked as he stared at his father.

Shane looked up from his plate. "Not that I know of."

169

"A-Train, table seem smaller to you?" he asked without shifting his eyes from his father.

My assigned position at the table had changed from being seated beside Ripp to across the table between Manda and Katie. I peered over the table toward him and shook my head.

"Same size," I responded.

Still staring at his father, and his father steadily staring back, Ripp released his piece of chicken dramatically and tossed his hands into the air as his chicken fell to his plate.

"How in the hell can I be crowdin' her when we're all sittin' in the same spots we've always sat in, Pop?" he growled.

"She needs more damned room," his father growled in return. "She got one in the oven."

"It's the size of a damned piece of rice," Ripp said as he reached for his piece of chicken. "And Vee's fine, aren't you, Vee?"

"I've got plenty of room," she said.

His father shook his head. "A piece of rice? Where in the Sam Hill do you get your information? That kid's the size of a damned orange."

Ripp sighed loudly, lowered his piece of chicken from his mouth and let it dangle from his fingertips. "Internet, Pop. Maybe you heard of it."

"Oh, Lord. You can't go believing everything you read on that damned interweb" he said as he glanced down at his plate and began to eat.

"It's true, Mr. Ripton. Rice baby. I've looked," Kace said.

Mr. Ripton raised his head, turned toward Kace, and lowered his chin. "Is that a fact? Never would have guessed it."

Ripp glanced at Kace, shook his head, and shifted his eyes to his father.

"So Kace says it and it's a fact. I say it and I'm an idiot?" Ripp howled.

"You *are* an idiot. Rice baby or not, you're a damned fool, Mike. Now, eat your chicken," his father said with a gesture from the tip of his fork.

"Don't call Michael an idiot, it isn't nice," Mrs. Ripton said.

I grinned and glanced around the table. Everyone in attendance acted as if this was typical, and from what I had seen of the dinners at the Ripton residence, it was quite normal for the family to act in the manner they were acting. Vee rarely spoke unless spoken to, and Shane never said a word unless asked a question or paying Mrs. Ripton a compliment on the food. Manda, Ripp and Katie's sister, seemed to have a hidden agenda, and attended the meals only to eat, never saying a word one way or another.

Ripp cleaned the meat from the bone he was chewing on and tossed it aside. "You need to treat everyone at this table the same, Pop."

"I do," his father said without glancing up from his meal.

"Don't either," Ripp responded. "I said *rice baby*, and I'm a damned fool. Kace said rice baby and you said *is that a fact*. Be fair. I'm not a damned fool, and stop calling me one. I'm excited about this baby."

"So am I, Michael," his mother said.

"So am I," his father said with a hint of love in his eyes. "But you're a damned fool, baby or no baby. And I call 'em as I see 'em."

"Like a fuckin' umpire, now, huh? Now you're a god damned umpire, callin' 'em like you see 'em?" Ripp snarled playfully.

Katie gripped my leg slightly above my knee and squeezed, causing me to jump, hitting my leg on the bottom of the table.

171

"Michael Allen. Not. At. The. Table," his mother said as she looked up from her meal.

"Sorry, Ma," Ripp said.

Kace turned toward Ripp and cleared her throat to get his attention. "If we're treating everyone the same, why do you always say Shane is kissing your mother's rear end when he compliments her on the meal, and you never say the same to Alec?"

Ripp turned toward her and furrowed his brow. "Dekk's the all-time biggest ass kisser ever. A-Train's just sayin' when he likes something. It's different," Ripp explained.

"Nicknames, Michael," his mother said.

"I can't win," he said.

Ripp reached for the platter of chicken. After digging through the platter and tossing each piece of chicken to the side without actually taking a piece, his father looked up, tilted his head to the side, and widened his eyes. Still tossing pieces of chicken left and right as if looking for the perfect piece, Ripp didn't notice his father's glare.

"What in the hell are you doing, fingerin' all the damned chicken? Nobody's going to eat it now, who knows where those damned hands have been?" his father snarled.

"I know where they been, and they're clean," Ripp said without looking up.

Ripp turned toward his mother. "You buy breastless chickens, Ma?"

She shook her head. "Two per chicken, just like always."

"No extras?" he asked.

She shook her head. "It was before the football game, and they were out."

He pushed his chair from the table and crossed his arms in front of

172

his chest, like a child throwing a fit.

After a few long seconds of no one caring about his act of defiance, he cleared his throat. "Where the hell did you go?"

"HEB, just like always," she said.

"Eat a damned thigh," his father said, pointing to the platter of chicken with his fork. "Thighs are good."

"I ain't looking to get fat just because Vee's gonna get fat," he said. *Oh shit.*

"Excuse me?" Vee said. "I'm pregnant. I'm not *getting fat*, I'm *giving birth.*"

Vee had a dark complexion, had dark hair, and was what I would guess to be Italian. She was all of a size two at the absolute most. If she doubled in size she wouldn't be the size of one of Ripp's thighs.

"Well, you know what I mean," he said. "I'm done. I'm full. Food was good, Ma."

"Thank you Michael," his mother said.

"We're going to have to get out another leaf for this table when those grandkids get here," Mr. Ripton said as he glanced around the table.

As our eyes met, I nodded my head in agreement.

"So, Alec. You like kids?" his father asked.

"Yes, Sir. I love 'em. They're our future, and there's not a thing on this earth more innocent and eager to absorb all we're willing to offer them. I look at a child as our opportunity to right the future wrongs of this earth – in how we raise them and the values we instill in them," I said.

He nodded his head and grinned.

"I like that. Be a lot of fixin' right here though," he said as he wagged his fork toward Ripp.

Ripp shook his head, stood, and stomped to the kitchen with his plate full of bones.

"Good answer," Katie whispered.

"No secrets at the dinner table," Mrs. Ripton said.

Katie squeezed my leg again, causing me to jump slightly, but not as much as before.

"I said it was a good answer. I didn't think the table needed to hear me," she said.

After a shallow breath, she tilted her head back slightly and shouted. "Good answer!"

"There, now everyone knows," she said as she pushed herself from the table.

Eating dinner at the Ripton residence was nothing short of a three-ring circus.

"Are you finished?" she asked as she reached for my plate.

I nodded my head and handed her my plate. As she walked away, I realized little by little she was coming out of her shell. Be it because she was more comfortable with me, letting go of her past, or that we were simply making progress in our relationship, I didn't care.

One Sunday dinner at a time, I was becoming human again.

And so was she.

CHAPTER TWENTY-FOUR

Fall 2014, Austin, Texas, USA

Several months into Kace's pregnancy and Shane disappeared. For those who didn't know Shane, maybe it wouldn't have seemed at all a shock or out of character. For me, however, I knew something was terribly wrong, so I went to his home and talked with Kace at length about his disappearance.

"So, the doctors did that test, you know, the amnio deal, and they said our baby was probably going to be special needs," she said.

"How'd he take it?" I asked.

She shook her head and tossed her hands in the air.

I nodded my head and reached for my glass of tea. "Well, for what it's worth, I'm sorry. I know sorry doesn't fix things, but it's out of our control, you know? This is all God's will. So, did you two discuss it?"

She shook her head. "He clammed up, Alec. He wouldn't talk. He freaked out. I just thought he needed some space, but then he was gone. He hasn't talked to Ripp or Kelsey or anyone. And he's supposed to be getting ready for that fight. I swear, when he does come home..."

"I'll find him," I said.

"How?" she asked.

"I have my ways," I said.

"Kick his ass, Alec. I mean it. You know, everyone thinks he's so nice, and this? This is bullshit. Who leaves their pregnant wife? Who?" she asked.

Someone who's scared, that's who.

"I don't know," I said.

Kace was a saint. She was barely five-foot tall, a blonde, and more full of spunk than any other woman I had ever met. Her husband, six-foot two and 200 pounds of undefeated professional boxer, was no match for her. She would challenge him in a moment, and argue with him until she was blue in the face if it was something she believed in.

For Shane to leave her at such a time was absolutely unforgivable, but I fully understood. His reasoning for doing so was similar to my reasoning for keeping my distance from my father. The space that separated Shane and Kace prevented him from dealing with the issues in life he took exception to.

But a man can't hide forever.

Sooner or later, we're all forced to face reality whether we like it or not. It's only a matter of time.

I stood from my seat. "Well, thanks for taking the time to talk. I'll be in touch."

She stood and waddled to my side. After a heavy sigh and kicking one of the pillows across the floor, she gave me a hug.

"I meant it about kicking his ass," she said as I walked toward the door.

"We'll see," I said.

I had yet to meet a man I was scared of. If push came to shove, I'd fight Shane over this, but I sure didn't want to.

First, I had to find him.

***

The entire thought of Shane leaving Kace, their child potentially being born with special needs, and not having the best of luck finding him, and I went to Mr. Ripton and requested my cigarettes back.

Six days, half a pack of cigarettes, and 600 miles after talking to Kace, and I rolled into the parking lot of a shitty little diner in Anthony, New Mexico. Spitting distance from the Mexican border, and miles from any real civilization, Anthony was a small town of 9,000 people and a step into yesteryear, with half of the residents still riding horses.

As I pulled my motorcycle alongside Shane's filthy Harley, I peered through the glass and caught a glimpse of him sitting at a booth facing the lot. I wanted to walk in, grab him by his thick hair, and drag his ass back to Austin. After smoking two long drags off the cigarette, I put it out, and placed the butt in my shirt pocket alongside the others.

"You might need a lesson or two in how to hide, Dekk," I said as I walked into the diner.

He gazed back at me as if I were a ghost. "I won't even ask."

I walked to the edge of his booth, pointed to the empty side of the seat and waited. After a nod of his head, I sat down.

"In the future, you need to use cash. That debit card of yours is like a flashing beacon of fucking light." I said.

Without speaking, he pulled his hood over his head.

I glanced around the diner, then fixed my eyes on Shane. "I'm going to tell you a story. Say my peace, so to speak. When I'm done I'm going to walk outside and smoke another cigarette then ride out of here. I hate shitty little dusty towns like this. They remind me of places I'm trying to forget about."

I glanced out the window at the dust blowing down the street in front of the restaurant. "You know, if God was going to give the world an enema, he'd more than likely stick the tube in this shitty little town."

"When I leave you can either head out with me or stay here, I don't care either way," I said as I pointed toward a full cup of coffee on my side of the table.

He nodded his head toward the cup.

I took a drink from the cup of coffee, and considered the analogy I was prepared to share with him. After another sip of the luke-warm java I began.

"During my first tour, we were looking for al-Zawahiri. Hell, we were searching for a lot of al-Qaeda officials, but at this point in time, *he* was our target. We received intel on where he was and why he was there. It seems he was having a summit meeting of sorts with every other high ranking Islamic militant within a three-hundred-mile radius. Without a doubt, on this particular night, we were going to bag this shit-bird and bring the war to a screeching halt. At least that's what we were told."

He sat and stared, his hood pulled over his head to a point I could barely see his eyes. A complete meal sat on a plate in front of him. Apparently, I had stumbled onto him during his morning breakfast.

I tossed my head toward his plate. "Go ahead and eat, this is going to take a minute."

"So, based on this intel, they assembled a handful of us; three Marines, and seven or so SEALS. They indicated al-Zawahiri had gone into some shit-hole home earlier on this particular day, and he hadn't come out. Hell, from what they said, no one came in or out after he arrived. It seemed his little meeting was underway, and all we had to do was get there before he left," I pause and removed a cigarette from the pack.

As I chewed on the end of the unlit cigarette, I continued. "Now this being my first tour, I didn't have much experience – and none in extraction to speak of – only training. All the brass wanted him alive if possible, so they'd preached protocol and rules of engagement to us all fucking day. We all sat around and waited for the cover of darkness while we planned what we were going to do. You know, studying the chicken-shit map they'd given us showing the supposed layout of the home, cleaning our weapons, and talking about how we were going to get this prick."

"So, it's zero dark fucking thirty, and we're all waiting. About oh two thirty they round us up, take us as close as they can get us, tell us good luck and god fucking speed. We surround the front of this little mud hut and blow the door off this place, toss in a few flash-bangs, and in we go," I paused and recalled the night of the raid, and what a cluster-fuck it ended up being.

"Needless to say, I'm as nervous as a fucking whore in church service. I've got diarrhea, my stomach is all fucked up, my head's full of all kinds of thoughts on what *may* happen to me or to someone else, and what I'm going to do when it does. I'd gone over every possible god damned scenario based on the intel we have and who's supposedly in this shit-hole. You see Dekk, men are just that; men. And men make mistakes. A man will give you an *opinion*, and portray it as an absolute fact. If you're either gullible enough or dumb enough to believe him, you then make a life changing decision based on the inaccuracies of his beliefs."

I gazed out into the parking lot, stared at our two motorcycles for a moment, and turned to face Dekk. "And you see, Dekk. It's just that. It's an opinion. It'll never be any more or any less. If I had all of the lives we lost based on one man's opinion of what was sure *not* to happen, I could fill this fucking diner with good god damned Marines. But I can't, because they're all fucking dead."

"The opposite happened on this particular night. The shit-hole home was empty. No hidden exit. No tunnels. No way out except the doors which were in full view. And we had eyes on every fucking corner of this place. And after an assurance he and his band of merry men walked in and never came out – we went in after him. I was mad as fuck. Let down, depressed, and I felt kind of betrayed. They were wrong Dekk. They're wrong more than they're right. You know why? Because they're fucking human and they gave their *opinion*."

"You see," I said. "If we're forced to make a decision that has the potential to have a profound effect on our life, and it's based on the *opinion* of one man, we must weigh the legitimacy of the man in question. And in my humble opinion, if the man in question is not God, his opinion is nothing more than an educated guess."

He pulled the hood from his head and stared. After a few seconds, his face washed with what I would have guessed to be shame. I said all I came to say, and I hoped my little speech was enough to convince him to come home. As he gazed at me blankly, I stood, flipped the cigarette into my mouth, and nodded my head.

"I'm going to go burn this. I've been chewing on it for too damned long. Come out and join me?"

He nodded his head and stood from his seat.

I walked to my bike, lit the cigarette, and waited for him to come outside. Half-way into my four puff limit, and he was standing in front of me with a blank look on his face.

"So, you riding out with me?" I asked.

He shrugged his shoulders. "I don't know. I just…"

I shifted my eyes to meet his and glared. "You just what?"

The more I studied him the angrier I became. I tossed the cigarette on the ground beside the motorcycle, stepped on it, and stepped in front of him.

"You wanna give me your honest *opinion* as to whether or not you think you can whip my ass?" I asked.

His eyes widened. "Excuse me?"

I spread my feet shoulder width apart, and tugged against the thighs of my jeans. "You heard me."

His eyes fell to my feet, back up to my face, and narrowed. I needed to make another point, and I had hoped it wouldn't come to this. Desperate times, however…

"I have an *opinion* you won't get one punch to make contact. *Not a fucking one.* You know why? Because you're a washed up piece of overweight shit who's scared to fight for the title fight. You're scared to be amongst your friends, and scared like a little bitch you might have to become a man and raise a child who doesn't fall within the limits what *you* perceive as perfect," I said as I raised my hands in preparation of what was sure to come.

I would give anything to have a relationship with a woman and have a child. If God so chose to have that child be born with special needs, so be it. I'd welcome him into the earth with all of the love, care, and hope for a future that he or she deserved. For Shane to run from his responsibilities made my temper flare to a point I really didn't care if I had to fight him to make my point.

As he stood and glared at me, I continued.

"Did I hit a nerve? You afraid if you and Kace raise a special needs child someone might eventually call him a retard?"

His eyes narrowed and the muscles in his jaw flared.

Good, it's working.

"You'd get mad if they called your little boy a fucking retard. Huh Dekk? Your little retard boy?" I asked, attempting to lure him into a fight.

His right hand twitched, and I swung my left arm upward in anticipation for one of his signature heavyweight right hooks. As I stepped into the punch, allowing his arm to go under my armpit, I turned, pulled my knife, and held it to his throat.

I chuckled a light laugh and pressed the knife to his throat. "You see Dekk, you threw the punch under the *opinion* you were going to teach me a lesson. But here's the thing. I made those comments about your child knowing – *absolutely knowing* – I had to do so to make my point. You swung because you're going to defend your child regardless. Special needs or not, he's yours. Subconsciously, you're already committed to him being your son. And you're his father. You're just fucking scared. And there's nothing to be afraid of."

I pressed the knife with slightly more force, just to make sure he was paying attention. "That doctor gave you his fucking *opinion* based on the amnio test they performed. He told you the kid *might* have some chromosomal disorder. He said he could be born with Down Syndrome, and you fucking disappeared. Well, I got news for you. My nephew *is* special needs. More specifically, he has Down Syndrome. And he's one of the best damned people you'll ever meet. *Ever,*" I growled.

"You see; special needs are nothing more than *that*. He has needs that are special. It doesn't mean he isn't deserving of anything and everything that every other person on this earth is deserving of. It only means he has a few needs unique to him – and they're described as special. *Special.* You know the definition of special?" I asked as I released my grasp and pushed him to the side.

He stood with swollen tear-filled eyes and stared.

"Better or more important than others," I said as I pushed the knife into the pocket of my jeans.

Without speaking, he began to softly cry.

"I didn't mean a word I said about your child, Dekk. I was making a point, you need to know that," I said.

He nodded his head.

"Now, you know what we're gonna do?" I asked as I patted him on the shoulder.

"We're going to get on our sleds and ride to Austin. You're going to apologize to Kace, Ripp, Vee, Austin, the old man, and everyone else who's been worried about you. I could give two shits whether or not you're going to fight for the championship, makes no difference to me. But you're going to support Kace through this. And the day will come when your little boy will be born. And every fucking one of us will love him – because he's part of you, and he's part of Kace. Now, you ready to ride or you want me to wad you up into another ball and cut you this time?" I asked as I bent down and picked up the cigarette butt.

"A-Train?" he asked.

I stood and shoved the cigarette into my pocket. "What is it, Brother?"

"I'm scared," he said.

I nodded my head. "Been there plenty of times, Dekk. Generally, I'll ask the man upstairs for spoon full of courage."

He bit into his lower lip and nodded his head.

183

"You know what? He hasn't let me down yet," I said as I wrapped my arms around him.

I held him in my arms until he finally stopped crying.

After I released him he gazed down at the ground for a long moment. While clearing his throat, he glanced up with swollen eyes.

"Let's ride," he said.

"You lead the way, Brother," I said. "I've got your back."

And, little did he know it, but I had the back of his unborn son, too.

CHAPTER TWENTY-FIVE

Fall 2014, Austin, Texas, USA

The soon to be births of the children of my best friends put a damper on the feeling of necessity to start a new chapter for our motorcycle club. Although Shane, Ripp, and I enjoyed riding our motorcycles together, I felt no real desire or benefit in devoting any amount of time to the idea.

In recent months I was happier than I could ever remember being. I was slowly seeing a side of myself I had never seen, and was quite pleased with the transformation. Still much the Marine I had always been, I was evolving nonetheless into a man with different desires, feelings, and hopes.

I realized my former relationship was not necessarily a relationship at all – only a person to unwind with after each deployment. My entire adult life had been spent at war, and my time with Suzanne had been roughly one month a year – most of which I spent recovering from the horrors of battle.

Now spending time with a woman for all of the right reasons, life seemed so much different. Sitting at the bar with Shane and Ripp, however, reminded me some things were likely to never change.

"I can't fuckin' wait for this kid, Dekk. I been goin' to the store, and when I go, I'm eyeballin' the aisles with kid shit in 'em instead of the aisles with guns and fishin' poles. Who'd a thought that?" Ripp said as he tipped up his bottle of beer.

Dekk shrugged his shoulders and grinned. "Not me."

"Hell, Ripp, I might be more excited about these two kids than both of you combined. I'm fucking giddy," I said.

Ripp wrinkled his nose and lowered his bottle of beer. "Giddy?"

"That's what I said," I said.

He shook his head, glanced at Dekk as if seeking support, and upon getting nothing in return, turned to face me. "High school girls are giddy."

I cocked my head to the side and widened my eyes. "Add me to the list."

"You alright, Bro?" he asked.

"Quite," I said.

"Sister of mine's got you all fucked up. Shit before long you two'll have a kid of your own," he said.

"Not yet," I said.

"Better be careful. Knock her up and Pop'll make you get married," he said.

"Don't have to worry about that," I said as I reached for my bottle of beer.

"Ain't shootin' blanks, are ya?" he asked.

I coughed a laugh. "No, as far as I know my ammunition's fine. We'd have to have sex first. That's what I meant."

He leaned forward and pressed his forearms onto the edge of the table. As he fixed his eyes on mine, he cocked one eyebrow and cleared his throat. "Couple a months and you two ain't fuckin'?"

Normally such a question would have been rewarded with an escorted trip to the parking lot or a punch in the face. As Katie was his sister, and he really meant no disrespect, I decided I would allow it.

"Listen. Most men ask questions after a guy dates a girl for a while like have you fucked her yet? Or is she good pussy? I don't ask those questions, and I don't appreciate them asked of me. Those things aren't my reason for being with her. If they're meant to be, they'll happen. If they're not, they won't. But when they do," I paused and reached for my beer.

I took a long drink, placed the bottle to the side, and leaned onto the edge of the table. As he met my gaze, I locked eyes with him.

"It'll be between Katie and me," I said.

After a few seconds of our eyes being locked, he leaned back in his seat and grinned. "Fair enough. It's nice knowing you ain't takin' advantage of my sis."

I nodded once and reached for my beer.

Ripp twisted in his seat for a moment as if uncomfortable, drank the rest of his beer, and leaned forward, resting his elbows on the edge of the table. As he rubbed his hands together, he fixed his eyes on mine.

"What?" I asked.

"You whack off all the time, don't you?" he asked.

Dekk choked on his turkey sandwich and I let out a long belly laugh.

"No, actually I don't," I said.

"Shit. I whack off while I'm getttin' ready to have sex. Sometimes after," he said as he leaned into the back of his seat.

"Good to know," I said with a laugh.

"You know why I like it so much?" he asked as he pointed at Dekk. "Don't answer, Dekk. Dekk knows, and I don't want him spoilin' it."

"Wasn't planning on it," Dekk said.

There wasn't anything to spoil. I didn't give a half-ounce of fucks why he whacked off as much as he did. But, as much as I fought against it, my mouth curled into a smile. "Why?"

"Because the whole fuckin' time, I'm in control. Speed. Passion. All of it," he said.

Passionate masturbation?

I stared at him in disbelief. "Passion?"

"Yep," he said as he waved his hand at the waitress. "I can make it rough sex, passionate, slow and easy, fast and light, fast and rough, hell the possibilities are endless."

I shook my head and laughed. "Well, I choose to exercise more control than that. Keeps me strong, alert, and more passionate about relationships."

He tossed his head toward Shane. "Sound like Dekk, now. He ain't much for whackin' off either."

"What can I get for you?" the waitress asked.

"Two things," Ripp responded. "Bring us a glass of water, and two more beers."

"Is that it?" she asked.

"No," Ripp said. "I said there was two, that's one. Here's the other. I got a question."

She placed her hand on her hip and glanced at each of us individually. "Okay."

"Who here has the most self-control?" he asked.

Without shifting her eyes away from him, she responded. "Those two. Probably a dead tie. My guess is you've got none."

"Seriously?" he asked.

"Yeah, seriously," she responded. "Is that it?"

"Yeah," he said. "That's it."

"Sharp girl," I said.

"Is it that obvious?" he asked.

"Just as well have it tattooed on your forehead," Dekk said.

Ripp shifted his focus to Dekk, and glared. "Shut it, Dekk. You ain't got that much self-control. You beat the fuck out of people for a living."

"So do you," Dekk responded.

Sitting at the bar with Ripp and Shane wasn't much different than being at Sunday dinner. It was anyone's guess what the topic of discussion would be, and there was never a doubt that Ripp would be the center of attention. He didn't do it out of necessity or desire, it was just that he was a very outspoken person with very little tact.

"Whatever, Dekk," Ripp said with a wave of his hand.

"Back to the original subject," I said. "I'm pretty excited about this kid thing. And if anybody needs a babysitter, I'm your guy."

"No shit?" Ripp said.

I nodded my head. "I'm serious. I love kids."

"Know anything about 'em?" he asked.

"Damn bit more than you, if I was forced to guess," I said with a laugh.

"Ain't never had any though, huh?" he asked.

I shook my head. "No, not yet."

"Got any nephews or nieces?" he asked.

I had never been a man to lie, and now wasn't the time to start. In some respects, I led myself into the question and needed to answer it, but I sat staring at my bottle of beer trying to decide just how to answer it without answering it in full.

"My sister had a little boy. I haven't seen him in years," I said.

"Must not like 'em too much," he said.

Now I have to answer….

"Actually, I do. She put him up for adoption. I don't have any right to see him any longer." I said. "Long story."

It wasn't a subject I liked to discuss with anyone, and it was the reason I hadn't spoken to my father – or my sister – in so many years. In front of Shane, who I had already shared my nephew being a special needs child, I hated to bring up the subject. Although we hadn't discussed the matter since I went to New Mexico and brought him home, I could only guess that he still struggled with the subject.

"Sorry to hear it, Brother," Ripp said.

"Not as sorry as I am to say it," I said. "It makes me sick."

And truer words had never been spoken.

CHAPTER TWENTY-SIX

Early Winter 2014, Austin, Texas, USA

Life, at least for me, had always been full of surprises. To say that things happen when they're least expected would be the understatement of a lifetime. Although Vee was further along than Kace in her pregnancy, Kace gave birth first, a little prematurely. I received a text message and multiple calls from both Shane and Ripp, but I was out for a ride on my motorcycle and didn't see them until I stopped for gas.

The ninety miles I rode from south of the city passed in less than an hour, and I came to a screeching halt beside the entrance of the hospital. After parking my motorcycle on the edge of sidewalk leading to the hospital, I rushed through the door and to the receptionist desk.

"Dekkar. Childbirth, they've moved them. I need the room number, please," I said.

"Spell the name," she receptionist said.

"D. E. K. K. A. R. Dekkar," I said excitedly.

She pecked at the keys, stared at the monitor, and glanced up. "Room 724. Down the hall, on the elevator on the left, and up to seven. It's on the right."

"Do you have a flower shop?" I asked.

"Right down the hall, on the way to the elevator. Third door on the left," she said.

I chose the perfect bouquet of flowers and ran down the hall to the elevator. As the door opened on the seventh floor, I clutched the flowers, gazed down at the toes of my boots, and exhaled. I calmly walked down the hallway, glancing at each of the numbers until I reached their room.

724.

I rubbed the palms of my hands against the thighs of my jeans and took a deep breath. On the other side of the door I could hear Ripp's voice over everything else. Another deep breath, and I pushed the door open.

"Uncle A-Train is here," I whispered as I walked into the room.

Kace's hair was an absolute mess, and she looked exhausted. Shane looked equally worn out, but was smiling from ear to ear. Ripp, dressed in his typical shorts, wife beater, and Chucks despite the fact it was winter, and Vee was wearing cotton pregnancy pants, a cute black top, and flats.

As I walked into the room, Kace's eyes shifted to the flowers I held, and she forced a slight smile as she tried to sit up.

"These are for you," I said as I leaned over the edge of the bed and kissed her cheek.

I placed the vase of flowers on the table beside the bed.

"Fellas," I said as I nodded my head toward Shane and Ripp.

"Congratulations," I said as I shook Shane's hand.

"Thank you," he said.

I did my best to contain my excitement, but it didn't last long. Beside the far side of the bed a bassinet sat with a heat lamp over it. I craned my neck and did my best to peer inside, but from the end of the bed I could see nothing.

I tossed my head toward the side of the bed as I edged my way past

Ripp. "Can I hold…"

My throat constricted and my mouth went completely dry. It was much tougher than I imagined it would be. I wedged myself between the edge of the bed and the small bed the baby was sleeping in. I glanced at Shane, shifted my eyes toward Kace, and met her gaze. She nodded her head and grinned.

I peered into the bassinet.

Innocently sleeping and undoubtedly developing into a man with each passing second, he was much smaller than I remembered my first nephew being. After admiring him for a few seconds, my eyes began to well with tears.

"Don't worry, Alec. You won't break him," I heard Kace say from behind me.

I turned away from the bassinet and faced the bathroom. "My hands. I need to wash my hands."

I walked into the bathroom, closed the door, and stared down at my boots as I washed my hands. After more than a decade of experiencing my fair share of death, embracing a new life being introduced to the earth was almost more than I could stand to witness. I dried my hands, inhaled a shallow breath, and stared blankly into the mirror. I couldn't let this nephew escape me.

You keep him healthy, Lord, and I'll keep him safe.

I reached for the door, pulled it open, and paused.

Thank you.

"Good to go," I said as I raised my hands in the air.

I quietly walked to the bassinet, reached inside, and carefully picked up my nephew.

Ripp continued to tell a story, Shane argued about the size of the man Ripp had challenged to a fight, and Kace quietly laughed.

For me, the room fell silent.

I gazed down at the child cradled in my arms and couldn't help but smile. A new life. Another chance for someone to grow into the next person to make a difference on earth. Potentially the future President of the United States, a doctor who may cure cancer, or possibly the man who just might convince the world to live in peace.

I turned away from the crowd, began to hum him a tune, and allowed a tear to roll down my cheek.

And for that moment, as I held my sleeping nephew in my arms, nothing else mattered.

CHAPTER TWENTY-SEVEN

Early Winter 2014, Austin, Texas, USA

"Do you have anything in white gold? I've never much cared for yellow gold," I said as I gazed at the display of jewelry he had placed in front of me.

"We certainly do, it's one case over, follow me," he said as he reached for the jewelry.

After securing the bracelets in the display I followed him to the next case, peered down at the jewelry, and grinned. They were exactly what I had in mind. The thought of giving Katie a gift she could enjoy for a lifetime was exciting to me, and although I realized life offered no assurances, I had no reason to believe we wouldn't be spending the rest of our lives together.

"Here are three that are my personal favorites," he said as he placed three velvet-lined boxes on the glass surface.

I picked up the one in the center, studied it, and slid the box to the side. The diamonds were larger, had better clarity, and the bracelet appeared to be of slightly better quality than the others. "These are custom, correct?"

"That is correct, our jeweler hand-crafts them all," he said with a nod. "That particular piece is 8 carats total weight. The stones are VS1 clarity and E color. We have less expensive pieces, but we do not have a better quality. If cost is something you're concerned with…"

I found it unnerving that because of how I was dressed and that I rode in on a Harley he would find me less capable to purchase his jewelry than anyone else who would happen into his store.

"Did I mention cost?" I asked.

"No, Sir. You did not," he said.

"I'll take this one," I said as I placed my hand over the bracelet I had set to the side.

I watched his Adam's apple rise and fall as his eyes shifted downward and recognized which one I had chosen.

"That particular piece is $21,000. There will be state tax added, increasing the total to $21,650," he said flatly.

"Put the others back in the case, I'll take it. Do you take cash?" I asked.

He swallowed heavily again. "We certainly do."

I nodded my head and lowered the pack from my shoulders. After checking over each shoulder and determining the store was still empty, I carefully lifted the pack to the counter. I wanted Katie to have something that would act as a constant reminder of my presence in her life, and it's been said *diamonds are forever*. Nothing would make me happier than to see her pleasure from a gift I had chosen for her.

"Safe to count it here?" I asked.

He glanced over his shoulder, flipped a switch on the wall, and nodded his head. "Yes, it is."

I counted 217 one-hundred dollar bills, placed them on the counter, and after his recounting and totaling the amount, he gave me fifty-dollars change.

"Would you like me to gift wrap it?" he asked.

I reached into my pack and removed a hand towel I had brought with me. "No, Sir. I'll take care of that myself."

After wrapping the box in the towel and placing it in my pack, I zipped the pack up.

"All secure?" he asked.

I pulled the pack over my shoulder. "Couldn't be safer if it was in Fort Knox."

He reached to the side and flipped the switch, deactivating the electronic door lock. "You're free to browse the store if you like, or the door's unlocked whenever you're ready."

"Appreciate it," I said over my shoulder.

"My pleasure," he said. "Glad we could be of service."

I pushed the door open, paused, and turned to face the store. "Do you make custom rings as well?"

"We certainly do," he said with a smile.

I nodded my head and turned away.

Good to know.

If things keep going my way, I may need one here pretty soon.

CHAPTER TWENTY-EIGHT

Early Winter 2014, Austin, Texas, USA

In Katie's presence, the events of my day disappeared, regardless of what they might be. I found her to be cleansing to me, and each time we were together I felt myself becoming a fractionally better man that I was when we saw each other last.

Our time together seemed to pass quickly, and I couldn't get enough exposure to her no matter how frequently I was able to see her. While we were in each other's arms or embraced in a kiss, my watch seemed to spin at a much slower pace; allowing me to always enjoy our intimacy for what I perceived as a longer period of time.

I positioned the steak on the plate beside the grilled vegetables and placed the small bowl of peaches to the side. As I carefully lifted a portion of the salad from the bowl to the plate, she shouted from the other room.

"You sure you don't want me to help?" she asked from the other room.

"Just about done. Be there in just a minute," I responded.

"But you don't want any help?" she asked.

"Sure don't," I said. "Just sit still."

"Preparing her a meal was more enjoyable than I ever would have imagined. Making something I hoped she would enjoy with my own hands gave me a sense of accomplishment I couldn't recall ever feeling. If it happened that she actually enjoyed eating it as much as I enjoyed preparing it, I would be an extremely happy man.

I lifted the plates from the counter and carefully walked to the dining room.

"Viola," I said as I lowered her plate to the table.

"Wow," she said. "It looks great."

"Unless you got the wrong plate, your steak should be medium-well. Mine's medium-rare, so if you cut into it and it's wrong, hand it over," I said as I sat down.

"Believe me, I will," she said with a laugh.

"Peaches?" she asked as she poked the peach with her fork.

"It's dessert, but I kind of had to do it at the same time on the grille. I was about out of gas. They're grilled with brown sugar sprinkled on them," I said as I motioned toward her plate.

"Well, it looks great," she said.

"I've got the right steak," she said as she lifted a piece of the meat to her mouth.

"That's good, because I don't think I could eat a piece of medium-well steak, even if I tried," I said.

"It seems like it's still almost alive," she said. "I don't get it."

I shrugged my shoulders as I poked my fork into my salad. "Maybe it's a man thing."

"I think so," she said. "And it's got something to do with life, death, and everything in between."

I'd never looked at it that way, but she had a good point. Men eating their steaks half-raw could very well have to do with something primal within us. As I cut into my meat and the little remaining blood ran onto the plate, I decided she was right.

We enjoyed our meal, and the peaches – as I had hoped – were a huge success.

"These peaches are *good*," she said as she shoveled them into her mouth.

"I'm glad you like them," I said.

"I don't like them, I *love* them. I'm going to have to tell mom about them. You just grilled them?" she asked.

"That's it. I bought 'em fresh at the store, cut 'em in quarters, and grilled them until they were slightly soft. Then I just sprinkled the brown sugar on them," I said.

"Well, they're great," she said.

"And this entire thing," she said as she waved her hand toward the table. "It's just. I don't know. It's too much."

"It's dinner. It's a necessary part of the day," I said as I poked my last peach with the tines of my fork.

"Well, most guys don't do things like this," she said.

Well, maybe they should.

I looked up from my plate to see her gazing into the small bowl hoping to find a peach that didn't exist. Finally, after she realized they were truly gone, she sat up straight and exhaled a sigh of frustration.

To anyone else she probably appeared no differently than she did on any other day. To me, she seemed to be more beautiful than ever. I didn't look at her with eyes more capable of seeing, or with a mind more open that it had ever been in the past, but she was truly different. I sat and admired her until she met my gaze. As she returned my smile and brushed her hair over her ears, I raised my fork and offered her my peach.

"It's not the last one is it?" she asked.

I nodded my head. "Last one in the house. I cooked them all."

"I don't want to take your last one, you eat it," she said.

I shook my head and wiggled my fork slightly, careful to keep the beloved peach from falling to the table.

"I want you to have it" I said.

"Share?" she asked.

"Sure," I said as I reached over the table and handed her my fork.

I fully expected her to eat half the peach and hand me the fork in return. Instead, she lifted the fork to her mouth, bit into the peach, and pulled it from the tine. With the peach half in her mouth and half out, she leaned over the table.

Without speaking, our mouths met. The sugar-coated peach was nothing compared to the sweet kiss of her lips, something I seemed to yearn for from the very moment our last kiss ended.

Resting on my elbows and hovering over the center of the table, I kissed her fully and passionately, while the sweet taste of the peach lingered throughout the length of the kiss. Long after the taste of the peach was gone, she broke the embrace.

I opened my eyes and gazed in her direction. She tilted her head, stared up at the ceiling, and mumbled to herself as I lowered myself into my chair.

"What?" I asked.

"I don't want this to end," she said.

I shook my head. "It won't."

"You make my stomach go crazy each time you kiss me. It's just too good to be true," she said.

"I think that's just what happens when two people are really meant to be together," I said.

I truly believed what I told her. Kissing her was more satisfying than anything to me. No other woman on earth could provide me the feeling of satisfaction that Katie provided me by simply kissing me, and not only did I know it, I wasn't afraid to admit it.

"Kissing you takes me somewhere else. Somewhere nice," I said.

"I feel the same way," she said as she stood from the table.

I stood from my seat. "Hand me your plate. I'll get it. I've got one more thing."

"I'll help you," she said.

I shook my head. "It's a surprise."

"Crap. I hate surprises. Okay," she said as she handed me her plate.

I carried the dishes to the kitchen, opened the freezer, and removed two dishes of raspberry sorbet, being careful not to mix them up. As I carried them to the dining room, I fought the urge to smile.

"Here, maybe it'll help you forget the peaches. It's just a small dish," I said as I handed it to her.

"It's cute," she said.

I sat in my chair and slowly ate my sorbet as I watched her eat hers. As her ball of raspberry-flavored dessert slowly disappeared, I wondered if I had possibly given her the wrong bowl.

"Theres..." she said as she shifted her eyes to her bowl.

"Something in here. It's..." she placed her spoon to the side, lifted the bowl and peered inside.

She shifted her eyes toward me.

I shrugged my shoulders and attempted to act preoccupied. As I caught a glimpse of her fishing in the bowl with her fingers, I glanced over the table.

She pulled the bracelet from the dish and held it between her thumb and forefinger, dangling it over the table. Raspberry sorbet dripped from the end of the string of diamonds as she stared at it, still obviously not knowing exactly what it was. It looked like a small string of red beads.

"What'd you find?" I asked.

Her lack of response prompted me to stand, grab my glass of water, and walk to her side.

"Here," I said as I reached for the bracelet.

I took it from the tips of her fingers, rinsed it in the glass of water, and wiped it as clean as I was able in her napkin. After drying it off fully, I placed it in my palm and extended my hand.

She gazed into my hand, gasped, and shifted her eyes upward. As she stood from her seat she turned to face me, opened her mouth and said nothing. She stood with her mouth agape and her eyes filled with surprise as I carefully clasped it around her wrist.

She didn't speak. She really didn't have to, her eyes said everything words would have been able to, and even more. As she leaned forward, I was fully aware we were about to kiss once again, and nothing, at least at that particular moment, could have made me happier.

The kiss was more magical than the kiss prior to it, and far more passionate than any kiss I had ever experienced. I think, on that night, Katie gave me a part of her that she had been reserving for when she realized I had given her all of me there was to offer. It had nothing to do with the bracelet or the diamonds, it had to do with my heart, and hopefully she realized I had given her no less than my heart and soul.

I had no more of myself to give, she was the recipient of all I had to offer her, and all I could do was hope having me in her life was enough to please her half as much as she pleased me.

As our lips parted and our eyes met, I was sure of one thing and one thing only.

I had truly been blessed.

CHAPTER TWENTY-NINE

Early Winter 2014, Austin, Texas, USA

The entire group paced the hospital waiting room floor, waiting for an answer. Ripp insisted on being alone with Vee during the birth of their child, and that the sex of the child be a surprise. After over two hours of no news whatsoever, the crowd was growing weary.

I walked to the car seat, gazed down at Casey, and shook my head. "Get that little Marine out of that shit you got him wrapped in Kace, you're smothering him."

Kace stopped pacing and turned to face me. "Keep your hands off of him, Alec. He's sleeping. You can hold him later."

She turned toward Shane. "How long are they going to be in there? I popped mine out in like ten minutes."

He might have been sleeping, but he looked uncomfortable. It appeared she had him dressed for a Canadian vacation, and although it was technically winter, it was winter in *Texas*, and the temperature outside was 65 degrees.

"I know he's hot, he's got to be," I said as I reached into the car seat.

Kace stopped pacing and pressed her hands to her hips. "Stop it Alec, you're going to wake him up."

As I pulled him from the seat his eyes opened, closed, and opened again. After a few more sessions of opening and closing, he opened them, did his best to focus on me, and gazed up at me with one eye looking directly at me and the other looking toward the wall.

"Stop that, or they'll stick," I said with a laugh as I wiped the tips of my fingers over his eye lids.

When they opened again, his eyes were right where they should be.

"That's more like it. Now, let's take a walk," I said as I walked to Katie's side.

"You ready to be an aunt?" I asked as I leaned forward and kissed her.

"I feel like I already am," she said. "But yeah, I'm pretty excited."

I nodded my head and smiled as I bounced Casey in my arms. After a few seconds, he began to fuss.

"He needs me to sing to him, I'll be right back," I said.

I walked to the windows, tilted him to the side so he could see the street lights outside, and began to hum.

"You ready for *our song*?" I asked.

His eyes said *yes*.

"Here we go…"

As we paced the floor, I began to softly sing the Marine Corps Hymn.

"From the Halls of Montezuma…"

"To the shores of Tripoli…"

"We fight our country's battles…"

"In the air, on land, and sea…"

"First to fight for right and freedom…"

"And to keep our honor clean…"

"We are proud to claim the title…"

"Of United States Marine…"

I continued to pace the floor, not paying much attention to anything other than the baby in my arms. After a few laps across the floor, I shifted my eyes down to Casey. He was fast asleep, but that by no means meant he wasn't listening to his favorite uncle.

"You see, as Marines, we're *first to fight*. Anytime, anyplace, anywhere. As soon as you wake up, I'll tell you a story about the night Gunny Marshall and I got drunk in Okinawa, Japan. You'll appreciate it when you're a little older," I said.

"You will not, Alec. Don't fill his head with stories about your drunken escapades," Kace snapped from across the room.

I glanced toward Kace and grinned, not realizing I had walked close enough for her to hear me. "Just reassuring him he's safe in my arms."

The unmistakable sound of someone running down the hallway echoed throughout the hospital. All eyes shifted to the door.

"You motherfucker's ready?" Ripp screamed as he stepped in front of the door.

"Michael!" his mother gasped. "Don't say that in the hospital."

"It ain't a church, Ma. And it ain't the dinner table, it's a fuckin' hospital," he said as his eyes darted around the room.

He tossed his hands in the air and widened his eyes. "So, you ready for the news?"

Apparently he didn't like the lack of response from the crowd and was attempting to develop interest.

"Ready!," Katie hollered.

"We've been waiting for three hours, spill it," his father bellowed.

Katie walked to my side, squeezed my arm, and waited for the report.

"Eight pounds and fifteen ounces. Almost a nine pounder," he said. "And both my little girls are doing just fine."

"A girl?" Kace shouted. "Vee had a girl?"

"*We* had a girl, she's *ours*," Ripp responded.

"Congratulations, Brother," I said with a nod.

"A baby girl," Katie whispered.

"What's her name?" Kace and Mrs. Ripton asked at the same time.

Ripp remained standing slightly inside the door, and looked like the ring leader for a circus who was making his announcement to the crowd. With his shoes covered in protective booties and still wearing the Tyvek paper suit, it was hard for me to take him seriously.

He waved his arms like an excited child as he responded. "Three at a time can come see her, and her name is Jessica Ann Ripton. We're gonna call her Jessie. Jessie and Casey, has a nice ring, huh?"

I held Casey with Katie at my side, not necessarily as interested in the birth of Ripp's daughter as much as I was in holding my nephew. It wasn't that I didn't care, or that I was even insensitive to the event, it was more a matter of prioritizing.

Katie was my first commitment, and she was the most important thing to me. Casey was my second, and he was equally important, but his needs were different. I had always done a pretty good job prioritizing my commitments, and the majority of my devotion was currently cradled in my arms.

"How's Vee?" Kace asked.

"Vee's doing great," he responded. "I need to get some cigars; we need to celebrate."

"Got 'em right here, Ripper," Kelsey said as he reached into his gym bag. "Brought several of both, just in case.

"Alec?" Mr. Ripton asked as he held a cigar in the air.

I grinned and shrugged my shoulders. "Still trying to quit."

He shook his head from side to side and tossed the cigar into the air.

I cradled Casey with one arm and caught the cigar with the other. As I shoved the cigar into my back pocket, I glanced around the room.

The excitement lingered heavily in the room. Hugging, talking, and Ripp's repeated telling of the birth continued until his mother complained about needing to see the baby. After a short argument, Ripp decided to take his parents and Kace in the first wave to see the baby.

I continued to cradle Casey in my arms, hoping Shane wouldn't object. As Ripp walked out of the room, I wondered how many babies were born throughout the course of a typical day and if that number exceeded the amount of men killed in a normal day during the war.

As Katie began to walk in my direction, her face covered with the satisfaction of being new aunt, I decided it didn't matter. All that mattered at that moment was what was in my arms, and what was walking toward me.

I was no longer at war, and I was no longer in charge of protecting Marines. My solemn duty, at least at the moment, was to protect the people gathered in the waiting room.

And I intended to do that at all costs.

CHAPTER THIRTY

Early Winter 2014, Austin, Texas, USA

In what was to be our pre-fight celebration, we left the kids with the grandparents and had gone out on the town the night before Shane's heavyweight championship fight. He was an extremely humble man, and he certainly didn't act like the celebrity he had become. He was soon going to be fighting in a match with tens of millions of people watching which would net him in excess of 50 million dollars if he won. To be in his presence, however, a person would have no idea he was any different than anyone else.

I couldn't help but admire his simplistic way of living life. His quiet and humble demeanor resembled mine in many ways. He was not one to tell stories about the events of his life, and didn't care to brag about what his accomplishments were. Ripp was a completely different person, and I felt that Shane and I both lived vicariously through him.

After a late night of drinking and listening to Ripp's stories, one of which was about him throwing up on his daughter after smelling her diaper, we decided to call it a night.

"Big fight tomorrow, Dekk," I said as I patted Shane on the back.

Walking down the sidewalk with his arm over Kace, he glanced over his shoulder and grinned. "Hope I don't embarrass myself."

"All you can do is give it your best, Brother," I said.

"He's gonna smash that dude," Ripp said.

Shane's opponent, 'Tick-Tock' Brock earned his nickname from knocking out his rivals in a matter of minutes. According to his camp, the clock ticked past the seconds until the inevitable happened.

He was massive, he was strong, and he was as mean of a boxer to ever step in the ring with anyone. But, in my opinion, he wasn't as determined as Shane. All Shane needed to do was get angry. And making him angry wasn't always an easy feat.

"It's not going to be that easy, Ripp. We'll see," Shane said as we walked alongside the parking lot where Vee had parked her SUV.

The bar we had been in was in a district labeled Dirty Sixth, which was the east side of 6th street in downtown Austin, and earned its name from being a filthy place to be. The area was filled with bars and other forms of entertainment but deciding what to enjoy and what to avoid wasn't always easy.

Parking was disastrous, and remote parking areas were generally the only option. Luckily we had found one close to the bar we were patronizing, and by the grace of God, Vee's SUV wasn't stolen while we were in the bar.

As we stepped into the parking lot, Vee, Katie, and I walked to the left side of the SUV, and Ripp, Shane, and Kace walked to the right side. Immediately after Vee pressed her key fob and unlocked the vehicle, the dirty side of 6th street emerged.

"Oh my God! Shane!" I heard Kace screech.

Her voice clearly conveyed her fear. I ducked down and peered through the windows toward the other side of the vehicle. Although I couldn't see everyone, I was able to see all I *needed* to see.

A man had a gun pointed directly at Shane's head.

"What happened?" Katie asked.

"Listen," I whispered as I shifted my eyes back and forth between Vee and Katie. "There's a man with a gun. Do *not* walk around the other side of the car. Is that understood?"

"Oh my God," Katie whispered.

"I'll be right back," I said as I leaned forward and kissed her.

She pulled away and glared at me. "Alec, no. He could kill you. I'll just call the police."

I glanced through the windows again. The man continued to hold the gun at Shane's head and seemed to be mumbling demands. There was no time to argue, and there was no time for the police. In a city like Austin, the police wouldn't arrive for half an hour, and a robbery like this ended – one way or another – in less than five minutes.

"I'll be right back," I said.

"Please," Katie begged.

"Go," Vee whispered as she wrapped her arm around Katie.

"Alec…"

"I'll be right back," I assured her.

As Katie began to softly cry, I slumped my shoulders and sauntered to the other side of the SUV.

As I walked around the back side of the vehicle, I could clearly see everyone and everything. Half of the parking lot lamps were broken, but the illumination from the adjacent building's lights was enough for me to see what I needed to. The man, wearing a dingy black hoodie and dirty jeans, appeared to be holding a semi-automatic pistol with an external safety. My intention was to take it from him without him shooting me or anyone else during the process. With his back slightly to me, and Shane, Kace, and Ripp facing me, I raised my right index finger to my lips as I slowly approached them.

"Give me all your muh muh money, boxer man," the man stammered.

"Give him whatever he wants," Kace shouted.

Quiet down, Kace.

Apparently he knew Shane was a professional boxer and had probably seen us going into the bar and recognized Shane. His two-hour wait let me know he was determined to get what he came for.

"Babe. Just settle down, I'll give him whatever he wants," Shane said.

"Well, get get get to givin', muh muh motherfucker," the man stuttered.

With the gun an inch from his forehead and his hands held in the air at each of his sides, Shane responded. "I'll give you what I've got but…"

I cleared my throat lightly to get his attention. "But, I carry the money. I'm his bodyguard. I've got all the cash."

You need to focus on me, motherfucker.

"Duh duh don't walk up on me, Mr. fuh fuh fucking bodyguard. I'll kuh kuh kill this boxer lickety split if you do," he said as his eyes darted back and forth between Shane and me.

As I continued to study the pistol, I walked in a wide sweeping pattern around the four of them and stepped beside Shane. I wanted the man to be as comfortable as he could be considering the circumstances. Having his attention diverted to behind him may have caused Ripp to attempt something, or possibly even Shane, neither of which would end well for anyone.

"Listen. I've got the money. So, you're going to need to talk to *me*. But we've got a little problem," I said as I shifted my eyes to the pistol he held.

Colt 1911 A1, cocked and locked.

Thank God.

He'll have to release the safety.

The pistol he held would require two steps before it could be fired. First, the safety would have to be flipped to *off*. Second, he would have to pull the trigger. The entire process, if performed by an absolute idiot, would take one second. A second didn't sound like much time, but it was all I needed. The extra step of flipping the safety provided me just enough time to do what I needed to do.

I shifted my focus from the pistol to his eyes. "He pays me to keep his money safe, you know, protect it. Now, I can't just give it to you or he's going to fire me as soon as you're gone – and I'll lose my fucking job."

"So for me to let you have it, I'm going to need you to point the gun at me and threaten me," I said.

I needed him to move the gun directly in front of me, preferably either at my chest or directly at my head.

"I ain't duh duh dumb. He'll buh buh box my ears when I muh muh move the gun," he stuttered.

His eyes told me he was long overdue for whatever drugs he intended to buy with his proceeds from the robbery. He was a time bomb waiting to explode.

Eliminate his perceived threat, Jacob.

I shook my head lightly. "No he won't. I'll make sure he doesn't do a god damned thing. It's my job to keep *him safe*, and keep *you happy*. You're just going to have to trust me."

His eyes remained focused on me while I spoke, which at least let me know he was more concerned with getting paid than anything else.

"He's got seventeen bucks in his wallet, and I've got ten thousand bucks, so you need to pay attention to *me*, not him," I said.

His eyes fell to my feet, quickly raised the length of my body, and eventually he met my gaze.

"Dekk, slowly put your hands in your jeans pockets. And I mean *slow*. Kace, I need you to take four steps to your left, babe. Just four. And stand there quietly. Ripp, Brother, don't you dare fucking move," I said calmly.

"Now, as soon as he gets his hands deep in his pockets, you're going to need to point the gun at *my* head," I explained.

"Alec, no!" I heard Katie scream from the other side of the car.

"It'll be just fine Katie," I said. "We'll all be sipping slurpies at the 7-Eleven in five minutes. I promise, Baby."

As Shane lowered his hands and pushed them into his pockets, the robber's eyes shifted downward and then quickly raised. As they darted back and forth between Shane and me, I gave my next command.

"Dekk, step four steps to the side slowly, and stand by your girl. He'll move the gun when you do. Just make it slow, Brother," I explained.

"I uhhm…" Shane began.

"Just move slowly. He doesn't want you, he wants me because I've got the money," I lied.

Shane slowly stepped to my left and wrapped his arms around Kace. Ripp, still standing to my right, was potentially in the danger zone. Normally, there would be a few ways I could disarm the man, but with the people I was trying to protect on my left, there was only one way to do it, and it was the least favorable.

"Ripp, move to my left and stand with them. I really need you to go over there, Brother. Being behind me like that makes me nervous, and I know it makes him nervous too. You're just too damned close," I said flatly.

"Wuh wuh what about thu thu the ten grand, fucker?" the gunman asked as he moved the gun directly in front of my forehead.

As he stood and stared at me with uncertain eyes, I slowly raised my hands as if I was scared, stopping them in front of my chest.

"I'm going to reach for my wallet with my left hand. I'll do it slow. Hell you got that piece pushed into my forehead, so you know I won't try a damned thing," I assured him.

Come on, Ripp, get your big ass over there.

As Ripp stepped beside Shane and Kace, I continued.

"I'm nervous as hell, but I need you to be calm, okay? You okay with that? Me reaching for my wallet?" I asked.

I needed a reason for him to allow me to move my hands, and hoped my movement in a direction he wasn't expecting would be much quicker than his mind could process a threat.

He nodded his head. "Yup. Suh suh slow."

Every combat trained Marine had learned the maneuver in CQC training. It wasn't always effective, nor was it an assurance of not being shot, but considering the location of the people I needed to protect, it was my only choice.

With my eyes fixed on his, I slowly began to move my left hand slightly forward. As soon as I noticed his eyes didn't follow my hand, I swung my open left hand into the barrel of the pistol, and my cupped right hand into his forearm.

Instantly, he was disarmed, and I held his pistol in my right hand.

I pushed the pistol into his face, flipped the safety off, and gave my command.

"Get on your knees," I demanded.

With wide eyes and shaking hands, he slowly lowered himself to the ground.

"Holy shit!" Ripp shouted.

"It's all good over here, Katie," I shouted as I followed the man's head with the barrel of the weapon as he crouched to his knees.

Katie and Vee came around the end of the SUV, and Vee gasped as she saw what was going on.

"I'll call the police," she said.

"Fucking punk ass bitch. Now, I'm going to beat your ass," Ripp said from behind me.

"Stand down, Ripp," I said over my shoulder in a stern tone. "And Vee, don't call the cops. Our man Dekk has to fly out for a fight in less than 48 hours, and he doesn't need to be on the ten O'clock news, or sit in an interrogation room for eight hours."

Katie stood and stared with her hands covering her mouth, clearly scared.

"Don't worry, Baby. Everything will be just fine. Vee, get everyone in the car and go around the block. Just go around slowly and come back and get me," I said.

"Go around the block?" she asked.

Without shifting my eyes away from him, I responded. "Just load everyone up and go around the block. Do it quick. I don't need to be standing here with a gun any longer than I have to be."

"I'll stay here with A-Train, just roll around the block. Nobody needs to see this guy get his ass beat," Ripp said.

"Just like you always say, Brother Ripp, *I got this*. Just go with them.

Give me ten, alright?" I asked as I glared down at the would-be thief.

Reluctantly, they got in the SUV and backed out of the parking stall. As they pulled away, I lowered the pistol, shoved it into the waist of my jeans, and sighed.

As he stared up at me, his eyes filled with wonder, I planted the heel of my boot into his forehead, knocking him onto his back.

"That's for pulling a gun on the father of my nephew," I said. "If you move, I'll break your fucking neck."

I reached down and helped him to his knees. Blood trickled down along his face from the massive cut on his forehead. There was no doubt he was half delirious, but I didn't have much time to make a decision, and I needed his undivided attention.

"You're going to need to listen, and listen carefully," I said.

He nodded his head eagerly. As with many people who terrorized others, he had obviously never been on the receiving end of a violent situation and it was apparent by the level of fear his eyes projected.

"As you might have suspected, I'm not new to this shit. I've killed motherfuckers like you and walked away without even giving it a second thought. But something tells me I don't *need* to kill you. I've always said I give everyone a chance, and I guess this is yours. If you'll give me your solemn word that you'll never do something like this again, I'll let you walk away. If you don't, or if for some reason I don't believe you, I'll blow a hole in your head the size of a grapefruit. Now, you haven't got much time, so I need an answer," I said.

He fixed his eyes on mine, swallowed, and responded.

"Wuh wuh wuh won't happen. Eh eh ever ah ah again," he said.

Well, he maintained eye contact.

"Will you ever do anything like this again?" I asked, wanting to see where his eyes went when he responded.

He shook his head from side to side and maintained eye contact. "No."

"Why?" I asked.

I didn't care to hear his stuttering response, but I needed a little more reassurance.

"Buh buh because I'm guh guh giving my word," he said, his eyes locked on mine the entire time.

It appeared he was being truthful.

"Stand up slowly and turn around with your fingers interlocked behind your head, just like you were getting arrested," I said.

He slowly stood and complied with my request. After patting him down and finding not even a wallet, I pressed my hand against his right shoulder.

"Turn around," I said.

He turned to face me. His eyes told it all. He was scared shitless.

"Go sit beside that truck, out of sight. Don't move until you're sure twenty minutes have passed. Not five, not ten, not even fifteen, but twenty, Understood?" I asked.

He nodded his head repeatedly.

"Go," I said as I tilted my head toward a truck parked thirty feet away.

He stumbled to the truck, walked to the far side of it, and hunkered behind it, well out of sight.

I gazed down at my feet as I waited, realizing it was the first time in my life I had let such a man walk away. I was undoubtedly taking a risk, but my objective was to protect the people I loved, and I accomplished it without resorting to killing a man.

A tremendous improvement on my part, I felt proud knowing I was a more compassionate man than I had been in the past. I realized I would probably never know if my decision to let him go was a good one, but it was my decision nonetheless. As the SUV pulled up in front of me I knew one thing for sure.

At least he would never harm one of the people who were important to me.

Although I realized that particular fact wasn't all that mattered, it was all that seemed to matter at the moment.

And I had lived one more day without taking a life.

CHAPTER THIRTY-ONE

Early Winter 2014, Austin, Texas, USA

At one minute and fifty-seven seconds into the third round of the fight, Shane Dekkar knocked out Tick-Tock Brock and became the new Heavyweight Championship of the World. Not once did I doubt his ability, I only questioned his devotion. From what he said, he won the fight for Kelsey, who claimed to have never trained a fighter as great as Shane, and had never trained a champion.

Shane's father was a former Marine who was killed in the line of duty in Afghanistan, a fact that may have played a part in my devotion to Shane as a friend and brother. His father, however, had abused his mother, and his mother left when he was as small boy. He was raised by his grandfather while his father was away at war, and his mother never returned.

His grandfather trained him as a boxer, and the sport was Shane's outlet for a lifetime of frustration, anger, and slight hatred toward the actions of his father for what he had done to his mother. Shane never forgave his father, which was something else I could completely understand, because I had never forgiven mine fully either.

One night, after one of his fights, Shane's grandfather had a heart attack and died, prompting Shane to move to Texas from Compton, California for a new start in his career.

Kelsey trained Shane, and in many ways, became the fatherly figure he always wanted but never had. I admired Kelsey for being exactly what each fighter needed, but never allowing them to understand he cared about them as deeply as he did.

He was, to the fighters in the gym, exactly what I was to my combat Marines.

A true leader.

"Listen up, Jarhead," Kelsey said. "This gym has people beating the door down to be trained by the great Shane Dekkar, and if you can't make a fighter of this Justin Bieber look-alike, we need to send his skinny ass down the road."

"He's getting there, Boss," I said.

Kelsey shifted his eyes into the ring, studied Austin for a moment, and shook his head in exaggerated frustration. "He needs to stick to dancing and sashaying around like a princess."

"Two more weeks, and we'll know," I said, referring to Austin's first scheduled fight.

Ripp met Austin one day in a street race, and the two became quick friends. Austin was a dance instructor, and agreed to trade Ripp dance lessons for boxing lessons. Somehow, after the birth of Ripp's daughter, I became Austin's trainer. I enjoyed training him to not only box, but to protect himself, and to have the proper mindset to compete in a match.

I had no doubt he had the ability to win against any comparable opponent, and the last thing he wanted to do was let any of us down, so I was quite certain when the time came that he'd apply everything he had learned when fighting.

"The kid's a fucking weirdo, you've got two weeks, Jarhead," Kelsey complained as he turned away.

I glanced into the ring. Austin's opponent connected a right uppercut, sending him reeling backward to keep from falling.

Turn your body, Kid. Just like I taught you.

He twisted away from the other fighter as he stumbled, making himself more difficult to hit.

Suddenly, he had his footing. He raised his hands slightly, obviously ready to continue. As the fighter approached him, certain he was a few punches away from a win, Austin lit into him with a barrage of jabs.

The punches caught the other fighter off guard, and as he fought to keep his footing, Austin swung a slightly wild but extremely effective uppercut. It was, without a doubt, his most effective punch.

The fighter collapsed onto the mat, flat on his back.

I shifted my eyes toward the locker room. Kelsey stood beside the entrance intently watching the fight. As my eyes met his, he flipped me his middle finger and turned away.

You grumpy old fucker.

I shifted my eyes into the ring. The fighter was unsuccessfully attempting to get onto his feet. Austin shifted his eyes toward me and shrugged his shoulders.

"Fight's over, fellas," I said as I ducked under the ropes and entered the ring.

Training Austin was not only good for him, but it was good for me. It gave me a sense of accomplishment, and a means of measuring my success through his wins or losses. To date, he hadn't lost a fight, but everything so far was nothing but sparring, and not an actual boxing match.

As I helped the other fighter to his feet, I shifted my eyes toward Austin.

"I had my doubts, Kid. You need to protect that chin of yours or someone's going to knock it off," I said.

He nodded his head.

"You alright?" I asked the other fighter.

Incapable of responding legibly with a mouthpiece in his mouth, he blinked his eyes and nodded his head.

"Alright, hit the showers," I said as I tossed my head toward the locker room.

Kelsey began to walk out of the locker room, noticed Austin walking in that direction, and quickly turned toward the door. As I watched him hustle back into the locker room, I laughed to myself.

Going to give him some pointers, Old Man?

Shane had earned almost 50 million dollars for winning the fight, and Kelsey made enough to make his life slightly easier to live than it had been in the past. The money, however, would never change either of the men regarding the sport itself, they enjoyed it far too much.

I walked toward the locker room and stood beside the door waiting on Austin to come out. Kelsey's unmistakable voice echoed from the concrete room.

"Keep that chin tucked, Kid. You're going to lose it if you're not careful. And turn that skinny little body of yours when you're on your heels, it's a smaller target," he growled.

Sounds familiar.

"You got it, Boss," I heard Austin say.

"Now listen to me," Kelsey said. "Whatever that Marine tells you, you listen to him. He's a good man, and he'll lead you to a championship if you let him."

Filled with a newfound pride and a slightly inflated state of being,

I walked toward the ring, proud that Kelsey felt my abilities were sufficient. I realized I was good at almost everything I devoted time to, but I rarely received recognition from anyone for anything I had ever done. As I gathered up the wet towels from around the ring, I swelled with pride.

I turned toward the dirty rag bin and tossed the towels inside. As I glanced up Kelsey walked by, flipping me the bird as he passed.

I didn't say a word, at least not out loud.

Thank you, Old Man.

I won't let you down.

CHAPTER THIRTY-TWO

Late Winter 2015, Austin, Texas, USA

The day was unseasonably warm, and I was glad to be riding the motorcycle. A thirty-minute ride had the ability to transform my mind to another place altogether, and allow me to release things I would never be able to let go without it.

It seemed the nation's perception of a man in Levis and boots riding a Harley was one of drinking, fighting, and the commission of crimes. From what I had learned of bikers – and I had been exposed to all walks of biker life – the exact opposite was true.

Bikers were the first to stop and lend a helping hand, the last to resort to violence without a reason, and although they were quick to protect their brethren, they typically didn't do so with any more force than was necessary to do so.

As I sat at the traffic light one block away from my destination, the woman beside me in the minivan stared straight ahead at the traffic light, seemingly petrified in fear of what may happen if she glanced in my direction.

In the back seat, her children waved and made faces.

I grinned at the children, stuck out my tongue, and waved one last time before pulling in the clutch as the light changed from red to green.

I pulled into the driveway, shut off the engine, and let the bike coast to a stop. After a short emotion-filled hesitation, I tossed my leg over the bike and walked to the porch.

On my third knock, the door opened.

"I heard you half way up the street. I didn't think any of those damned things were louder than Mike's, but yours sure is. Got a distinct sound, too. Come on in, Son." he said as he opened the door.

"So, you called and said to get the pack of cigarettes ready. What's going on?" he asked.

"Can we go out onto the back deck?" I asked.

"Hell, we can go anywhere you like, Son. This is just as much your home as it is anyone's," he responded with a light laugh.

"You go on out there, and I'll grab those smokes," he said as he turned toward his bedroom.

I walked out onto the deck, glanced around the back yard, and inhaled a long slow breath through my nose. As I opened my mouth and tilted my head back, he opened the door to the deck. I exhaled and turned toward him.

"Great day, Sir," I said.

"Sure is. Damned near eighty degrees. Spring is almost upon us," he said as he handed me the pack of cigarettes.

Since I gave them to him, I had been back on three occasions. I took one from the pack, reached into my pocket, and removed my lighter. As I flipped the lighter between my fingers and toyed with the cigarette, he sat down in the chair beside me.

"Now I'm gonna guess because you're here and you're wanting a smoke that this is a tough day for ya, Son. Just what's going on?" he asked.

I sat down across from him, flipped the cigarette into my mouth, and bit into the cotton filter. As I clenched it lightly in my teeth, I shifted my eyes toward the large maple tree in the corner of the yard. I imagined each of his children attempting to climb the tree as they grew old enough to reach the lowest of the branches. I laughed to myself, took another breath of courage, and turned to face him.

I had no way of knowing how he was going to react to what I had to say, but I'd never been one to sugar-coat subjects or dance around the truth. There was one way and one way only to do what it was I came to do, and spitting out what I had to say was a far better alternative than chewing on it.

I raised the lighter to the tip of the cigarette, lit it, and inhaled a long pulled deep into my lungs. As the smoke from the stale cigarette burned my lungs, I fought not to cough. I tilted my head to the side, exhaled, and took another long drag, watching the paper burn as I mentally prepared to speak.

"Well, I'll tell you," I said as I exhaled the smoke toward the yard.

The deck was concrete, covered, and a very peaceful place to sit. I found it quite relaxing, and although Katie and I often used the space for relaxation and make-out sessions, the remainder of the family rarely came out onto the deck.

"I have a question for you," I said.

"Something's eatin' ya, I can see that. What happened?" he asked.

"Nothing happened," I said as I leaned forward, resting my forearms onto my thighs.

I fixed my eyes on his, swallowed, and said what I came to say.

"I've got something I feel like I need to do, and although I'm not planning on doing it for a while, I need to see if it's acceptable to you before I make any plans to do it," I said.

I was clearly beating around the bush.

He narrowed his eyes and stared, revealing the wrinkles beside his eyes that generally remained hidden. "Well, I can't help you if you don't tell me what it is, Son. Say what you've come to say, and we'll go from there," he said.

Katie's mother carried out two glasses of tea, handed them to us, and turned toward the house without speaking a word. As the door slid open, she spoke over her shoulder.

"Good afternoon, Alec," she said. "It's sure nice to see you."

"Good afternoon, Ma'am. And likewise." I responded as I raised the glass of tea to my lips.

I lowered the glass to the table, shifted my eyes to the cigarette, and then to Mr. Ripton.

Just say it, Jacob. Say it quickly

I locked my eyes on his. "I'd like to ask your permission to marry your daughter."

His eyes widened slowly as his mouth curled into grin. "Well, I'll be go to hell. That's what's eatin' you?"

I nodded my head. "It's not something I want to do right away, and I'll know for sure when the time is right, but I don't want to plan on doing it without your getting approval first."

At some point in time, the application of traditional values escaped the minds and lives of the residents of the nation, and although I firmly believed in old-fashioned traditions, there were not many people who shared my opinion.

Perform every task to the best of your ability.

Respect your elders by addressing them as Ma'am and Sir.

Open the door for anyone who's within eyeshot.

Don't lie, steal, or cheat.

If you have anything to say to someone, say it to their face or don't say it at all.

Ask a man's permission to marry his daughter.

Save sex for marriage.

Always remain true to the one you love.

"Damn it, Son. This heat's drying out my eyes," he said as he reached up and rubbed his eyes with the tips of his fingers.

After a few seconds, he stood from his seat, lowered his head, and coughed. As he looked up, he lowered his hands and nodded his head.

"It'd be an honor to have you as a son-in-law. It surely would," he said as he extended his hand.

I tossed my cigarette to the side and reached for his hand. "Thank you, Sir. I won't disappoint you. Or her for that matter."

"Now, you're not thinking of one of those runnin' off deals, are ya? You know, when the time comes, that is," he asked. "We'd sure like to attend."

"No, Sir." I chuckled. "I'd like for it to be something we could all enjoy."

He grinned a prideful grin, wiped his swollen eyes, and nodded his head. "That'd sure tickle the wife and me."

I reached down, snuffed the smoldering cigarette, and pushed the butt into the pocket of my jeans.

"Well, that's all I had," I said with a laugh as I patted him on the shoulder.

"Well, I don't know if I could handle any more in one day, so I suppose that's a good thing," he said. "You mind if I tell the wife?"

"Not at all," I said.

"That's good, I hate the thought of keeping secrets from that woman," he said as he shrugged his shoulders. "Call me old-fashioned."

"You and me both," I said with a laugh.

"Wouldn't want you any other way," he said as he draped his arms over my shoulder.

And, I couldn't have agreed with him more.

CHAPTER THIRTY-THREE

Late Winter 2015, Austin, Texas, USA

I had been blessed with an opportunity to babysit Casey while Shane and Kace went out to eat dinner and see a movie. For the first hour and a half, Casey slept and had absolutely no interest in waking, regardless of how much I wanted him to.

As he began to stir in his swing, I rushed to it and reached down to pick him up.

"Listen up, Little Man," I said as I pulled him from the swing.

As I raised him even with my face, he smiled. Seeing him smile was one of the best rewards life had ever offered me. With an adult, it was always anyone's guess whether the smile was genuine or not. With a baby, I knew it was always genuine. Babies don't lie and tell a man what he wants to hear, and they're always honest.

And a smiling baby is a happy baby.

"Your old man is a good fella."

He gazed off in the distance, well beyond me and toward the wall.

I carried him to the changing table, lowered him onto it, and opened his dirty diaper.

'Do you hear me?" I asked him as I changed his diaper.

His mouth curled into a slobber-covered smile as if he fully understood every word I said.

"He's a good solid dude, and you need to be sure and make him proud of you as he teaches you about life. Is that understood?"

Again, he grinned and cooed, apparently understanding each and every word. I picked him up, cradled him in my arms, and began pacing the house as we spoke. Having Casey in my life allowed me to look at things not necessarily differently, but with a more open mind. He provided me what the Ferris wheel provided me, an entirely different perspective on life.

A view from an alternate vantage point.

My exposure to him allowed me to develop a better relationship with God, as I was now sure God was looking down on all of us with compassion and understanding, which was something I had always worried about in the past. In short, Casey was damned good for me.

His eyes followed mine as I admired his ability to maintain focus not only on me, but on what I said each time I spoke. I realized he didn't understand me, but it was nice telling myself he did. One day, without a doubt, he would, and when that day came, I would be a very proud uncle.

"That's what I thought," I said with a nod. "I knew the minute you were born you'd be a good listener. You see, we grow up a product of our environment. Violence breeds violence, and a loving family teaches compassionate behavior. Your parents are as good as gold. They love you. And Ripp and I love you, Little Man. You need to know if you ever want someone to just kick it with you can always come to uncle A-Train. Remember that. I'll keep telling you, just in case your little baby brain forgets. But I'll be here for you, Little Man. Always."

"You see, my old man was a pretty good dude, but he didn't so much care for kids. Me? I'm different. I like little fellas like you. One of these days, I just might have to have one of my own. Maybe make a little brother for you. Some might call him a cousin, but that's not the case."

I shifted my eyes from the window down to his face. His eyes were drifting closed. "Are you paying attention to me, kid-o?"

The tone of my voice changing caused him to open his eyes and smile. As his gaze met mine, he giggled, opened his mouth, and released a little bit of baby slobber onto his cheek. I reached down to wipe off his mouth, and his eyes attempted to follow my finger, but he soon lost focus.

"We'll need to work on that, wont we?"

I moved my finger back and forth in front of his face slowly. As I did, his eyes followed it for the entire time.

"That's better. We'll tell your old man when he gets home you're going to be a good baseball player. He'll be excited. You'll just have to remember to always keep your eye on the ball, little man."

He grinned, got excited, and spit up a little bit. After I wiped his face with a burp rag, we got back to our discussion.

"Brothers are brothers, and don't ever let anyone tell you differently. Your aunt Katie and I might just make you a little brother or sister someday. If she'll marry me, that is. I asked her father for permission, and he gave me the go ahead, so it's all up to me now. I just need to make sure I'm ready for everything."

I heard the garage door open as we finished talking about the possibility of a marriage proposal. From the sound of the voices, Dekk and Kace had returned from the movie.

"Keep that marriage stuff quiet little man. Got it?" I asked.

"Right here," I said as I cradled him in one arm and held out my clenched fist with my free hand. "Pound it."

Babies invariably have clenched fists. Further proof they're always ready to make a promise and have every intention of keeping it. As I pounded my fist against his, he laughed.

"I know, the thought of it makes me giggle too," I grinned.

As I carefully placed Casey into his swing, I wiped his mouth one last time and kissed him on the cheek.

"We don't want your folks thinking I held you the entire time they were gone, so keep that quiet too."

Filled with gratitude and appreciation for everything Casey provided me, I bowed my head and closed my eyes.

If you let me make Katie a part of my life, I'll make you proud, Lord. I certainly will.

CHAPTER THIRTY-FOUR

Early Spring 2015, Austin, Texas, USA

Immediately following high school, I joined the military. Soon thereafter, I met Suzanne, and quickly got married. My deployments overseas to the war began as soon as my military training was complete, and they continued for over ten years. In short, my only exposure to the real world as an adult without the atrocities of combat, battle, and war, had been since my return from The Middle East.

The time I spent in Wichita following the war was unhealthy for me, and allowed me little, if any, recovery from post-war emotional and mental complications. My decision to move to Texas proved to be an excellent one, the elimination of stress alone allowed me to proceed through life with wide-open eyes. My new home allowed me, for the first time, to begin my journey not only to recovery, but to becoming a civilian responsible for his own actions.

Although I had been in combat for 12 years commanding troops, and home from the war for almost three years, I was experiencing the situations and making the same decisions that a high school senior would be forced to make upon graduating high school. My time in the Marine Corps did little to prepare me for living civilian life, and everything from housing, meals, and even medical provisions were provided for us.

I was cautiously proceeding through life no differently than if I was walking through a minefield.

And, since I had been in Texas, I had stepped in all the right places.

"I am so relaxed, it's crazy," she said.

With the tip of my index finger I traced along her skin lightly, from her shoulder to her wrist. Her skin was tanned from exposure to the Texas sun, yet silky smooth and without flaws. As she remained motionless, I slipped my finger under her hand and lifted it from the cushion.

I softly gripped the tips of her fingers and lifted her hand toward my face. Her eyes followed the movement of her hand, and as my lips pressed against the surface or her skin, she shifted her eyes to meet mine.

"Your skin," I said as I gazed along the length of her arm. "It's so soft."

"So are your lips," she responded. "I love it when you kiss me. It gives me goosebumps."

"Scoot in here and lay down with me," she said as she patted her hand against the cushion.

Comfortably positioned on the couch, seated beside her hips, I stared down at her and shook my head. "Not yet. I like it here."

She nodded her head and closed her eyes. As she lay motionless, I admired depth of her true beauty. To me, in many more ways than her looks alone, she defined perfection.

Each time I looked at Katie at for any length of time, it raised wonder as to why she would choose to find interest in me. I felt undeserving of her attention, unworthy of her love, and often uncertain that her love for me could last a lifetime.

"On a scale of one to ten," I said. "How happy are you right now? Not *right* now, but in general. With me?"

"Ten," she responded without opening her eyes.

I feel the same way.

I lifted her hand to my lips again, paused, and shifted my eyes to her waist. Her shirt had moved slightly, exposing a few inches of her stomach. After an extensive period of time, I reached for the bottom of it with the intention of pulling it down to meet the waist of her shorts. With my free hand half-way there, I hesitated and shifted my eyes to her face.

Her eyes were still closed.

As I lowered my hand into my lap my eyes quickly fell to her waist. The slight guilt I felt for admiring such a remote and sensual portion of her body slowly faded away, leaving me feeling rather curious.

I gazed blankly at the four-inch section of exposed skin for some time, wanting time to jump forward to a day when we were married – a time in which I would naturally feel that my exploration of her would be without limits, free from reservation, and filled with nothing but pleasant memories.

"Touch me," she said softly.

The guilt which had faded away quickly came rushing back. Almost as if I was a child again, caught for doing something I had been warned not to, I shifted my eyes to meet hers, only to find her smiling softly with her eyes opened ever-so-slightly.

"I thought you were going to. It's okay, Alec. Touch me," she said.

"I…"

As I began to explain, I stopped, realizing that my desire to feed my curiosity was being fed fuel by her approval to proceed. I smiled, shifted my focus to her waist, and convinced myself touching her could be harmless as long as my intentions were pure.

With the backs of my knuckles I brushed her shirt upward slightly, exposing yet more of her silky smooth skin. As I admired the contour of her stomach and the slight depression into her naval, I flattened out my hand and raked the tips of my fingers ever-so-lightly around the surface of her skin.

Softly, she began to moan. Her state of mind was unmistakable. The sound escaping her lips was derived from pleasure, not pain. I continued, hoping to feed her desires without causing her any discomfort whatsoever.

Fed by each of her rather vocal releases of delight, I continued to trace my fingers along her skin in a circular motion, raising the bottom of her shirt ever so slightly each time my fingers passed by the fabric.

Soon, the curved portion of the bottom of her bra was exposed, and although I initially – and naturally – felt the need to pull her shirt down to cover the undergarment, I fought the urge, and continued to enjoy softly touching her skin – my reward being her repeated outbursts of pleasure in response to my touch.

With my eyes fixed on her stomach and following the pattern my fingers outlined on the surface of her skin, I watched as she arched her back and lifted herself from the surface of the couch slightly.

She removed her hands from behind her back and flattened herself onto the couch.

"Take it off," she said.

I swallowed heavily and shifted my eyes upward until they met hers.

"My bra," she said. "Take it off."

I gazed down at her body for what seemed to be an eternity, not quite sure of what to do next. As I sat alongside her thighs on the edge of the couch peering down at her, I felt rather foolish and slightly immature.

Slowly, she sat up, reached into her shirt, and pulled her bra from underneath.

With the bra dangling from her fingertips, she lowered herself to the couch, draped her arm over the edge, and dropped it onto the floor. I shifted my eyes to her mid-section. Her shirt once again covered the skin I was so eager to caress.

As I stared down at her shirt, afraid to make any sort of advancement, I wondered exactly what prevented me from doing what it was I knew she found pleasure in. I decided, after a long pause, that it was nothing other than the guilt of moving too quickly or in a manner that brought her something other than pleasure. Frankly, I had no idea of what it was she wanted or how to proceed.

As I continued to stare, dumbfounded and confused, she sat up, pulled her shirt over her head, and tossed it onto the floor. Still sitting up and facing me, she leaned forward and reached for the bottom of my shirt. With our eyes locked on one another, I leaned in for a kiss. As our tongues explored what our minds desired and our mouths were either too innocent or too protective to say, I reached down and helped her pull my shirt over shoulders.

As we continued to kiss, I pressed my chest to hers, leaving the shirt draped over my shoulders. With my hands and mind at battle over how to proceed, my hands soon won, and found their way to the underside of her breasts.

I softly kneaded her flesh in my hands as we continued to kiss, finding the vibration of her pleasurable gasps against my lips to be rather sensual. Eventually our mouths parted, and she leaned away from me, fully exposing her bare chest to my exploration. My eyes admired the fullness of her breasts, and my hands soon followed. As I softly squeezed, she groaned in pleasure, arching her back a little further each time.

Cupping the bottoms of her breasts in the web of my hands, I lowered my lips to her erect nipples and opened my mouth fully. I pressed my face against the surface of her skin, circling her nipple with my tongue.

The repeated moans that filled the room left little doubt as to her pleasure, and I continued based on the sound of her expressed excitement alone.

I realized as I continued that we had done very little speaking, and further understood doing so wasn't at all necessary as long as I was receptive to her manner of communicating to me.

I lifted my mouth from her swollen nipple, leaned toward her bicep, and kissed my way to her shoulder. With my hands softly squeezing the upper portion of her arms, I lifted my lips from her shoulder, met her gaze, and grinned.

I reached out and lifted her chin slightly. After a few seconds of admiration, I kissed her again, softly and slowly, only to pull my lips from hers and move my mouth along her jaw and to her neck. As I nibbled and kissed her neck, her writhing against me became more intense and passionate. I continued for some time, and eventually slowed my pace until she became calm.

After a long moment of regaining my senses, I kissed her passionately and fully. As our lips parted, her eyes met mine and we shared a silent moment of admiring each other.

"I love you, Alec," she said.

My response was immediate.

"And I love you," I said.

And, for the first time in my life, I had no doubt that it was genuine.

CHAPTER THIRTY-FIVE

Late Spring 2015, Austin, Texas, USA

In what I suspected was the only way he saw an opportunity to assemble the family that he had lived so long without, Shane bought three adjacent lots in an upscale neighborhood with his proceeds from the fight; and as the winter came to a close, the three homes he was having constructed were completed.

I couldn't help but admire his newfound desires – and the reasons behind them – even if he didn't admit what the driving force was behind his spending habits. As far as I was concerned, he didn't need to, it was apparent.

A man who had spent his adult lifetime pinching every penny he earned seemed to now enjoy spending at least a portion of his fortune on the things and people he truly found valuable. A block from his home, a school was being built for special needs children, all funded by him entirely.

I sat in a lounge chair on the deck of my new home staring blankly at the massive swimming pool in Shane's back yard. According to him, the pool was a community pool for all of us to share; and since we moved into our homes, we had done just that. Barbeques, gatherings, parties, and discussions happened on the deck of the pool on an almost daily basis.

Initially, being in Texas wasn't an easy thing for me. Regardless of the animosity I felt toward my father for coercing my sister to give up her child for adoption, leaving him wasn't a simple thing for me to do.

Sitting there gazing at the area where I had spent countless hours playing with my new nephew, I had a slight epiphany.

God is not only understanding and forgiving, he places in front of us all that is necessary to live a peaceful life. At times he may take from us, but he also provides. It is up to us, however, to see exactly what it is he is offering.

I stood from my seat. As my eyes continued to linger toward the pool, I was filled with a newfound gratitude for everything and everyone in my life. My mind took a short pause as well, acknowledging how both Katie and Casey were a tremendous blessing to me, each providing me unconditional love on varying levels. The two loves of my life were gained as a result of friends, not family. People I had met who were selfless, willing to offer themselves and the ones they loved all in an effort to become closer to a man who just happened into their lives.

I was now living in the polar opposite location from where I had spent the majority of my life. Learning how to live a life filled with love wasn't a natural task for me, and as I turned away and began to walk toward the house, I chuckled at the similarities between Casey and me. In some respect we were each learning how to live life for the first time, neither of us fully understanding what was around the next corner.

As I opened the door leading into the house, I paused and turned back toward my lounge. My phone was on the table beside the chair, sitting idle, as always. It was a device I had never really become accustomed to, but appreciated nonetheless. I reached over the chair, picked up the phone, and typed a text message to Katie.

Thinking of you

I pressed *send* and turned toward the open door knowing no matter what happened, I would spend the rest of my life doing so.

CHAPTER THIRTY-SIX

Early Summer 2015, Austin, Texas, USA

The state of Texas was unique in many respects, but one in general that pertained to me. The state was occupied by a 1% MC who claimed the state as theirs sixty years prior. Any club who wanted to be respected, even non-1%ers, needed to get authorization from the Banditos to open a chapter in the state. It wasn't as much a matter of necessity as it was a matter of respect.

Although our club was not going to be an outlaw club, we respectfully set up a meeting with all of the local clubs to assure there were going to be no surprises after the club began to operate in full force. Shane, Ripp and I went to the meeting with high hopes of their being little if any resistance to our starting the club.

The three of us were seated on one side of the room, with the entire group seated across the room glaring at us. More than a dozen various clubs, primarily 1% clubs, each had their respective presidents in attendance, with the exception of one local club, the Selected Sinners.

Their support came from my home town of Wichita, due to the local chapter being on a mandatory run. As Wichita was the parent chapter for the Sinners, no exception was taken to their representative or their participation. Although their representative showed up late, I was glad he did, because he seemed to be the only sensible man in the group.

With Shane on one side and Ripp on the other, I did my best to respond to the questions as they were asked.

"So you ain't even gonna have a bottom rocker?" one of the men asked.

Jesus, how many times are you going to ask this question?

"That is correct. Our colors will employ an upper rocker, club logo, and an "MC" patch with no lower rocker. We claim no territory," I responded.

"So you ain't claimin' the state of Texas as your territory?" another man asked.

The president of the Selected Sinners cleared his throat and turned toward the man who asked the question.

"That same question has been asked a dozen fucking times. Asked, and answered," he said.

He continued to glare at the man, and continued. "They're a fucking do-gooder club."

Well, I wouldn't call it that, but...

He turned to face me, met my gaze, and stared. After a moment of our eyes remaining locked, he leaned forward slightly and cleared his throat.

"What's your hustle?" he asked.

He was asking what, if any, criminal activity the club was going to participate in to support themselves. Not all, but some 1% MCs ventured into a criminal enterprise.

I shook my head. "We don't have one, nor will we. Simply some local fellas that have a common love for bikes, riding, and enjoying the open road. I'm a former Marine, and the brotherhood a club offers is important to me. We don't need a hustle to support the club."

He leaned back into his seat and nodded his head once.

"I say we vote," he said. "They're not claiming territory and they aren't going to interfere with the business of any of the clubs in attendance. If a club isn't here, as far as I'm concerned, they don't care, and therefore have no say. We've been here thirty minutes, and that's about twenty-eight too fucking long."

He paused and turned his head toward the left and then toward the right. The meeting was a fly by the seat of your pants affair that no one was really in charge of, and although many had asked questions over the last thirty minutes, the Selected Sinners President seemed to be the one in charge, or at least he was taking charge.

"All in favor?" he asked.

"Aye," voices from the group rang out.

"Opposed?" he asked.

Silence.

I glanced at Ripp and Shane and grinned. "There you have it, fellas. It's official."

"Appreciate all your time," I said as I stood from my seat.

As a matter of respect, I waited for the men to stand up and either come speak to me or show their lack of interest and go speak to someone else. The first man to come speak was the president of the Selected Sinners.

"Slice," he said as he stepped in front of me. "Welcome to Texas."

"A-Train," I said as I shook his hand. "President."

I tilted my head to the side. "Dekk, the V.P., and Ripp, Sergeant-At-Arms."

"Pleasure to meet you fellas. I'm pretty tight with Doc back in Wichita, he said you're originally from there, speaks highly of you," he said.

"Damned fine man," I said.

"Couldn't agree more," Slice responded.

"Well, if you fellas don't have plans, we're headed out to a bar for drinks and a little food. Love to have you ride with us," he said.

Being asked by a 1%er to ride with their club wasn't unheard of, but it certainly wasn't common, either. Even if I had other plans, I would have cancelled them out of respect to him and his club. In short, it was an honor to be invited, and it spoke volumes about Slice's respect for us as a club for him to invite us.

"We'll ride. Know where you're going?" I asked.

He shrugged his shoulders. "Hoping you'd know a place."

"Red Shed," Ripp said. "Best biker bar in town, and they're 1%er friendly.

"Sounds like my kind of place," Slice said. "Come on, I'll introduce you to the fellas."

"Be right there," I said. "Just going to go shake a few hands."

Ripp and Dekk followed Slice outside and I wandered the inside of the facility giving anyone an opportunity to speak or introduce themselves. After shaking two hands and being eye-fucked by the remainder of the wannbe gangsters, I stepped outside and peered along the length of motorcycles that had parked outside since we walked in.

"Ripp's over there," Dekk said as he tossed his head toward Ripp.

He stood forty feet away with four men, all who wore Selected Sinners colors. As my eyes attempted to adjust from the darkened building to the Texas sun, I noticed one of the men had a USMC tattoo on his forearm, which immediately caught my attention.

"Staff Sergeant Jacob!" he yelled.

I shifted my eyes from his bicep to his face.

My mind began to spin.

They told me you were dead.

I stood and stared. It couldn't be. There was no way. He had to be be someone else.

I slowly walked in his direction. The closer I got, the clearer it became. I blinked my eyes. It had been ten years since I had seen him, but he looked exactly the same.

"Sergeant Todelli? The fucking Toad? Holy shit, Brother, I thought you were dead," I said.

He shook his head and grinned. "Fuck, I got medevaced out, treated, handed a Purple Heart, and went right fucking back. But I watched you get killed."

Although I was told by the Lieutenant Colonel that there were no men killed in action in my platoon, Sergeant Todelli was the only casualty my platoon had later suffered from the Second Battle of Fallujah, or at least I had thought.

Seeing him opened a part of me that had long since been closed off, and I felt as if I had truly accomplished my task the day I was shot into a piece of Swiss cheese.

He opened his arms and we embraced. A whirlwind of emotion that had long since left me quickly returned, and I recalled the last battle I had seen him in. As I released him from my arms, I leaned back and studied him.

"Shit, that bastard didn't kill me. Shot me a few times, but that's it. They told me you died. I was out six months, handed a couple of medals, and went back. Longest six months of my fucking life. Had to beg those bastards to send me back, and when I got to battalion they said you were dead. I asked around, and no one remembered what happened to you. I guessed you died, but I didn't know if it was the second in Fallujah or somewhere else," I said.

"Alive and well," he said. "But when they transferred me to first platoon in Charlie, I heard you died. Died a fucking hero," he said.

I shook my head and grinned. "Shit, the medevac chopper flew out, and I laid in the fucking street returning fire until a Corpsman drug me behind that building. Fucking sniper shot me twice, but your chopper hadn't made it out yet. Hell, I had to stay and make sure my Marines got out of there safely. And he had to shoot me one more time for before I got him," I said.

"*Ready for anything, counting on nothing*," he said with a laugh.

It was the motto of the 2/7 Marines.

"Isn't that the truth. Damn, it's good to see you," I said with a nod.

He grinned and nodded his head. "Good to be seen. And fuck it's good to know you're alive."

Axton crossed his arms in front of his chest and leaned back slightly. "I'm guessing you two fuckers don't need an introduction?"

"Not at all," Toad said with a laugh.

"So what the fuck are you doing *here*?" he asked.

"Trying to start a new chapter for our club. Just trying to make sure we don't step on any toes," I said.

"One percent club?" he asked.

"We're not a 1%er, club, no. We don't claim territory, and we don't have any hustle. We just ride and have a deep brotherhood. It's a nationwide group of firefighters, military, and friends of. We can talk about it at the bar," I said.

Finding out he was alive and well was a huge relief, and quite a boost to my military ego. The emotion I was filled with was unexplainable, and would be the equivalent of someone learning their brother was alive after mourning his death for more than a decade. I stood there admiring him feeling better than I had felt since the war ended, and most definitely more accomplished than I had felt throughout all of my experience in combat.

I shook my head, still incapable of believing it was him. "Damn it's good to see you. Let me introduce you to the soon-to-be Vice-President and Sergeant-at-Arms. Two of the best motherfuckers to ever grace this earth."

"Big bastard here is Mike Ripton, but just call him Ripp," I said as I extended my arm toward Ripp.

"Ripp, this is Toad, a Marine brother of mine. Toad, this is the one and only Ripp," I said.

"Nice to meet you," Toad said as his eyes fell to Ripp's Chucks.

Most bikers rode their bikes in boots and jeans, but Ripp wasn't most bikers. Dressed in his typical cargo shorts, wife beater, and Chuck's he looked like he was going to the beach, not on a motorcycle ride.

Toad coughed a laugh. "Do you ride in those fucking tennis shoes?"

"Pleasure to meet ya," Ripp said as he reached down and grabbed his foot. As he lifted his foot to his chest, he continued. "But these ain't tennis shoes, Brother. They're fuckin' Chuck's."

Toad's eyes widened as Ripp released his foot.

"And fuck, yes, I ride in 'em. Hell, I even keep 'em on when I fuck," Ripp said.

I shook my head and pointed to Shane, who, as always, had stood silently.

"Ripp's going to be the SAA. And this fella here…"

"You're Shane fucking Dekkar," Toad said excitedly.

Shane pulled his hood from his head and extended his hand. "Sure am. Pleasure to meet you, Sir. And call me Dekk."

Toad glanced over his shoulder and quickly turned around. "You've got to be fucking shittin' me. You've got the Heavyweight Champion of the fucking World as your Vice President? Otis, did you see this?"

A man standing behind him who was no less than six foot six nodded in our direction. "Sure as fuck did. Axton introduced us while you were zoned out."

"Pleasure to meet you, Mr. Dekkar, call me Toad. And that fight a while back, against Brock? Best fucking fight I've ever seen. We all watched it in our clubhouse. Son-of-a-bitch that was a good fight," Toad said.

"Thank you, Sir, I appreciate it. He was a tough opponent," Dekk said.

"Fellas, I want you to meet Staff Sergeant Jacob. Known by his Marine brethren as *The A-Train*, because when he's coming, not a fucking thing can stop him," Toad said to the group of men as he stepped between where we were standing and the building.

The group was standing alongside the motorcycles, facing the building, and Toad was facing the group, waving his arms as if he was announcing the arrival of a celebrity. It was easy to forgive his excitement, because I felt exactly the same way, I only did a better job of hiding my emotion.

Slice stood from the side of what I assumed was his bike. "Well, if all you fuckers are done swapping spit and hugging each other, maybe we should head out to the bar."

"Axton, my two o'clock," Toad said.

258

I glanced over my shoulder to see what he was shouting about. A car slowly pulled into the parking lot. I turned around and shifted my eyes back to Toad, who was looking behind me and now clearly appeared to be concerned.

I'd seen the look a thousand times. Something was wrong, and when something was wrong with one of my Marines, something was wrong with me. With the car being the only thing I knew of that was behind me, and Toad's eyes widening, I glanced over my shoulder again.

"Axton, *behind you,*" I heard Toad shout.

The driver of the car was no other than the one piece of shit in my life I allowed to walk away. The man who attempted to rob us before Shane's title fight. The man who I kicked in the head.

And he was pointing a pistol out the window of the car.

Fuck.

I should have killed your sorry ass.

"Remember me, Motherfucker?" he asked.

The barrel of his pistol was pointed directly at my chest, and there was no time to react. I tensed my muscles and prepared to be shot once again.

But this time at point blank range.

At the same instant the sound of the weapon firing filled the air, Toad jumped between me and the car.

The shock of the bullet impacting my body never came. As the car sped away, Toad fell into me, and slowly began to collapse to the ground.

No.

No.

No!

Immediately, I reverted back to my training, and became the

commander of my men.

"Dekk, get a plate number of that car, move!" I screamed as I fought to prevent Toad's body from falling to the pavement.

"Ripp! Run that motherfucker down and yank his ass out of that fucking car!" I screamed.

I glanced at my watch and quickly shifted my eyes toward the men. Dekk ran toward the speeding car, and Ripp hopped on his motorcycle. As the car sped toward the on ramp, I saw Ripp's motorcycle shoot across the lot, over the curb and through an adjacent yard, and onto the ramp behind the shooter's car.

Get him, Brother Ripp.

I shifted my eyes to Sergeant Todelli.

He was losing blood with each beat of his heart.

A tourniquet was impossible.

"Corpsman!" I screamed.

I shook my head as I realized I had no support and I wasn't at war. "Call a fucking ambulance!"

I slapped the palm of my hand against Todelli's face as I lowered him to the ground. "God damn it, Sergeant, hold on."

His eyes opened and closed repeatedly. If an ambulance didn't show up within minutes, I was going to have a dead Marine on my hands.

Your will, not mine, Lord.

But we both know who that bullet was meant for.

He lived through that hell hole trying to make this world a better place, don't take him now.

I'm begging you.

"Open those eyes for me, Todelli," I said as I slapped his face again lightly. "Talk to me."

He opened his eyes and grinned. "We're…you and me…we're…"

I could hear the blood in his lungs. We needed a medevac, and we needed it immediately.

"Hold on Sergeant Todelli. Medevac's en route," I lied.

He opened his eyes.

"Hear that chopper, Brother?" I asked. "Corpsman's on his way."

He opened his eyes fixed them on mine. There was no doubt in my mind he wasn't going to live much longer.

"You and me," he said. "We're even."

Obviously, he felt I saved his life the day I laid in the street and shot the three snipers. But I wasn't ready to lose one of the Marines I almost died saving.

Not in that parking lot.

And not by the hand of the piece of human shit I chose to let live.

As the ambulance came screeching around the corner, I carried my Marine to the street.

"Gunshot wound to the chest, his lung is collapsed," I said.

I glanced at my watch. "Fourteen minutes."

They strapped him to a gurney and began to attempt to prevent his lung from collapsing completely. As they began to load him in the back of the ambulance, I pulled myself inside.

"Sorry, you can't…"

"There isn't one of you that's going to stop me," I said. "Now get my Marine to the hospital."

As the ambulance sped away, I lowered my head and prayed.

Only you know what lies before him, Lord. If his life has meaning, and his soul has purpose, and I do believe it does, I ask that you spare his life.

And, if you must, take another of this earth, but not this man.
Not now.
Amen.

CHAPTER THIRTY-SEVEN

Early Summer 2015, Austin, Texas, USA

I kneeled at the edge of the hospital bed and held his hand in mine as Katie's hand rested against my shoulder. Cambio Todelli was in a coma, and there was no consensus on his potential recovery. According to the doctors, he may come out of it, and he may stay in it forever.

I had no idea of what to expect, and left the outcome in the hands of God. Mentally, spiritually, and physically, I attempted to release myself from the feeling of responsibility to keep him alive, realizing my health and sanity was far more important than anything.

As Otis, Slice, and Ripp walked into the room I stood and turned to face them. "We're going down to get something to eat."

"Hell, I'll go with ya," Ripp said.

"I'm going to stay up here. His girl is supposed to be here pretty quick," Otis said.

"Mine's coming with her," Slice said. "I'll wait up here 'till they get here anyway, then I'll be down."

Ripp had followed the shooter in a high speed chase down the highway for several miles. While a traffic jam slowed the vehicles to a halt, he dumped his bike, ran to the car, and pulled the guy through the window.

One of the stopped motorists called police, and when the police arrived, Ripp was still beating on the guy.

I walked to Ripp's, patted him on the shoulder, and nodded my head toward Otis and Axton. "We'll be back up as soon as we're done. If you're not down first."

"See ya in a bit," Otis said with a nod of his head.

Axton nodded his head toward us and slapped his hand against my back as we passed.

We silently walked to the elevator, got inside, and independently stared at the closed elevator doors as we rode to the first floor. I was truly blessed to have Katie in my life, and seriously doubted I would have had the state of mind or the spirit to accept Toad's condition as God's will if it had not been for her.

The elevator doors opened and as we stepped from the elevator, Katie gasped.

"What?" I asked.

She grinned and shook her head. "Did you see that?"

"See what?" I asked.

"The light. When we were getting out," she said as she peered over her shoulder toward the elevator.

I shook my head and glanced toward Ripp.

"Come on," he said. "Dekk's in there with Austin."

"What happened?" I asked as I turned toward Katie, confused as to what had startled her.

"The elevator light, it flickered," she said.

I shrugged my shoulders. "Fluorescent lights do that sometimes. Probably a bad ballast."

She grinned, grabbed my hand, and proceeded to skip down the hallway toward Ripp.

"Well," she said as she tugged against my arm. "I said a prayer on the elevator. And I asked for a sign. God answered me. So, he's going to be just fine."

"I don't think it's that easy," I said.

"I do," she responded.

As we walked to the cafeteria hand-in-hand, I hoped she was right. After getting a plate of fruit and a few muffins, we sat down at the table with Austin and Ripp.

"So, any changes?" Austin asked.

I shook my head. "Not yet."

"Made a few calls." Dekk said. "Seeing if we can get a specialist in here."

"Appreciate it," I said with a nod as I reached for a banana.

"He's going to be fine, I'm sure of it," Katie said.

"You shouldn't say stuff like that," Austin said. "You never know. It's not good to get your hopes up."

"Shut up, Austin. What the fuck do you know?" Ripp growled.

"Why do you say he's gonna be fine, Bug?" Ripp asked.

"I said a prayer, and God gave me a sign," she said cheerily.

"Can't argue with that," Ripp said as he glared at Austin.

"I'm not going argue God with you," Austin said, waving his hand toward Ripp as he spoke.

"Not a believer?" I asked.

He shrugged his shoulders. "Don't really know."

I glanced toward the entrance of the cafeteria as Otis, Slice and who I assumed was Slice's girlfriend walked into the cafeteria. I turned to face Austin again.

"I'm not going to argue God, either. And I'm damned sure not going condemn you. But let me ask you this. Why not?" I asked.

He shrugged his shoulders. "Never really had a reason to believe."

I nodded my head. For me, it wasn't a difficult thing to believe. All I had to do was look around me. For others, however, it wasn't always that easy. I said a quick prayer for Austin as Slice, Otis and the girl with them sat at the adjacent table.

Axton cleared his throat, placed his hand on the woman's shoulder, and stood from his seat.

"Fellas, this is my Ol' Lady, Avery. Avery, this is Toad's friend and former Marine commander, A-Train. And the one on his right is Ripp, the man who ran down Toad's shooter and damned near beat him to death, and the one on the left is Shane Dekkar. Ripp's sister, Katie, and the other fella is Austin. How'd I do?"

I nodded my head. "Perfect."

He grinned a shallow grin as he lowered himself into his seat.

"Nice to meet all of you," Avery said.

"He's awake! He's awake!" Someone shouted from the cafeteria entrance.

I spun in my chair toward the screaming. As everyone jumped from their seats, I followed, not knowing for sure who it was who was doing all of the screaming.

"Come on!" Otis shouted as the woman turned away and ran toward the door.

As we all ran for the exit, I glanced toward Austin.

Reason enough?

CHAPTER THIRTY-EIGHT

Early Summer 2015, Austin, Texas, USA

It wasn't surprising that a broken collarbone and punctured lung didn't keep Toad down for long. After his continuous demands to be released from the hospital, they complied, and he stayed in my home for the remainder of his recovery. I found his stay to be a pleasant change for me. I had been living alone for several years, and although I constantly found myself looking forward to the day that Katie and I lived together, actually sharing my mornings and evenings with someone was nice.

Two weeks after his release from the hospital, he went back to Kansas. Seeing him in a healthy relationship provided reassurance that a full recovery from the war was not only probable, but quite possible.

"I know I don't have to, I want to," I said. "It's something I think needs to be done."

"Tell you what," she said. "I'll make a trade with you. I'll agree to it as long as we get to eat some of those peaches when we get done."

I glanced toward the kitchen counter. I found it surprising that she noticed I had purchased them.

"Deal," I said.

"Okay," she responded as she walked into the living room and sat down.

My new home was an open floor plan with a kitchen that faced the front of the house. Directly behind the kitchen sink was a large island and bar, and beyond it, the large open living room that faced the back deck. The entire back wall was lined with windows, providing not only a view of the spacious back yard, but of Dekk's pool.

I grabbed my coffee, followed her into the living room, and sat across from her in a chair.

"I struggle, not as bad as I used to, but I still do. You know, with everything I did, and even some things I didn't do. My mind struggles with the men I've killed, and it's weird. It's not that I wonder if it was necessary, because it was. But there's a part of me somewhere that isn't completely convinced of it. So I have dreams, moments of pause, and sometimes I just sit and think about it," I said.

She cupped her hands around her coffee cup as she rocked back and forth lightly on the cushion of the couch. After a moment she leaned forward and rested her elbows on her knees.

"But you don't dwell on it?" she asked.

"No, I mean, I'm fully functional. So, no. I don't dwell on it," I said.

"And it's getting better? It's better now than it was when you came home?" she asked.

"Much better. I used to sleep about three hours a night. Hell, when I was in Wichita, I'd get up at night and check the doors, go outside, check under the cars before I drove them. It was pretty bad," I said.

"But none of that now?"

I shook my head. "None of *that*, no."

"I'm sure it just takes time," she said.

I inhaled slowly as I gazed down at the floor. As I shifted my eyes to meet hers, I continued. "Well, that's not all of what I wanted to talk about. I've uhhm. Since the war, I've done some things. Things I'm not ashamed of, but I haven't uhhm. I haven't admitted them to anyone but God."

I felt the need to be truthful with her. I had not, nor would I ever lie to her, but not telling her everything about me, at least in my mind, was the same as not telling her the truth. In my opinion, for her to commit to spend a lifetime with me, she needed to know exactly who I was.

She leaned to the side, placed her cup on the end table and folded her arms in front of her chest. "Bad things?"

"In my mind, not so much. In most people's eyes, I'd say so," I said.

"Are you going to get arrested some day?" she asked.

I shook my head. "No."

As she nodded her head softly, I decided to expand my response.

"I could be, but I won't," I said.

She tightened her grip on herself as if she were cold. "Are you sure?"

I was talking in a circle, and not giving her the information I had intended to. It was all too easy for me to give minimal information and convince myself I had actually discussed – at length – whatever the subject was I intended to discuss. It was typical of the Marine in me.

"Katie," I said. "I've killed men."

"I know," she said. "You had to."

I shook my head. "Since the war."

Her eyes widened slightly, and she shifted them to the side, gazing beyond me. I studied her as she stared blankly at the kitchen behind me, her eyes eventually narrowing into slits as she drifted deep into thought. After a moment, she shifted her eyes to me, inhaled a slow breath and dropped her gaze to the floor.

"Like Ripp did? Guys like that?" she asked.

"Worse," I responded.

"Do you want to talk about it?"

"Do I need to?"

"I guess…"

"Let me say this," I interrupted. "I have no idea how or why my mind works the way it does. I'm not saying I'm always right, but I sure think I am for some reason. Whether I'm an active duty Marine or not, I'm a protector. I feel like it's my duty to protect the people on this earth from what is evil, because I am able. And, believe me, not everyone is able."

"Now I don't plan on scouring the nation looking for any and everyone who is evil, but when evil threatens the ones I love, I'll take care of it," I said.

She unfolded her arms, reached for her coffee, and took a drink. As she lowered her cup, her eyes followed it.

"So you're protecting your loved ones from harm," she said as she shifted her eyes to meet mine.

"Exactly," I said.

"I'm not agreeing with you just to agree with you," she said. "But you know, when I think about what happened to me, and what Ripp did…"

Her eyes dropped to the coffee cup and she hesitated for a moment before continuing. "I wish someone would have done that to him a long time ago. You know he told Ripp that he had done that before to several women, and no one would testify against him. So he just kept doing it."

She lifted her eyes from the cup and continued. "I mean, you're a good guy. A great guy. I've lived in Texas my entire life. This state is full of vigilantes. People walk around with guns on their belts. Ripp was robbed at gunpoint a year ago, and a guy tried to take his car. We were almost robbed that night at the bar, and then that guy shot your friend, Toad. I guess I trust you."

It seemed all too easy. I didn't expect her to agree with me, but having her do so was comforting. I pressed my forearms onto my knees and leaned forward.

"Trust me to what?" I asked.

"Make good decisions," she said.

"So, you're not upset about it?"

She shook her head. "Really? I've lived with Ripp my entire life. He's beaten up guys for looking at girls cross-eyed. And Shane? Yeah, he might come off as a really mellow guy, but he's not. When he first got here he was going out to bars and beating the crap out of guys who he thought were shitty. And I know what Ripp did to Kace's old boyfriend. He got drunk and told us. No, I'm not upset."

I felt relieved, but I was still not convinced she had accepted me for who I was.

"That night the guy tried to rob us?" I said.

"Yeah?"

"Well, I wished I wouldn't have let him go," I said.

There. I said it.

Her mouth twisted into a slight smirk. "Alec, we all talked about it when we drove around the block. I was sure you *had* killed him. So was everyone else."

I scrunched my brow and stared. "Really?"

"You know," she said. "There's a huge difference between people like me and Vee and Kace and people like you and Ripp and Shane. We might not be able to always tell you what we want or even what we expect when it comes to things like that, but that doesn't mean we don't want them. Deep down inside, we want them. We just don't want to talk about it."

She stood from the couch and picked up her coffee cup. "One reason, one *big* reason I was originally attracted to you? Because I knew you'd always protect me. And I knew you were able."

I followed her with my eyes as she walked toward the kitchen. Halfway there, she glanced over her shoulder.

"I just don't want to hear the details," she said.

I stood from the chair as she poured another cup of coffee. There wasn't a person on the entire earth who could claim to be perfect in a complete sense, but for me, Katie was as close as a person could be.

All I could hope for was that one day I could be the same in her eyes.

"Alec," she said over her shoulder.

As she realized I was walking in her direction, she continued. "We all have flaws. But as far as I'm concerned, you're perfect."

And, at that instant, I realized the day I had waited for arrived.

CHAPTER THIRTY-NINE

Summer 2015, Austin, Texas, USA

Austin had won his first three fights, proving not only that he was a great boxer, but that I was capable of teaching him. The pride I felt in his abilities was probably similar to what a child's father felt when his son accomplished a difficult goal.

Shane paid to have a new gym built, and we were all enjoying the size, new equipment, and additional boxing rings. Waiting in line to be able to spar was a thing of the past, and although the old gym was still available, it was becoming more of a museum than anything.

My life, entirely, was as in order as it had ever been. In the grand scheme of things, I exhaled, paused, and inhaled a long slow breath of appreciation.

"You're just going to have to get used to it. You're a father now, and being a father is about makin' sacrifices," Mr. Ripton said.

He had Jessie balanced on his knee, holding her in place with one hand and was eating a hamburger with the other.

Ripp crossed his arms in front of his chest. "Since when do we not have chicken?"

"Since now," his father responded.

Ripp turned his head to face his mother and sighed. "Seriously, we're not going to have any chicken?"

"Meal's been served, Mike. Look around you," his father said sternly. "Everyone's about done eatin'. You been bitchin' about it for fifteen minutes."

"The burgers are really good," Kace said as she held her half-eaten burger in the air.

I shifted my eyes toward Mrs. Ripton. She glanced up from her plate and nodded her head toward Kace. "Thank you, Kace."

"Burgers are really good," Ripp repeated sarcastically as his eyes darted around the table for something satisfactory to eat.

Ripp's eating habits were similar to that of a teenage girl. He refused to eat hamburger, claiming it would make him fat. Although I wasn't as big as Ripp, I was certainly in better physical condition, and I ate beef on a regular basis. Despite Shane's and my attempts to convince him otherwise, he wouldn't eat a hamburger if we tried to force him.

It was now apparent even his parents couldn't convince him to.

"I say we go the next year and eat Sunday Burgers. I'd like to watch you wither away. You don't fight anymore anyway," his father said as he reached for another burger.

Ripp furrowed his brow and glared at his father. "I still fight. I fought last weekend."

"Fightin' in Rundberg doesn't count, Mike. Bare knuckles fights are for kids and thugs. You need to grow up," he said.

Katie choked on her food and began to laugh. I pursed my lips and shifted my eyes toward Ripp, fully knowing he would respond with some type of smart-assed remark.

"Grow up?" Ripp howled as he waved his arm toward his father. "I've got a house, a kid, and a wife. How much more can I grow up?"

"Shane bought you that house, you ain't got a wife 'cause you ain't actually married, you're still fightin' bare knuckles matches in Rundberg for cash, and I'm holding your baby. I'd say you could stand to grow up plenty," he responded.

"Gimme the baby," Ripp demanded.

"Eat a burger," his father said as he nodded his head toward the platter of hamburgers.

"I ain't eatin' a burger," Ripp said. "Gimme the baby."

Mr. Ripton shifted his eyes from Ripp toward me. "What do you weigh, Alec?"

"Hundred ninety-five, Sir," I responded.

"You get on that machine at the gym? The one where they test your fat?" he asked.

"Body fat percentage? Yes, Sir, I do," I responded.

He took a bite of his burger, shifted his eyes to Ripp, and glared at him as he chewed. After swallowing, he placed the remainder onto his plate and began to bounce the Jessie on his knee, but never moved his eyes away from Ripp.

With their eyes locked, he continued.

"So, Alec. What's your fat? How much fat you got?" he asked.

"Eight point two percent this morning, Sir," I responded.

"Huh," he said, still staring at Ripp. "So, Mike. What do you weigh?"

"What's your point?" Ripp asked.

Vee chuckled. "Answer your father."

"Two-forty, give or take," Ripp said.

"And the fat?" Mr. Ripton asked.

Ripp clenched his jaw and stared.

"Alec, you eat hamburgers?" his father asked as he shifted his eyes from Ripp to me.

"Yes, Sir," I responded, fighting not to smile as I did.

"This is funny," Katie whispered.

I nodded my head.

Ripp sighed, reached for the plate of burgers, and picked one up.

"None of your business," he responded.

"I'm thinkin' you could learn a lot from Alec," Mr. Ripton said.

"Alec ain't perfect, Pop," Ripp snapped back.

"More so than you," his father said as he reached for his burger.

"He's got a different metabolism," Ripp snarled.

"Sure does," his father said as he finished his burger. "It's called devotion."

Ripp had already eaten half the burger. As he glared at his father, he dramatically opened his hands and dropped the remainder onto his plate. "You sayin' I ain't devoted?"

"I said all I got to say," his father said.

"That's about enough," Mrs. Ripton said softly. "It's Sunday, we should all get along."

Katie grinned as she squeezed my knee. When we gathered on Sundays, I'd become accustomed to her having her hand on my leg for almost the entire meal, which was something that developed over time.

I glanced around the table as everyone quietly ate and realized I was amongst my family. Since moving to Texas, my old habits had faded away one by one, leaving a void within me. The void, entirely, had been filled with new events, new people, and new purpose.

There was no doubt in my mind I was exactly where I belonged.

After everyone finished their meal and began to tell stories of bare knuckles matches, changing diapers, and babies learning to eat solid food, I lowered my head and said a one-word prayer.

Courage.

I lifted my head, glanced at Mr. Ripton, and as he met my gaze, winked. In response, he furrowed his brow and glared back at me. I stood from my seat.

"Since I've moved to this fine state of yours, I've learned a lot. I've grown considerably, and not in size, but in my ability to become human again. I look at each and every one of you as family, and I appreciate all you do for me," I said.

"But something's missing," I said as I turned to face Katie. "Something I'm afraid I can't go any longer without at least attempting to fix it. There's a huge hole in my soul, and I feel empty sometimes. So, tonight, I'm going to take a step toward repairing that one part of me that remains broken."

I lowered myself to kneeling, reached into my pocket, and pulled out the ring.

"Katie, would you consider filling the void within me by agreeing to be my wife?" I asked.

Her mouth curled into a smile. She glanced toward her father. I did the same. He grinned and nodded his head. She gazed down at me with her beautiful blue eyes and responded.

"Yes," she said excitedly.

As I slipped the ring onto her finger she reached for the back of my head with her free hand. I'd never been one for public displays of affection, but as she pulled me into her for a kiss, I didn't resist at all.

I closed my eyes, kissed her, and allowed myself to become lost in the moment, but not so much that I wasn't able to hear her father.

"Yeah," her father said. "I'm thinkin' you could learn a lot from Alec."

CHAPTER FORTY

Summer 2015, Austin, Texas, USA

Regardless of my attempts to separate myself mentally or physically from my family, they were, and would always remain, my flesh and blood. No amount of effort, or lack of the same, would ever be able to break that bond.

I stared at the text message, reluctant to respond, but fully knowing I needed to.

It's dad. Wherever you are, you need to come home. He's bad.

As much as I despised some of the decisions my father had made, he was still my father. He was the man I once admired, and always looked up to. He was the one who taught me how to shoot a rifle, how to hunt, and how, at least initially, to defend myself. He made his values my values, and instilled a belief system within me that allowed me to become a hero in the eyes of many and a remarkable man in the eyes of at least one woman.

"Who was it?" she asked.

I glanced up from my phone and gazed blankly in her direction. The possibilities of what could have happened to him were running through my head, and it wasn't so much that I didn't want to face him, I really didn't want to face the problem – or the unmistakable truth that he was getting older.

"Huh?" I murmured.

"Your phone. You didn't answer. Who called?" she asked.

"My sister," I said.

"Oh," she said, narrowing her eyes slightly.

"I guess I knew you had a sister, but…"

"I need to call her back, she sent me a text message," I said.

"Is everything okay?" she asked.

I shrugged my shoulders. "Hard to say with her."

I pressed *redial*, and paced the floor as the phone rang. Four rings into the call, and one ring away from me hanging up, and she answered.

"Alec?" she asked. "Is that you?"

"Who else would it be?" I asked sarcastically. "So what happened?"

"He had another heart attack. His COPD is pretty bad and his heartbeat is irregular. They uhhm. They said if you want to see him alive, you better get here in in the next few hours," she said.

"They don't know shit," I snapped back.

"Alec, he's at the heart hospital. *Galleta*. A specialist has been assigned to him. He's had a lot more heart attacks than you're aware of, and he's had all the bypasses they can give him. They were talking about an ablation, but they don't think he'll live through the procedure. It's complicated. Come home," she said softly.

After my second tour, she had given me her promise to keep her son. Raising him without a husband certainly wasn't an easy task for her, but it wasn't impossible, either. After giving up on herself and her ability to raise him without assistance, she had moved back in with my father. Before my tour ended, he talked her into giving the child up for adoption.

I'd never forgiven her for doing so, and I had my doubts as to whether or not I would ever be able to. Since I turned my back on her and my father, it wasn't uncommon for her to stretch the truth regarding my father's medical condition – all in an effort to get me to be closer to her – and to him.

"I am home, Alicia. I live in Texas now. I tell you what. I'll drive up there, but if this is another one of your bullshit…"

"The doctor's given him a few hours to live, Alec. I don't know how long it will take you to get here, but if it takes too long, I'm afraid…"

"Be there in eight hours," I said.

And I hung up the phone.

CHAPTER FORTY-ONE

Summer 2015, Wichita, KS, USA

I stood in the waiting room with my sister, the doctor, and Katie. Everything he was telling us was not at all what I had hoped for, expected, or was prepared to process. No child, regardless of the relationship they have with their parent, wants to hear that their death is not only certain, but imminent.

There are few certainties in life, death being one of them.

Knowing when the exact moment will be that we are going to draw out last breath is something everyone seems curious about, but no one really wants to know the answer to.

"So, if the ablation isn't done, it's your professional opinion that he won't make through the night?" I asked.

"That is correct. His defibrillator receives a signal from the heart, if you will. That signal is processed, and recorded. If the signal is irregular or becomes irregular, the device shocks the heart, much like the paddles I'm sure you've seen in the movies that they rub on someone's chest to shock them back to life. The shock is intended to correct the heartbeat."

He paused and gazed down at the floor. As he shifted his eyes upward he continued. "Your father's heart has a spot on it which is sending false or inaccurate signals to the device. We monitor the device remotely, and it had gone off over a two-dozen times in 24 hours. In short, your father has suffered half a dozen heart attacks in the last day."

"And the ablation procedure corrects that?" I asked.

"It *may*," he said. "In a sense, we burn the heart, causing it to scar, and remove that section of heart from sending false signals. The process is a timely one, and *that* is my concern."

"The anesthesia?" I asked.

"Not the anesthesia itself, but the length of time he would be required to be under anesthesia. My guess is six hours or more," he said.

"And the decision is mine to make?" I asked.

"You're listed as the next of kin, and there is no wife, so yes," he said.

I had watched his eyes the entire time he had been speaking, and although it came as no surprise, and it was my opinion that he believed every word he said. I stared down at the toes of my boots and held my gaze there for some time, wishing twenty-four hours had passed, so it would be tomorrow already.

I lifted my head, glanced at my sister, and my eyes were immediately drawn to my mother's diamond bracelet she was wearing. A gift from my father on their 25th wedding anniversary, he had said buying her the traditional silver wouldn't serve as any form of justice to commemorate the quality of woman she was. Diamonds worn around the wrist, according to him, would draw attention to the fact that he perceived her as valuable.

She wasn't valuable.

She was priceless.

After my combat training and before I deployed the first time to Iraq, my mother was diagnosed with ovarian cancer. Four short weeks later, under the care of the best staff money could buy, she passed peacefully while in her sleep. She was a saint of a woman, always placing others before herself, and never turning her back on someone in need.

Growing up, I admired my father; but I adored my mother.

She died without ever having an opportunity to meet her grandson.

I shifted my eyes from my sister's wrist to the doctor. "Do the ablation procedure."

I reached up, gripped Katie's wrist, and lowered her hand from my shoulder to my side. As Alicia's eyes followed the path of my hand, I nodded my head toward her wrist.

"We'll get it started right away, I'll keep you up to speed as the procedure makes progress the best I can, but don't expect any progress reports for at least two hours," he said.

I nodded my head.

"You know that should be kept in a safe deposit box or a safe," I said as I tilted my head toward my mother's bracelet.

"I think she'd want me to enjoy it," she said.

"That was for someone who was priceless," I said as I gripped Katie's hand. "You heard the story. Priceless."

"Alec, please. Don't..."

I raised my hand between us to silence her.

"We'll be over there," I said as I tilted my head toward the corner of the waiting room.

"I'd appreciate it if..." I paused and shook my head, unwilling and almost incapable of continuing. Seeing her was much more difficult than I would have imagined.

"Are you okay?" Katie asked as I turned away.

"I'll be fine," I said, realizing I had acted inappropriately toward my sister in front of her. "I'm sorry. There's just a lot of animosity between us."

"I can see that," she whispered.

We walked to the corner of the room and sat down on a small sofa. I dug through the magazines at the table beside the arm of the couch, hoping to find answers to questions I had yet to ask, but instead found nothing. I lifted my boot, and propped it onto my knee as I gazed toward the far end of the room. Alicia sat on the far sofa with her head in her hands.

"You told me you always give people a second chance. Did you give your sister one?" she asked.

I lifted my boot from my knee and let my foot drop to the floor. I turned to face her, mentally prepared to answer, but incapable of doing so without admitting I had excluded my sister from a fundamental rule I had applied to all walks of life.

With the exception of Alicia.

"No," I responded.

"Well maybe you should," she said.

I was the first to admit when I was wrong, but I was rarely wrong. It wasn't that I believed I was without fault, or that I was arrogant or egotistical, because I wasn't. But my actions always came as a result of deep thought, and contemplation of any and every possible scenario that may arise as a result of my decision.

I was left living a life with few mistakes.

My eyes fell to the square tiles on the floor and I counted the years since my sister and I had acted as loving siblings.

Twelve.

I had never considered myself a stubborn person, but as I shifted my focus to the other end of the room, I came to realize I had yet to walk in my sister's shoes.

My forgiveness wouldn't act as an acceptance of her behavior, only an admittance on my part that I, too, wasn't without fault.

I stood from my seat and humbly walked to where she was seated, thinking the entire time of what she must have gone through in her decision to allow her only child to be placed up for adoption. Her choice, although unfathomable to me, had to be extremely difficult for her.

"Come sit with us," I said.

She glanced up, wiping her eyes as she did. She had obviously been crying long before I arrived, and looked ten years older than she probably would have on any other day.

Alone.

"Come on," I said as I reached for her hand. "You can come cry with us."

"I miss him so much," she said as she cupped my hands in hers.

"Who?" I asked, and then immediately realized I knew the answer.

"Derek," she said.

I gripped her hand firmly in mine. "So do I."

"That's a beautiful ring," she said as we stepped in front of Katie.

Katie reached for the ring and rubbed it between her thumb and forefinger as she responded. "Thank you,"

"And I love the bracelet," Alicia said.

"Yours too," Katie said as Alicia sat down.

"Let me tell you a story about it," Alicia said as she glanced at the bracelet. "My father said every day that my mother wore it, no one would question her value to him. He said the bracelet would prove to all who saw it that she was priceless. And she was."

Katie shifted her eyes to meet mine.

I shrugged my shoulders and grinned.

In case Katie didn't already know, she now realized that to me, she was priceless.

The talking and story-telling continued for some time, and I agreed to go get us a cup of acceptable coffee from the coffee bar by the cafeteria. As I walked from the room and turned down the hallway, I realized not only did I have a family in Texas, I had another in Kansas.

And the thought of having both let me feel just a little closer to becoming human.

CHAPTER FORTY-TWO

Summer 2015, Wichita, KS, USA

As he walked into the room, the first thing I noticed was how he wouldn't make eye contact with any of us. With his head hung low, he continued to walk in our direction.

"Come on." I said as I stood.

We met in the center of the room, and he raised his head slowly. "Well, he's one of the most stubborn men I've ever seen."

"Alive and stubborn?" I asked.

"Yes, he's alive," he said. "I guess telling you now causes no harm, but we lost him twice."

Alicia gasped. "Oh no."

"It's irrelevant now," he said as he raised his hands in front of his chest.

He poked himself in the lower portion of his chest with the tip of his finger. "The portion we worked on was here."

"It ended up being a much larger part than I had anticipated. The procedure took six hours," he said.

"He's in recovery now, and I suspect you'll be able to see him in an hour or so," he said. "I'll let you know as soon as we have him in a room."

"Thank you," I said.

The six hours had passed like minutes. Sitting with my sister talking about our childhood, my new life, her new job, and Shane's son went rather well, and I enjoyed it immensely. As the doctor left the room we turned toward the couch we had been seated on.

"Have you ever eaten Pho?" I asked Katie.

"What?" she asked.

The food was my sister's favorite, at least the best I could remember. She and her friends would drive repeatedly to a Vietnamese soup kitchen when they were 16 years old and devour the soup, and she would come home without enough appetite to eat dinner. I refused to even try the stuff as a kid, and although many years had passed, I still had yet to try it.

"It's a noodle soup," I said.

"I *love* noodle soup," she responded.

"You eat it now?" Alicia asked.

"Never tried the stuff. You still like it?" I asked.

"Love it," she said.

"Well, Erik Ead brags on the shit like it's gold. Let's go grab a bowl before they get him to a room, I'm hungry," I said.

"Who's Erik Ead?" she asked.

"A good friend," I responded. "So, do you want to?"

"I'd love to," Alicia responded.

I raised my arms and wrapped them around the two women's shoulders who I cared dearly for.

One bound to me by blood, and both by love.

As we walked to the door, I realized Alicia reminded me of my mother. By the time we reached Alicia's car, I admitted I resembled my father in many ways, one of which was described accurately by his

290

doctor.

I was stubborn.

CHAPTER FORTY-THREE

Late Summer 2015, Wichita, Kansas, USA

As a child, I made a decision on my own to believe in God. I don't think children require much convincing to believe, for most I suspect it comes rather easily. Believing there was a mighty being in charge of the universe pulling the strings from above like a talented puppeteer continued for me until I was a teenager. I gave considerable thought to the subject as a teen, and as I became more and more intelligent about my surroundings, I decided not only that I believed in God, but that God wasn't a puppeteer.

God was real.

My mother was outspoken about her belief in God and was a religious woman. Although Alicia and I went to service with her on almost every Sunday as children, I never saw my father step foot into a church. Initially, I though fathers in general were too busy for church and probably didn't attend, especially after working as hard as they did for the entire week to provide for their families. As time passed, and I grew older, I determined my father wasn't sure about the existence of God.

It wasn't something he talked about, nor was it something he ever admitted. He didn't have to, we just knew.

As a believer, I often wondered what would happen to my father when the clock ran out. When his heart beat its last drop of blood through his veins what would be next?

Would there be some means of forgiveness for stupidity?

Would he receive a free pass for being stubborn?

Did he really believe and was simply too afraid to admit it?

With the series of tubes taped to his mouth and extended into his throat, it was impossible for him to speak, and our only means of communication was by writing on a pad of paper with a pen. Clearly frustrated and growing angrier by the minute, communicating with him was similar to playing a game of charades.

"Need me to scratch somewhere? Alicia asked.

He shook his head from side to side frantically.

"Want a drink?" she asked.

He widened his bloodshot eyes and stared.

I turned toward her and glared. "Jesus, Alicia. He can't drink."

Although he was alive and they expected a full recovery, he was extremely frail at the moment. Regardless, I placed the pen in his shaking hand and held the pad close to his chest. I was fairly certain he wouldn't be able to write, but he didn't seem to be in agreement.

He glanced at the pad, raised the pen slightly, and upon realizing he was incapable of writing, closed his eyes and released it. The pen fell on the edge of the bed, rolled to the floor, and Katie bent down to pick it up.

I glanced at Alicia and shrugged my shoulders.

"Let me see the pad," Katie said.

I reached for the pad, handed it to Katie, and patted him lightly on the shoulder. "It's just going to take time."

He blinked his eyes.

Alicia, standing at the foot of the bed, reached out and squeezed his feet. "They said maybe tomorrow they'll take the tube out."

He blinked his eyes again. They were covered in a light film of grease, which made him seem even less able to exist on his own. As I studied him and wondered just how much longer he would actually live, Katie handed me the pad and pen.

"Here," she said. "The entire alphabet. Point at the letter and have him blink his eyes or something."

I felt like an idiot.

"Thank you, Baby," I said as I accepted the pad.

I held the pad in front of him and pointed at the letters one at a time, starting with "A".

When I got to "G", he nodded his head.

I repeated the process, and when I got to "O", he did the same.

"Good to see you?" Alicia blurted, attempting to guess what it was he was trying to say.

He shook his head and did his best to glare at her with his grease covered eyes.

"Just let him finish," I said.

The next letter was learned rather quickly, and surprised me somewhat. In choosing "D", he had so far spelled *God*, but I was quite certain we weren't done yet.

When he chose the letter "W", I wasn't sure where he was leading us, but we continued, each of us eager for our own reasons to see just what it was he was determined to say.

After a matter of a few minutes we had all of the pieces to the puzzle.

A chill ran down my spine.

I suppose I was relieved by the answer, but I was also shocked. I wanted to know more, but realized I would just have to wait. For now, I was satisfied that my father's life would probably be changing in some respects. Or so I hoped.

I placed the pad beside him on the bed and patted him on the shoulder. "I love you, Pop."

He blinked his eyes, closed them, and fell asleep.

I guessed, at least for the time being, he had said all it was he felt he needed to.

"Let's go get a cup of coffee while he's sleeping," I said.

As Katie and Alicia turned toward the door, chatting as if they were long lost friends, I tore the sheet of paper from the pad and gave it one last look before I folded it and placed it in my pocket.

God was there.

CHAPTER FORTY-FOUR

Late Summer 2015, Austin, Texas, USA

"There should be two options, but according to him, there's only one. I guess I see his point," I said.

"The attachment to home?" she asked.

"Basically. That's the home he married my mother in and raised his children in. There aren't many people who stay in a home that long, and he has. He doesn't want to leave," I said.

My father was going to require someone to be with him at all times, at least for a while. Although Alicia had been with him for the entire time he had been out of the hospital, it was time for her to return to Ohio, or she was going to lose her new job.

I realized using a home healthcare company was an option, but I felt it would be insensitive and selfish on my part. Going to Kansas, however, seemed impossible. My options, however, were limited. It was Friday, and Alicia had to be to work on Monday. I had dodged the subject as long as I was able and it was time for me to make a decision. I sat across from her and buried my head in my hands.

"What do you want to do?" Katie asked.

I raised my head from my sweaty palms and glanced in her direction. Sitting on the couch smiling, it was as if she was immune to my concerns and worries. Either that or she knew something I didn't.

"Want to do? Stay here and not have this problem," I said.

She narrowed her eyes slightly. "Don't call it a problem, Alec. It's not a problem. Look at it as an opportunity."

I choked on the thought. "An opportunity?"

"Yes. You've been separated from him for what? Ten years? And now you've finally either forgiven him or yourself, however you want to look at it. It's an opportunity for you to get to know him again, and for him to catch up on everything with you," she said.

I leaned into the back of the chair and crossed my arms. "And what about you?"

"What do you mean what about me? I'm going with you. What else would I do?" she asked.

The night I asked Katie on a date, her father's message to me was clear. *You're not from here. And I ain't lookin' to have my daughter taken from me, Mr. Jacob. Not now or ever. As far as I'm concerned, she can leave Texas when I'm dead, but not before.* Taking her with me, even for what I believed to be a temporary resolution to his condition, would likely be met by a *hell no* response.

"Your father made it clear that he didn't want me to take you from here. He was adamant about it. Me staying here in Texas, and you never leaving. He said you could leave when he's dead." I said.

She chuckled. "Sounds like something he'd say. But, is your father going to require your assistance forever?" she asked.

I shrugged my shoulders. "I don't think so."

"Neither do I. So, you're not taking me from here. Or from him. We'd be going there for a while to take care of your father. We'll be back," she said.

I nodded my head in agreement, knowing damned well it wasn't that easy. I was going to have to talk to her father, and I was quite sure his opinion wasn't going to be the same as hers. The thought of leaving, in general, had kept me from sleeping for the last ten days. The thought of leaving her, even on a temporary basis, seemed impossible for me.

But taking her seemed equally impossible.

I felt sick to my stomach.

"I'll talk to your father," I said. "Either way, I'm going to have to be there Monday."

"*We'll* be there Monday," she said.

She stood from her seat and walked into the kitchen, not seeming to understand just how much leaving was bothering me, even if it was on what we believed to be a temporary basis. She poured a cup of coffee, sauntered back into the living room and sat down.

"What?" she asked as she sat down. "You're making a big deal out of nothing."

"We'll see how he takes the news, I guess," I said.

She sat and studied me for several minutes as she drank her coffee. As she lowered her cup to the table beside the couch, she maintained eye contact with me.

"It's Casey, isn't it?" She asked.

"What?" I asked, even though I heard her clearly.

"Casey. You don't want to leave him," she said.

She was right. All things considered, I knew I could leave Texas. As a combat Marine, I learned not to become too attached to anyone or anything, because in a moment's notice, things can change. People disappear. Some change units, others get killed, and, as time passes, yet others are discharged. I loved Shane and Ripp as brothers, but I could leave them if need be. Leaving Casey, however, seemed to be an impossibility.

I felt if I left I would be doing what I had condemned my sister for doing.

I crossed my arms in front of my chest, fully realizing she was correct in her assumption about Casey, but not willing to discuss it. "I don't want to leave. It's that simple."

"I guess we need to go talk to my dad," she said.

"We'll go as soon as I'm done with this cup of coffee," I said.

I stood from my seat and walked into the kitchen. I only had two days to decide whatever it was we were going to do. Talking to her father was the next step, and something we had to do without exception. His response to our request may very well allow both of us to travel to Kansas on a temporary, or semi-permanent basis.

And I knew as sure as I was standing there that of everything I had to do throughout my entire life, leaving that child was going to be the most difficult of them all.

CHAPTER FORTY-FIVE

Late Summer 2015, Austin, Texas, USA

Unconditional love is something I had always believed was shared between parents and children; and at times, between two people who fell in love. I never expected it to exist between friends, or between a parent and a child who weren't related.

"Your father needs ya. There ain't a damned thing I can do to fix that, other than offer my love and understanding. You know, we take care of you when you're little, and there comes a time when it's your turn to return the favor," he said.

I was completely shocked by his open-minded acceptance of what it was that I felt I needed to do. His insistence that Katie went with me was equally surprising, and although I was relieved, I realized my next step was to actually go through with it and leave.

"I'll see how things go, and we'll hope for the best," I said. "I appreciate your understanding, Sir."

He wrinkled his brow, narrowed his eyes and glared at me. "You appreciate my understanding? What the hell did you expect, Son? Resistance? Did you honestly think that I was going to stand between you taking my daughter – your future wife – with you to take care of your sick father? I might seem like a mean son-of-a-bitch, but I ain't. Well, 'less I have to be. Hell, Alec, I love you like you're my own.

Whenever you get the gumption to go ahead and get married, you'll be just as much family as she is. Hell, to tell you the truth, you are right now. Appreciate my understanding? Shit, that's almost funny."

My throat constricted and my mouth went dry. I didn't know how to respond. I shifted my eyes toward Katie and met her gaze. As we shared a silent moment, she grinned.

"Stand up," her father said in a demanding tone.

I looked up and realized he had stood from his chair and was hovering over me. I stood, only to be immediately pulled into a hug. As he held me in his arms and patted my back with his hand, he gave me all of the reassurance I needed to understand what he was allowing us to do came from deep within his heart.

"I love you, Son," he said.

As his words sank in, I realized I was an extremely fortunate man.

A month prior, as far as I was concerned, I had no parents.

And now, I had two loving fathers.

CHAPTER FORTY-SIX

Late Summer 2015, Wichita, Kansas, USA

I hadn't spent any time in my father's home to speak of since I was eighteen years old. Being there at length brought a rush of memories with it, some good, and some not-so-good. As he slept and Katie cleaned the house, I looked through cabinets, boxes, and drawers for memories of my mother.

The deepest memory came not only of her, but of Suzanne.

I pulled the egg-shaped bottle from the bathroom cabinet and removed the lid. It became my mother's signature scent, and the bottle was something I remembered seeing on a regular basis as a child, but I hadn't associated the smell with my recollection of the bottle – or with my mother – yet.

I pressed the tip of the nozzle and sprayed some of the fragrance into the air. As I watched the small droplets fall toward the floor, I craned my neck toward them and inhaled slowly.

Immediately, I pulled my head back and wrinkled my nose.

The scent reminded me not only of my mother, but of Suzanne.

Confused, I turned the bottle to the side and lowered my nose to the tip of the nozzle. The perfume, without a doubt, was what Suzanne wore. It angered me that she wore my mother's perfume, but what eventually caused me to feel enraged was that I had spent my entire time in combat associating Suzanne with the scent of my *mother's* perfume.

It was as if I had been robbed of a memory of my mother, or that somehow it had been replaced with a new one. Maybe it was something that happened over time, I decided, and wasn't a conscious thing at all. In the end, as I carried the bottle to the trash, I decided the only reason I liked Suzanne in the first place must have been because of how she smelled, not the person she was.

I walked through the kitchen, past Katie, and out the back door. I tossed the bottle of perfume into the trash container, slammed the lid, and walked inside.

"I like the way you smell," I said as I walked past her.

I paused at the doorway leading to the living room and turned to face her. "What is it?"

"Flowerbomb," she responded. "And, I like the way you smell, too. What is wrong with you?"

"Nothing," I said. "Just getting rid of some stuff."

"Okay. I'll have lunch ready in about fifteen minutes, you should probably wake up your dad here pretty quick," she said.

"Just let me know when you're done," I said. "I'll wake him up when it's ready."

"Okay," she said as she turned toward the sink.

I walked through the bedroom, past the bathroom, and into the walk-in closet. On one side, my mother's clothes hung, no differently than they had for years. On the other, my fathers. As I shifted my eyes along her outfits, memories of her wearing the clothes came rushing back, and I grinned at the thought of her.

I dragged my finger along the shoulder of the clothes, watching them wave in my wake, each one bringing a separate memory with it.

The dresses she wore to church. The dark suit she wore to my uncle's funeral. The tomato colored jacket that I detested, and I was certain she wore for no other reason than to irritate me. The bottom of the closet was lined with her shoes, dusty, but still just as they were fifteen years prior.

I glanced at my father's side of the closet. His clothes weren't as plentiful as my mother's, but with them, too, came memories. His Carhartt work jacket that he wore on a daily basis to and from work. His one suit he owned. Several jackets hung side by side, none of which that he wore, all of which were gifts.

I chuckled at the thought of his stubborn nature.

My eyes fell to the floor, and immediately I noticed two boxes at the back of the closet, somewhat hidden underneath his clothes. I knelt down and gazed at the ends of them. One clearly marked *good stuff* and the other marked *shit*, my curiosity soon got the best of me.

I slid the box marked *shit* from underneath the clothes, glanced over my shoulder, and removed the top.

A quick check of the documents inside produced receipts, tax forms from what appeared to be his lifetime, and a handful of letters regarding overdue medical bills from years gone past. I grinned at his labeling of the box, placed the lid on top and carefully slid the box back into place.

I shifted my hands to the other box, slid it in front of me, and removed the top.

A folded newspaper sat atop the large assortment of documents. The headline immediately caught my attention, and as I reached for it, I was quickly overcome by emotion. I swallowed heavily, carefully removed it, and peered down at the page.

Local Marine, 23, A True Hero

Although difficult at times, I read through the entire article. Reading about myself wasn't easy, and along with the resurrected memories came a tremendous amount of emotion. The article was about the Second Battle of Fallujah, and when I had hidden behind the truck to kill the three snipers.

I lowered the article to my lap, wiped the memories from my cheeks, and peered into the box with swollen eyes and a dry throat.

Local Marine, 21, Awarded Second Purple Heart

I stared down at the newspaper and tried to remember when I was 21 years old. As I read the article, the spotter who was shot and killed on the rooftop seemed as if he was with me. I could smell the cordite from the sniper rifle, the coppery stench of the dried blood, and the smell of our sweat.

I wiped my runny nose, brushed the back of my hand against my eyes, and placed the article beside the other.

One by one, I removed the newspapers and placed them on the floor beside each other.

Local Marine Single-Handedly Saves Army Special Forces Platoon in Afghanistan

Local Marine in Military Spotlight

Wichita Marine Awarded Bronze Star

End of the War is Near, Says President

Local Marine, 19, Awarded Purple Heart

Hijacked Airliners Destroy Twin Towers and Hit Pentagon in Day of Terror

I stared down at the articles and swallowed heavily. As difficult as it was to read about my actions in combat for the first time, it was rewarding in many ways. In my father's eyes, I was the man depicted in the articles. A boy who quickly became a man, did what he had to do at a time of war, and emerged – by the grace of God – as a hero.

In my eyes I was nothing more than my father's son.

I gathered up the articles and neatly placed them in order. As I began to lower them into the box, I noticed a small box of photographs, something my mother had always truly loved, and my father refused to stop taking.

My father never accepted digital photography, and for as long as I could remember, used a 33mm camera to take his photographs. As stubborn as he was, the majority of them were developed at home, in the basement. I gazed down at the photos, the majority of which were black and white, and stared.

On the top, a picture of Derek I didn't recognize. I picked up the photo, studied it, and realized it must have been taken on his birthday when I was deployed. I picked up another. And another. And another. All of Derek. Eventually, I got to photos of my sister and me, my mother, and some relatives.

Several of the photos of Derek were with my father, obviously either taken by my sister. I spread the photos on the floor and stared at them, trying my best to etch the memory of my nephew into my mind as indelibly as my memories of the war. As my mind began to drift to memories of his first birthday, I realized that soon it would be Casey's first birthday.

The sound of Katie's voice startled me.

"Alec, lunch is ready," she said.

"Be right there," I said as I began to pick up the photographs.

One by one, I carefully placed the items back into the box. As I slid the box into its place in the closet, my mouth curled into a smile.

HARD CORPS

There was no doubt my father loved me.
And it was time for me to love him in return.

CHAPTER FORTY-SEVEN

Present Day, Wichita, Kansas, USA

Two months had passed since our arrival in Wichita, and my relationship with my father was surprisingly better than I could ever remember it being in the past. I desperately missed Casey – and my other Texas brothers as well – but Ripp and Shane had both ridden and driven to Wichita to visit on more than one occasion. Each time Shane drove he brought Kace, and with them, Casey.

My father seemed to enjoy having Casey around, but I wondered just how much his visits reminded him of his only true grandson. For me to consider Casey to be my nephew was easy. I thought for my father to consider him as a grandson would be a stretch, but the excitement on his face and the smile in his eyes was impossible to hide.

Katie's parents had yet to drive to Kansas, which didn't surprise me. It was my guess getting her father to ever leave the state of Texas would require nothing less than our refusal to return. She had, on two occasions, driven down and seen them, but I stayed in Wichita with my father.

I realized the day would come when he was able to be alone, but further realized the day hadn't arrived. For the time being, I was enjoying my time with my father, and viewed it as making up for lost time.

I truly missed Katie's Sunday dinners, the family in general, the feeling of participating, and training at the gym, but it was her father I seemed to miss the most.

"Too damned bad about the club," Jackson said.

"Bound to happen," I said as I tightened the exhaust bolts. "With me gone and that state as fucked up as it is with clubs? It was just a matter of time."

Our MC in Texas dissolved for a few reasons. One was my absence. But the primary reason was the string of recent problems in Texas with 1% clubs, violence, and the categorization by police of all MCs as being outlaw regardless of their intentions. Harassment and incarceration of men in cuts was becoming common, and it seemed a reason wasn't always behind the incarceration. Out of respect for Shane and Ripp as parents and as good citizens, I decided to dissolve the club.

"Well, the Sinners don't accept applications, but we do invite men to prospect as long as they're vouched in by a fully patched member. And, if a man has already paid his dues, so to speak, he may be vouched in without prospecting on a 100% vote. I know you can go back to your old club, but we discussed it in our last meeting…"

He paused as I stood up and tossed the wrench to the side.

"I feel like I owe you. For what you did for me," he said.

"Don't owe me shit," I said flatly.

"I don't mean owe you like that. Owe you respect," he said.

"Give it, get it," I said.

"Show respect," he said. "Get respect."

I shrugged my shoulders. "Same difference."

I was anxious to hear what else he had to say about the club's meeting. As we were eventually going to go back to Texas there was no real way I could be a member, but the thought of riding with a 1% club in Kansas appealed to me. I stood out with Bones, Doc, and Crash's club as being a little too much of an outlaw, and maybe an outlaw club was where I truly belonged. The thought, at least, was appealing.

"So, you were saying. You guys talked about it," I said as I flipped the ignition switch *on*.

I pressed the start button as he began to speak.

"Club would love to have ya," he said over the sound of the exhaust.

I revved the engine a few times and listened for exhaust leaks. The dull drone from the new pipes sounded great, and there seemed to be no leaks. Only an open road test of hard accelerating and rapid decelerating would tell me for sure, but for now, I was convinced.

I flipped the ignition switch to *off*.

"No prospecting bullshit?" I asked.

He shook his head. "Not one single day of it."

"Fully patched the day I show up?" I asked.

"Fully patched," he said.

I was flattered. As much as the thought of such a close-knit bunch of bikers appealed to me, and as much as I knew the brotherhood would help me feel at home, there was no way I could disrespect the club by being a member for six weeks, two months. Or whatever length of time it would be before we left.

"I'm honored, but we're leaving some day, just don't know when. Can't disrespect you guys like that," I said.

He grinned and nodded his head. "Club's already discussed it. There's an Austin chapter of the Sinners. If you go back, you'll just transfer to that chapter."

"Hell, I knew there was an Austin chapter, but I had no idea..."

"Toad's our Sergeant-At-Arms, and he's not only my fucking

brother-in-law, he's one of the best motherfuckers in the MC. He's solid as a rock. Hell, we've talked about it, Axton, Biscuit, Otis and me. Only thing we can come up with that makes him different is that he isn't afraid of anything on earth, and he always thinks before he acts. It's a result of his training. He was a Marine. You were a Marine. Hell, you were his fucking Platoon Sergeant."

He slapped his hand against my shoulder and shrugged his shoulders. "I know you don't want to hear it, but you're his fucking hero. He spent a lifetime thinking you were dead, and now that he knows you're alive, he can't stop talking about you."

My knee-jerk reaction was to say no, but for some reason I couldn't seem to bring myself to it.

"Let me think about it," I said.

"Sounds good." He responded.

The side door of the house creaked as Katie opened the door. "Lunch is ready."

She had proven to be one of the most caring, kind, and compassionate women to ever exist. She stayed up at night playing Scrabble with my father – an old tradition of him and my mother's – and listened to every bullshit story he tried to tell her. She spent her days doing laundry, cooking, and folding clothes, and as much as I believed tasks like those should always be shared, she refused, and insisted I let her do what she described as *her* work.

Having her as my wife would truly make me the happiest man on earth.

I turned toward the doorway and pressed my hands against my hips. "What would you think about me becoming a Sinner?"

She lifted her head slightly. "Hi, Jackson."

As her eyes fell to meet mine, she responded. *"Becoming* a sinner? You're the devil himself, Alec."

"Katie," Jackson said with a nod.

"A Selected Sinner," I said.

"Sounds good to me," she said. "You staying for lunch, Jackson?"

"I am now," he said.

As we walked toward the house I thought of what it would be like to be reunited with my old squad leader, Toad. Riding with him, doing my best to protect him, all the while knowing he had my back...

"So no prospecting?" I asked as I stepped through the door.

"Not a bit," he responded.

Tight knit bunch of fuckers, aren't ya?" I asked.

"Devil looks after his own," he said.

"That the club's motto?" I asked.

"Sure is," he said.

Sounds like a place I could call home.

CHAPTER FORTY-EIGHT

Present Day, Austin, Texas

My chest heavy with medals, ribbons, badges, and commendations, I stood erect in my Marine dress blues with my Squad Leader at my side. I glanced over my right shoulder. Dressed in his dress blues, the left side of his uniform covered in medals and his right with various ribbons, he stood arrow straight and stared directly in front of him.

As the music began to play, I turned slightly to my left. Redefining beauty, she walked down the aisle, her dress flowing six feet behind her footsteps. In the front row, her mother, brother and sister were seated on one side, and my father, sister, Shane, and Kace were seated on the other.

"Who gives this woman to be married to this man?"

They were words I had longed to hear.

"Her mother and I."

"Sir, Ma'am, will you bless me with your approval to move forward with this ceremony of marriage?"

"I will."

"I will."

"We have come together at the invitation of Alec and Katie to celebrate the uniting in Christian love, their hearts and lives. This is possible because of the love God has created in them, through Jesus

Christ," he said.

"Katie and Alec, no other human ties are more tender, no other vows are more sacred than these you are about to assume. You are entering into that holy estate which is the deepest mystery of experience, and which is the very sacrament of divine love."

"Alec, will you have Katie to be your wedded wife, to live together after God's ordinance in the holy estate of matrimony; will you love her, comfort her, honor and keep her, in sickness and in health, and forsaking all others, keep yourself only for her so long as you both shall live?"

I lowered my head slightly. "I will."

"Katie, will you have Alec to be your wedded husband, to live together after God's ordinance in the holy estate of matrimony; will you love him, comfort him, honor and keep him, in sickness and in health, and forsaking all others, keep yourself only for him so long as you both shall live?"

"I will.," she responded.

"Alec, repeat after me. I, Alec, take you, Katie, to be my lawful wife, to have and to hold from this day forward, for better, for worse, for richer, for poorer, in sickness and health, until death do us part."

I recited from memory. "I, Alec, take you, Katie, to be my lawful wife, to have and to hold from this day forward, for better, for worse, for richer, for poorer, in sickness and health, until death do us part."

He turned to Katie. "Katie, repeat after me. I, Katie, take you, Alec, to be my lawful wife, to have and to hold from this day forward, for better, for worse, for richer, for poorer, in sickness and health, until death do us part."

She recited the vows without flaw.

"Will rings be exchanged?" he asked.

"They will," I responded.

"The rings?"

I glanced over my shoulder.

"Come on, Little Man," I said as I curled my arm toward Katie.

Casey stumbled up the aisle, spent a few minutes climbing the steps, and held the pillow as high as he was able.

I pulled the rings from the strings they were fastened with and handed them to the pastor.

Casey stood between Katie and me and hugged my left leg.

"Please remember, a ring is more than a symbol of your marriage. It is a seal of the vow you have made to one another. The circle of the ring is, as far as human eye can see, a perfect circle – with no beginning or end – so God too, has perfect love for you and wants you to love one another in His grace--never, never ending. This ring is made of precious metal. You also are precious in God's sight and now in the life of Alec. When you are absent one from another, the presence of the ring reminds you to be faithful and to fulfill your vows to Alec. Rings have historically been the sign of authority, used to seal documents and proclamations, you now accept this authority in your life."

"Alec, you may now place your ring on Katie's finger."

I slid the ring onto her finger.

"Katie, what symbol do you bring as a pledge of that sincerity of your vows?"

"A ring," she said.

"Alec, this ring is a seal of Katie's vow to you. She presents this to you as a token of her submission to you in Jesus Christ. This is a symbol of leadership and privilege. God has placed you as head of the family. You must lead in worship, works and fellowship. As the weaker vessel she depends upon you for strength."

"Katie, you may place the ring on Alec's finger."

"For as much as Alec and Katie have consented in holy wedlock, and have thereto confirmed the same by giving and receiving each one a ring; by the authority committed unto me as a minister of the Church of Jesus Christ, I now declare you husband and wife, according to the ordinance of God, and the laws of the state of Texas, in the name of the Father, and the Son, and the Holy Spirit, Amen."

"You may kiss the bride," he said.

I tilted my head to the side and kissed Katie for the first time as my wife.

We turned to face the crowd. Five Marines lined each side of the aisle, and as we stepped down the steps, they drew their swords. Under their raised swords we walked, and took the traditional kiss. I turned from the kiss and faced the rear of the church.

Selected Sinners lined the back of the church, all dressed in their cuts.

With my Marine brethren beside me, and my MC brethren in front, I cupped Katie's hand in mine and held it high in the air. After the cheers slowed, I picked her from her feet and carried her toward the door.

"I love you," she said.

"I love you, too," I responded.

As we approached the two long lines of men in their cuts, Axton lowered his chin.

"Get that Marine shit hung up in your closet where it belongs, and get on your cut, A-Train," he growled.

Soon enough, Brother Slice, soon enough.

"You ready to take care of some long overdue business?" I whispered as I carried her between the two aisles of Sinners.

"We have a reception," she responded.

"Doesn't start for thirty minutes," I said.

"Sounds good to me," she said with a smile.

I had no intention of having sex with Katie in the thirty-minute window we had before the reception started, but it was fun to joke about.

For her, it was going to be the first time, and I was going to make it special.

I glanced around the church. It was filled with my family – all facets of it. They surrounded me on all sides. Family by blood, family by oath, and family by choice.

And with God's blessing, I was ready to get started making my own family.

One special moment at a time.

EPILOGUE

I had waited my entire life to find the man of my dreams, and now I had him. I couldn't really call myself pleased or happy, or even elated – not if I wanted the word to accurately describe how I felt.

Alec took me to an entirely different place than anything life had offered me before meeting him, and I truly appreciated him for it. Since I had been a small girl, my dream had been to have a prince come riding up, sweep me off of my feet, and take me to his castle.

I didn't expect at the time that he would be riding a Harley-Davidson, or that his castle would be two houses down from my brother, but I wouldn't have it any other way.

One definition of a fairy tale is *a story in which improbable events lead to a happy ending*. So, by definition, I was living in a modern day fairy tale. It didn't seem to matter much if we were together or we were apart – although I preferred when we were together – I had a smile permanently etched upon my face.

I dug my fingernails into his chest, arched my back, and moaned into the otherwise silent room as I reached climax. A few electrically charged seconds later, and I opened my eyes only to find them focused on his muscular torso. I drew a deep shuddering breath, exhaled, and gazed into his eyes.

"Are you okay?" he asked.

"I'm better than okay," I said, still trying to find my breath.

"You sure?" he asked.

"Uh huh."

"I just…"

"Alec, *I'm fine*."

"I don't want to hurt…"

"Alec. Really. The doctor said. Oh. Wait. Let me see your hand. Hurry," I exclaimed as I reached for his hand.

"There," I said as I pressed his flattened palm to my stomach. "Feel it."

The baby rotated slightly, and although I wasn't sure, my guess was that it was his knees that Alec was feeling.

"He's active today," I said.

His eyes widened. "He?"

I went to the doctor for a normal checkup and they did an ultrasound to check the baby's heart. Although we had both agreed not to find out the sex of the baby, I glanced at the screen at the wrong time.

Apparently the baby and his father shared at least one trait.

"I'm sorry," I said. "They did an ultrasound today, and I really didn't even try to see, but he was. Well, let's just say you and him are a lot alike in one respect."

He sat up slightly, his mouth curled into smile from ear to ear. "A boy. I thought I didn't want to know, but now that I do…"

"Are you sure?" he asked.

I burst into a laughing fit at the thought of the sight on the monitor at the doctor's office. Even the technician gasped at the sight.

"I guess it was one of those you had to be there moments, but yeah.

I'm sure," I said.

He continued to stare at me with face filled with pride.

"At least it'll make picking a name only half as hard," I said.

His sister and I had become great friends, and I saw her almost daily. Shane gave her a job at the gym working as his CPA. Although she and I had already discussed names, I had yet to really talk to Alec about it.

"What do you think about the name Derek for a boy?" I asked.

He sat silently for some time and just stared.

I really liked the name and I had hopes he would to. About the time I was going to suggest my second favorite name, his bottom lip began to quiver. Soon thereafter, a tear rolled down his cheek.

"It's…it's uhhm…it's perfect," he said as he wiped the tear from his cheek with the back of his hand.

And so are you, Alec Jacob.

So are you.

www.ingramcontent.com/pod-product-compliance
Lightning Source LLC
Chambersburg PA
CBHW020907200626
46814CB00001BA/219